P9-BYY-873

# rome in love

## Also by Anita Hughes

*Monarch Beach*
*Market Street*
*Lake Como*
*French Coast*

# rome in love

## ANITA HUGHES

 St. Martin's Griffin ☷ New York

This is a work of fiction. All of the characters, organizations, and events portrayed in this novel are either products of the author's imagination or are used fictitiously.

ROME IN LOVE. Copyright © 2015 by Anita Hughes. All rights reserved. Printed in the United States of America. For information, address St. Martin's Press, 175 Fifth Avenue, New York, N.Y. 10010.

www.stmartins.com

Designed by Steven Seighman

The Library of Congress Cataloging-in-Publication Data is available upon request.

ISBN 978-1-250-06413-4 (trade paperback)
ISBN 978-1-4668-6933-2 (e-book)

St. Martin's Griffin books may be purchased for educational, business, or promotional use. For information on bulk purchases, please contact the Macmillan Corporate and Premium Sales Department at 1-800-221-7945, extension 5442, or write to specialmarkets@macmillan.com.

First Edition: August 2015

10  9  8  7  6  5  4  3  2

*To my mother*

# chapter one

Amelia stood on the balcony of the Hassler Hotel and gazed at the twinkling lights of the Spanish Steps. She could see the dome of Saint Peter's Basilica and the dim outline of the Vatican. She took a deep breath, inhaling exhaust fumes from the endless stream of yellow taxis, and tried to remind herself she was in Rome.

Amelia smoothed the folds of her pink satin Balenciaga evening gown and checked that the borrowed Harry Winston diamond clip still held back her hair. She stroked the white silk gloves and fingered the diamond and sapphire choker around her neck. It was all a fairy tale: the ivory Bentley that picked her up from Rome Airport, the elegant suite at the Hassler with its black-and-white marble floors, the Spanish Steps at her feet and all the places she read about in guidebooks: the Sistine Chapel with its intricate frescoes, the Via Condotti with its string of elegant boutiques, the Colosseum and the Pantheon and the museums with long, flowery names.

Amelia tried to recapture the thrill when the concierge welcomed her with a bouquet of two dozen yellow roses and her own personal butler. She tried to remember the first glimpse of her suite: the silver ice bucket, the gold tray of chocolate truffles and petit fours, the mahogany four-poster bed. But her legs were shaky from jet lag, her head throbbed from too much champagne and not enough food, and her mouth was frozen in a permanent smile.

For the last two hours she stood in the grand ballroom, her large brown eyes coated with thick mascara, her cheeks powdered, her lips painted with pink lipstick, and answered the journalists' questions.

"How does it feel to go from being a complete unknown to being nominated for a Spirit Award for best supporting actress for your first role to starring in the remake of *Roman Holiday?* Warner Brothers invested a hundred million dollars in this picture, do you feel the pressure with your name above the title?"

Amelia had tilted her head and answered in the way Sheldon Rose, her producer, taught her.

"Why, Mr. Winters"—squinting so she could read the reporter's name tag and then waiting so the journalists focused on her white shoulders and creamy skin instead of her words—"when you put the question like that, I don't feel any pressure at all."

The room erupted into polite laughter but the questions kept coming.

"*Variety* quoted you as saying 'Audrey Hepburn is my idol and I can't imagine ever hearing my name in the same sentence.' Are you nervous about playing the role that made her famous?"

"Is it true you were premed at USC and Spike Jonze discovered you when you drove a friend to an audition?"

"Are you and Whit breaking up? Does he really wish you'd give up acting and pursue a career in medicine?"

Amelia paused again, longer so that she didn't say what she was thinking: it's none of your business how Whit feels, I could never give up acting, we're madly in love, he bought me these gorgeous teardrop earrings before I left for Rome. Instead, she touched her earrings gently, smoothed the folds of her gown and smiled.

"There's a reason why they call it one's 'private life,' Mr. Gould"— again reading his name tag, trying to look him in the eye so he wouldn't fire off some scathing article that she refused to answer personal questions, and finally a slow genuine smile—"because it's best to keep it private."

Then more champagne plucked from the trays that floated past carrying crystal champagne flutes and silver goblets filled with plump prawns and slices of melon. She smelled tomato sauce and garlic and longed to sit down to a plate of steaming ravioli and thick bread dipped in olive oil. But her dress was so tight it was almost spray-painted to her hips, and it was impossible to answer questions with a mouth full of pasta, so she guzzled champagne and waited for Sheldon to say, "Thank you all for coming, Miss Tate cherishes each and every one of you, but if she doesn't get her rest she'll miss her six A.M. call."

But Sheldon seemed to have disappeared and Macy Smith, editor of *Vogue,* came gunning down the Oriental runner. Amelia remembered her vicious critique of her choice in Oscar dresses and desperately needed some air. She ran out of the ballroom, down one flight of marble stairs and onto the balcony. Now she stood, wishing she had grabbed a puffed pastry or at least a stone wheat cracker, and gazed at the ancient, glittering city.

Amelia had always been fascinated by Rome: the elegant restaurants opposite cramped trattorias, the modern stores flanked by stone arches, the women wearing sleek dresses and smooth pageboys and large gold earrings. She had only been once, on a school chorus trip in the eighth grade, but she loved the creamy fettuccine and sweet gelato and the boys wearing leather jackets and driving Vespas. She remembered standing in the middle of the Via Appia and a boy with curly brown hair driving around her in circles and never wanting to leave.

Now Rome was her home for two glorious months. They were shooting the whole movie on location, at the Trevi Fountain and the Piazza Navona and the Castel Sant'Angelo. Sheldon had given her the Villa Medici suite—the same hotel room where Audrey Hepburn stayed more than fifty years ago. Amelia remembered standing in front of the gilt mirror in the pink marble bathroom and picturing Audrey Hepburn brushing her hair and fixing her lipstick and slipping on a floral dress with a tiny waist and full flared skirt.

Amelia heard laughter on the street below and heels clicking on the sidewalk. She imagined late-night dinners of spaghetti and red wine and brisk morning walks to the Colosseum. Then she remembered everything she heard about Sheldon Rose: he arrived on the set when the sun came up and didn't release anyone until nighttime. She thought of the paparazzi who would trail her after hours, hoping to catch her without makeup in sweats and sneakers. Suddenly she had a desperate desire to slip out of the borrowed Balenciaga gown, unstrap the jeweled Prada sandals, and disappear into the street.

She ducked into the hallway and down the staircase. She walked quickly to the back of the hotel, past the sumptuous Imago restaurant and ornate conference rooms and dark, elegant library. She ran through the kitchen door, past the huge granite islands and giant chrome refrigerators and double sinks. She took the back stairs to the basement and searched for a door that would empty into the street.

Amelia blinked in the dark and realized she was in the laundry. She saw massive washing machines and dryers and rows of silver irons. She saw tall lockers and piles of neatly pressed uniforms. She stopped to catch her breath and suddenly had an idea.

She unzipped her gown and carefully folded it into a square. She slipped it into a laundry bag and added her sandals and sequined evening bag. She buttoned the starched black maid's uniform and tied a white apron around her waist. She covered her hair with a cotton scarf and stored the laundry bag in a locker. She found the back door and ran onto the street.

The night air hit her like an electric current. The air was damp and the clouds hung low over the rooftops. She glanced around to make sure no one was looking and dashed down the Spanish Steps and onto the Piazza di Spagna.

Amelia skipped along the cobblestones like a child released from Sunday school. She pictured Macy Smith waiting to grill her about her wardrobe and wanted to collapse on the sidewalk in a fit of giggles. She smelled espresso and cinnamon and amaretto and longed to sit at a café until her head stopped spinning.

She saw a couple leaving a restaurant; their heads pressed together, the man's arm looped around the woman's waist. Suddenly she missed Whit so much, it felt like an invisible weight pressed against her chest. She remembered their last dinner before she left for Rome, at Alembic in the Haight. She flew up from Los Angeles and they had two glorious days in San Francisco.

Whit took a whole day off work and they rode bicycles in Golden Gate Park and visited the Legion of Honor. Amelia gazed at the paintings by Leonardo da Vinci and Raphael and shivered. She couldn't believe in forty-eight hours she would be surrounded by Italian art and architecture.

Amelia remembered sitting across from Whit and holding hands in the candlelight. Whit wore a white collared shirt and a navy blazer and tan twill slacks. His dark hair touched his collar and he smelled of Hugo Boss cologne.

"Do you remember our first date?" he asked, eating a garlic baked potato fry. "We lined up to see *Titanic* at the campus theater and laughed that an engineering major and a premed student could never sit through a three-hour movie. We'd fall asleep before we finished our first bucket of popcorn."

Amelia looked at Whit's clear blue eyes and remembered the first time she saw him. She was camped out in her usual corner of the science and engineering library cramming for a physics exam. Her calculator clattered to the floor and she reached down to pick it up. When she looked up she saw a young man with eyes as clear as a lake. He wore a baseball cap over curly dark hair and had a day's stubble on his chin.

"Just think," Whit mused, eating chicken pavé with beet gnocchi, "if you stayed with medicine you'd be finishing your residency at San Francisco General. We'd eat Chinese takeout every night and you'd be living in Gap sweatpants and my Adidas T-shirts. Instead we live in different cities and you own couture gowns by Valentino and Dior."

Amelia's stomach clenched and her throat closed up. She remembered when Whit received his first round of funding. It was a year after graduation and they lived in a studio apartment in Santa Monica. Amelia just finished filming *Hannah's Secret* and Whit spent his days trying to secure investors for his electric car company.

"I met with Caufield Perkins." Whit dropped his briefcase on the coffee table. "They're ready to write us a check."

Amelia glanced up from a pile of scripts and saw Whit's navy suit and white shirt and black leather shoes. She smiled, thinking she still wasn't used to seeing him in anything except Adidas T-shirts and running shorts.

"They want us to move our operation to San Francisco," Whit continued, loosening his tie.

"San Francisco?" Amelia raised her eyebrow.

"We looked at an industrial space in Potrero Hill, they want to keep an eye on their investment." Whit shrugged. "We can rent an apartment on Russian Hill and eat at Italian restaurants in North Beach."

"I'm an actress." Amelia bit her lip. "I need to live in Hollywood."

Whit drummed his fingers on the coffee table. "I thought after this movie you might go back to medicine."

"Why would you think that?" Amelia asked.

"It was all just a fluke," Whit mused. "You got it out of your system."

"I love acting, I don't want to give it up," Amelia said slowly.

"We haven't gotten any other offers," Whit replied. "This is our one shot, I need to be in San Francisco."

Amelia pictured a quaint apartment on Russian Hill. She saw sidewalks filled with bougainvillea and corner groceries stocked with gourmet coffees and cheeses. She imagined preparing dinners of spinach salad and stuffed ravioli and sourdough bread. She saw nights spent on the roof-deck, sipping a Kenwood Cabernet and gazing at the twinkling lights of the city.

She loved visiting San Francisco. She loved the steep hills and the white houses and the wide views of the bay. She loved the outdoor markets in Chinatown and the vintage clothing stores in the Haight. But if she was going to be an actress she should live in Hollywood, where producers could bump into her at Coffee Bean & Tea.

"I'll fly up every weekend." Amelia blinked away sudden tears. "We'll go wine tasting in Napa and eat at Chez Panisse in Berkeley. We'll spend Sundays in bed with the *New York Times* and mugs of Peet's coffee."

The first few months were one long honeymoon. They flew kites on Crissy Field and hiked to the top of Mount Diablo. They ate at trendy new restaurants on Union Street and in the Castro. But then Whit started working longer hours and complained he was tired of playing tourist. He wanted to curl up with Amelia in front of the television and eat pizza and watch *CSI*.

"The lead in *Roman Holiday* is the chance of a lifetime." Amelia brushed her brown hair behind her ears. She wore a green cotton sweater and beige capris and flat Tory Burch pumps. Her face was free of makeup except for mascara and a hint of clear lip gloss. "After the movie wraps I'll take a month off. We'll drive up the coast and stay in a bed and breakfast in Mendocino."

"I'm proud of what you do." Whit cut beef tendons with white truffles. "I just wished we didn't live five hundred miles apart and the paparazzi didn't write down our orders at Starbucks."

"They'll find some new ingenue." Amelia nibbled shishito peppers with anchovy salt. "Soon I'll be newspaper wrapping for old fish."

They drank vodka gimlets and listened to soft jazz and Amelia turned the conversation to Whit's new prototype.

"I think it's ready for the road." Whit stirred melting ice cubes. "We're going to drive from San Francisco to Santa Barbara without recharging."

Amelia gazed at Whit's bright eyes and hard cheekbones and thought he was lit by some inner fire. She sipped the bitter vodka, feeling his fingers press into her shoulder, and wished he understood how much she loved acting.

They paid the check and walked onto the sidewalk. They passed sushi restaurants and smoothie cafés and oyster bars. Amelia felt Whit's hand on her back and suddenly wished she wasn't going to Rome. She wanted to spend every weekend at dark restaurants sharing plates of baked fries. She wanted to listen to Whit's dreams of a whole fleet of electric cars.

They drove Whit's Prius to the underground garage and took the elevator to his apartment. Whit opened the door and Amelia saw her Coach luggage stacked neatly in the entry. She saw her light winter coat and her Burberry umbrella and her carry-on packed with an Italian dictionary and a stack of magazines. She gazed into the small living room and saw a ceramic vase filled with pink roses. She saw a bottle of champagne and two crystal champagne flutes and a silver tray of chocolate truffles.

"What's this?" Amelia asked.

"You didn't think your last dinner would be beef tendons and vodka gimlets in a smoky bar?" Whit drew a black velvet box out of his pocket. "This is for you."

Amelia sat on the navy Pottery Barn sofa and snapped open the box. She saw sparkling diamond teardrop earrings and her eyes misted over. "They're beautiful! But you can't afford this, they must cost a fortune."

"We got our second round of funding." Whit poured champagne into chilled champagne flutes. "You're going to be playing a princess, you have to look like one."

Amelia felt Whit's lips on hers and her shoulders relaxed. She reached for Whit's shirt and slowly undid the buttons. He kissed her harder, biting her lower lip and tracing her mouth with his fingers.

Amelia leaned against the cushions and felt Whit's mouth on her breasts. She unzipped her capris and let them slip to the floor. She sucked in her breath, guiding Whit's hands between her thighs. She slid off his shirt and buried her face in his chest.

Whit put one hand under her panties and slid his fingers inside her. He pushed his fingers in deeper, sending shivers down her spine.

Amelia strained toward him, rubbing his chest with her palm. She gripped his shoulders, feeling the deep throbbing and the long, infinite release.

Whit took her hand and led her to the bedroom. He unzipped his slacks and slipped off his socks. He pulled Amelia's sweater over her head and unsnapped her bra. He turned down the white cotton sheets and lay down on the bed.

Amelia kissed him on the lips, tasting champagne and chocolate. She wrapped her arms around him and drew him on top of her. She dug her fingers into his back, catching his rhythm, feeling the slow build, the delicious pause and then the final bolt of pleasure.

Amelia tucked herself against his chest and thought about the brochure of the Hassler Hotel. She pictured the Villa Medici Suite with its marble bathtub and gold brocade curtains and wide stone balcony. She heard Whit's soft breathing and closed her eyes, wishing they were lying in the four-poster bed with the windows open and the sound of music and laughter floating up from the piazza.


Amelia felt a raindrop on her forehead and shivered. She had been walking for an hour and didn't recognize any street signs. She wanted to ask directions to the Spanish Steps but suddenly the rain fell harder and the sidewalks were deserted.

She hurried to a taxi stand and stood next to a man wearing a trench coat and holding a large black umbrella. She searched for her purse and realized she left it in the laundry bag with her evening gown and her jeweled Prada sandals.

"You take the cab," the man said when a yellow taxi pulled up and the driver honked impatiently.

"I don't have any money." Amelia bit her lip. "I forgot my purse."

The man shrugged and got into the cab. The driver was about to pull away when the man put his hand on the driver's shoulder. The taxi skidded to a stop and the man opened the door.

"You look like a drowned rat. We'll share the cab, you can pay me later."

Amelia climbed into the back and smelled wet vinyl and stale cigarettes. Suddenly she felt sheepish for running away. She should be relaxing in her suite at the Hassler, wearing a silk robe and drinking hot tea and eating scones with butter and strawberry jam.

"Where are you going?" the man asked. He was in his early thirties, with dark brown hair and a slightly crooked nose. He carried a black briefcase and had an American accent.

Amelia gazed at the damp maid's uniform and frowned. She could try to slip in the kitchen door but someone might see her. She imagined her picture plastered over tomorrow's papers and shuddered.

"I don't know."

"You don't know where you live?" The man wrinkled his brow.

"I don't know where I left my purse," Amelia hesitated. "Could we drive around until I remember?"

The man shrugged and said something to the driver in Italian. The driver mumbled under his breath and slammed on the accelerator.

Amelia shut her eyes, suddenly woozy from the champagne and jet lag. She pictured Sheldon and the throng of journalists waiting for her at the Hassler. She felt a great weight pushing her down, like a strong current carrying her out to sea. She fell sideways and everything went black.

# chapter two

Amelia opened her eyes and tried to sit up. She saw a rectangular room with a tile floor and a bright red rug. There was a round glass table and a brown sofa and a tall wooden bookshelf. She glanced around and saw a trench coat hanging on a peg and a black umbrella resting against the door.

"Oh, my God." She instinctively pulled the sheets around her. "Where am I?"

"You're awake." A man crossed the room and perched on the edge of the bed. He wore a white shirt with the sleeves rolled up and tan slacks.

"I remember you." She wrinkled her brow. "You let me share your cab."

"You wouldn't tell me where you wanted to go," the man explained. "The meter was running up higher than a month's rent so I brought you to my apartment. You've been asleep for ten hours."

"I'm so sorry." Amelia bit her lip. Her head ached and her eyes watered and her skin felt like sandpaper. "I had too much to drink and not enough to eat. I've always had a love-hate relationship with champagne."

"You don't need to apologize." The man grinned. "Though you were pretty insistent that you sleep in the bed and I got the sofa. Something about being fired if you didn't get your beauty sleep."

Amelia blinked and looked down at the wooden bed frame and blue cotton sheets. "Did we . . ." she asked, her cheeks turning pink.

"Nothing happened, we didn't even exchange names." The man extended his hand. "I'm Philip Hamilton, it's a pleasure to meet you."

Amelia touched his hand and froze. If she told him her name he might leak it to the press. She imagined the headlines: "Amelia Tate spends the night with a mysterious stranger."

"Ann," she replied, searching her brain for a last name. "Ann Prentiss. I'm so sorry I caused you trouble."

"No trouble." Philip shrugged. He stood up and his head almost touched the ceiling. He went to the window and opened the shutters, letting in the mid-morning sun. "Your clothes should be dry in a few minutes."

"My clothes?" Amelia glanced down and saw she was wearing a man's shirt. She peered under the sheets and saw white tube socks with yellow stripes.

"Don't worry, I didn't look," Philip replied. "Though you did say you were voted best legs in high school."

"I said that?" Amelia blushed.

"Among other things." Philip nodded. "Something about fettuccine Alfredo and vanilla custard."

"When I'm hungry I dream about food," Amelia groaned.

"Then you'll join me for breakfast," Philip replied. He walked to the narrow counter and put two pieces of bread in a silver toaster. "I'm making my specialty: pigs in a blanket with poached eggs and a side of bacon. Breakfast is what I miss most about America. Italians think you can start the day with espresso and a pastry. I need eggs and sausage and lots and lots of bacon."

"I'm late, I really have to go." She tried to stand up, but her knees buckled and she sunk onto the bed. Her stomach felt as if it had been carved out with a knife and she was desperate for a glass of water.

"Where ever you have to go, it won't help if you faint when you get there." Philip's eyes narrowed. "Have a piece of toast and a cup of coffee. You'll feel like a new woman."

Amelia walked unsteadily to the glass table and sat on a wooden chair. She resolved to gulp a quick coffee but when she saw the bowls of muesli and fresh fruit, the platters of poached eggs and sausages and crisp, juicy bacon, her resolve weakened.

She poured milk into a bowl of muesli and added strawberries and sliced banana. She took a bite and tasted nuts and oats and cinnamon. She didn't look up until she finished the bowl and washed it down with a cup of milky coffee.

"I'm glad to know your appetite wasn't affected by the rain." Philip drizzled ketchup on his eggs. He buttered a slice of toast and poured sugar into black coffee.

"I haven't eaten in . . ." Amelia stopped. She couldn't mention the terrible jet lag or the elaborate gala, or being afraid to eat in the pink Balenciaga gown. "In a long time. This is delicious. Do you make breakfast like this every day?"

"Food in Rome is so expensive." Philip ate sausage wrapped in flaky pastry. "On Mondays and Tuesdays I eat breakfast, on Wednesdays and Thursdays I eat lunch, and on Fridays and Saturdays I eat dinner."

"And Sundays?" Amelia asked curiously.

"On Sundays I sit at Canova and dream about roast beef sandwiches on dark rye with dill pickles and a side of sauerkraut. God, what I'd give for a root beer float and a slice of New York cheesecake."

"You're from New York?" Amelia asked, nibbling a slice of toast.

"The East Village." Philip nodded. "I've been in Rome for three years. I've learned Italians are great at napping but terrible at working, they like their coffee strong enough to glue wallpaper. . . ." He stopped and looked at Amelia. "And have more than their share of beautiful women."

Amelia looked down at her plate and blushed. "I'm American."

"I thought the dark hair, the brown eyes, the maid's uniform . . ." Philip stumbled.

"I came to Rome to study Italian." Amelia crossed her fingers behind her back. "It's so expensive, I took a job as a maid."

"I can't walk down the street without feeling like I've been pickpocketed," Philip agreed. "Ten euros for a cup of coffee. I pay more for this place than a one bedroom with a roof garden in the East Village."

"Why are you here?" Amelia asked.

"Why are we anywhere? Work." Philip's eyes darkened and he snapped a piece of bacon in half. "Why don't we work off this meal with a stroll around the neighborhood? If we're lucky we might hear Signora Griselda singing in the shower."

Amelia spilled hot coffee on her saucer and jumped. She should be on the set ready for her first day of shooting. But she had been so hungry and the muesli and fresh fruit were so delicious. She would call Sheldon as soon as she got back to the Hassler and tell him she was terribly sorry and it would never happen again.

"I really have to go." Amelia stood up and walked to the door. "Thank you for everything. If you write down your address I'll send you some money for the taxi."

"You might want to change first." Philip grinned. He walked to the balcony and brought in the black maid's uniform and white apron. "You can dress in the bathroom." He pointed to a door. "The door has a lock, it's perfectly safe."

Amelia carried the clothes into the bathroom and leaned against the sink. What was she doing eating breakfast with a strange man in his studio apartment in Rome? She pulled the shirt over her head and thought it had been nice to talk to someone who didn't want to know her favorite brand of lipstick or if she really met Tom Cruise and was he taller in person? Maybe Whit was right, they'd be happier if she worked fifteen-hour days at a hospital. Then she imagined the crowded movie set: the big cameras, the noisy technicians, the moment when the director yelled action and she felt as if she were walking on air.

She opened the bathroom door and found Philip sitting at the table. He was reading the newspaper and drinking a second cup of coffee.

"Well, you don't quite look like a drowned rat." He smiled.

Amelia touched her hair and fiddled with her apron. She glanced at the dirty breakfast dishes and the rumpled bed and suddenly felt embarrassed.

"Thank you." She held out her hand. "You've been very kind."

"It's nice to meet a fellow American." Philip nodded. "They say the French are snobs but the Italians give them a run for their money. They think the only good thing that came out of America is spaghetti Westerns."

Amelia ran down the cement steps and onto the street. It was almost noon and the cobblestones were bathed in sunshine. Amelia saw tourists lugging cameras and Italian men wearing silk suits. She saw street vendors selling warm pretzels and roasted chestnuts wrapped in newspaper.

Amelia saw the Spanish Steps rising in front of her and realized that last night she must have been walking in circles. Philip's apartment was only a few blocks from the Piazza di Spagna. She ran up the steps two at a time, passing couples basking in the sun and women selling bunches of daisies.

She approached the Hassler Hotel and pulled the scarf tight around her hair. She slunk around to the kitchen door and slipped quickly inside. She ran down the staircase to the basement and entered the laundry.

Amelia gingerly turned on a light and breathed a sigh of relief. The laundry bag was stored safely in the locker and the vast room was empty. She peeled off the uniform and folded it neatly. She stepped into her pink satin evening gown and strapped on the Prada sandals.

She grabbed her phone and called Sheldon's number. She reached his voice mail and left a message explaining she overslept. She was never good at time changes and was terribly sorry.

She was about to run up the stairs when she heard footsteps. She ducked behind the lockers and saw a woman enter the room. She had white-blond hair and wore a white lace dress and leather sandals. She glanced quickly around and climbed into a laundry basket.

Amelia held her breath and watched the woman cover herself with towels. She heard voices and saw two men race down the stairs and burst into the room. They spoke over each other in rapid Italian, gesturing with their hands. They shrugged their shoulders and disappeared into the hallway.

"*Merde,*" the woman exclaimed, tossing the towels on the floor. She climbed out of the laundry basket and lost her footing. She tumbled headfirst and landed hard on the wood floor. She lay with her arms sprawled and her ankle jutting at an odd angle.

"Are you all right?" Amelia rushed from behind the locker. She knelt down and saw a purple bruise forming on the young woman's forehead.

*"Merde alore!"* the woman moaned. She had pale blue eyes and alabaster skin. Her hair was knotted in a low ponytail and she wore a gold necklace around her neck.

*"Êtes vous blessé?"* Amelia asked, trying to remember her high school French.

"I think I twisted my ankle," the woman replied in accented English. "And my head feels like it's been attacked by a flock of seagulls."

"I'll get the hotel doctor." Amelia stood up. "Concussions can be serious."

"No!" The woman put out her hand. "Help me up, I'll be fine."

Amelia gingerly pulled her up and let her rest on her arm. The woman took a step forward and sunk abruptly to the floor.

"My ankle is crap," she said miserably, sitting in a heap on the floor.

"Why don't you want me to call the doctor?" Amelia frowned. "Were those two men following you?"

"I don't know, I don't think so," the woman mused. She looked at Amelia and her eyes were watery. "There's a clinic down the street. Help me get there and I'll explain."

Amelia gazed at the growing bump on the woman's forehead and the blue bird's egg on her ankle. She thought of Sheldon impatiently waiting on the set and photographers lurking in the alley. Perhaps the two men had seen her slip in the back door and were looking for her. But why did the woman climb into the laundry basket unless she was hiding from something?

"I really have to be somewhere." Amelia hesitated.

"Please." She touched her hand. "It's very important, you'd be doing me a huge favor."

Amelia sighed and took the woman's hand. She couldn't just leave her on the floor of the laundry room. "All right, but I don't even know your name."

"It's Sophie." The woman accepted her hand and her face broke into a small smile. "It's a pleasure to meet you."

They walked down a narrow alley onto the Via Gregoriana. Sophie stopped in front of a brick building with a bright yellow awning. She opened the door and entered a waiting room. There was a thin gray rug over white linoleum and two red vinyl chairs. Fluorescent lights shone from the ceiling and a plastic plant stood in the corner.

"Thank god it's run by Americans." Sophie sat gingerly on the chair. "Or it would be closed for the noon siesta."

"Do you come here often?" Amelia frowned at the worn magazines and the half-empty coffeepot.

"Only once, I have asthma," Sophie explained, twisting her ponytail around her fingers. "They have two doctors, they're both ancient but they're kind and they don't make you wait for hours."

The receptionist said something to Sophie in Italian and handed her a metal clipboard. A nurse ushered them into a small room with a gray stool and a plain white table.

"I can wait outside." Amelia hesitated.

"Please, stay." Sophie winced, leaning against the table. "I'm a baby when it comes to pain."

The nurse took the clipboard and closed the door. Amelia gazed down at her pink Balenciaga gown and her jeweled Prada sandals and stifled a giggle. She hadn't expected to spend her second day in Rome in a spartan clinic lending moral support to a stranger.

A man entered the room. "You look pretty banged up." He had blond hair and green eyes and a cleft on his chin. He wore a white coat and couldn't have been more than thirty.

"I tripped down the stairs," Sophie said, avoiding Amelia's eyes. "I've always been a klutz."

"You've got a pretty healthy bump." The doctor pressed her forehead softly. He shone a light in Sophie's eyes and placed his fingers on her wrist. "But I don't think there's serious damage."

"What about her ankle?" Amelia asked. "She can't walk."

The doctor maneuvered Sophie's ankle and she let out a sharp moan. He wrapped it in a thick white bandage and secured it with tape.

"I'll write a prescription for the pain." He scribbled on a white notepad and handed it to Sophie. "I'd spend the next few days with my feet up reading romances." His eyes sparkled and his face broke into a smile. "But I think you'll be good as new."

Sophie limped to the waiting room and Amelia opened the front door. They were about to walk into the street when the doctor appeared with the clipboard.

"You didn't fill in your name." He waved it at Sophie.

"You didn't tell me yours either." Sophie smiled and shut the door behind her.


"That was miserable," Sophie said when they reached the alley behind the Hassler. "I'm starving and dying of thirst. We deserve a bottle of red wine and a plate of spaghetti marinara."

"You shouldn't drink if you're taking medicine," Amelia replied, taking her phone out of her purse and glancing at the screen.

Sheldon had left a message saying the wardrobe hadn't arrived and filming would start tomorrow. Amelia let her shoulders relax and followed Sophie to a trattoria with round tables covered with checkered tablecloths and bottles of wine hanging from the ceiling. She smelled tomato and garlic and realized she hadn't eaten since Philip's break-fast.

"If I drink I won't have to take anything for the pain." Sophie grinned. "Don't worry, one glass is my limit. I promised I'd explain and it will be a lot easier over a platter of shrimp scampi and a bottle of Chianti. I know the perfect place, it's called Trattoria da Giggi. The waiters are horrid but they serve the best bruschetta in Rome."

"Why would we want to eat in a restaurant with rude waiters?" Amelia wrinkled her brow.

"Trust me." Sophie grabbed her hand. "You won't forget it."

They walked slowly down the Spanish Steps and onto the Via Belsiana. They entered a small restaurant with brown leather booths and smoky mirrors. Amelia gazed at the open kitchen and saw huge plates of prosciutto and mozzarella. There were bowls of rigatoni with porcini and spaghetti tossed with clams. She saw round pizzas topped with artichoke and spicy sausage and round red tomatoes. There was a tray of bruschetta with a dozen different toppings.

"The waiters take pride in being rude to tourists because they'd rather serve the locals," Sophie explained, nibbling a breadstick. "I ordered in Italian, they brought me double servings of anything I wanted."

"I would think tourists tip better," Amelia replied, deciding between the tortellini con Parma and the lasagna al forno.

"Italians don't care about money." Sophie signaled a waiter. "They'd rather feel superior."

Amelia watched Sophie converse with the waiter, pointing animatedly at the menu. Amelia studied her upturned nose and creamy white skin and thought she looked like a character in a Disney movie. Her hair was so blond it was almost white and her blue eyes were rimmed with thick lashes. She wore a gold necklace with the letter "S" around her neck and a heart-shaped diamond watch on her wrist.

"How long have you been in Rome?" Amelia asked when the waiter brought white porcelain plates of ravioli with ricotta and spinach and osso buco with wild mushrooms. He poured glasses of a full-bodied red wine and left a basket of fragrant olive bread.

"Three weeks," Sophie sipped her wine. "It's the most glorious city. Everyone sleeps until noon and eats and drinks until midnight. I've seen the Villa Borghese and the Roman Forum and Saint Peter's Basilica. I can't possibly take the doctor's advice and keep my foot up." She frowned, eating a forkful of ravioli. "I still have to visit Palatine Hill and the Colosseum and Hadrian's Villa."

"I'm here for two months." Amelia sighed. "But I probably won't see more than the Trevi Fountain."

"Why not?" Sophie asked.

Amelia put down her glass of wine and looked at Sophie. She had been so concerned with getting her to the clinic and making sure she was all right, she hadn't thought about the paparazzi. Now she glanced around the cramped restaurant to see if anyone was hovering with a camera.

"You don't recognize me?" Amelia asked.

"Should I?" Sophie raised her eyebrow.

"I'm Amelia Tate. I'm playing the lead in the remake of *Roman Holiday*. The producer is brilliant but he's a slave driver. I don't think sightseeing tours are in my contract."

"My father doesn't let me see movies," Sophie mused. "Or eat at restaurants or shop at department stores."

"He sounds like a dictator." Amelia frowned.

"He's a king actually." Sophie patted her mouth with a napkin. "Crown Prince Alfred of Lentz."

"I don't understand," Amelia replied.

"My full name is Princess Sophia Victoria de Grasse. In December my father is stepping down and I'm going to be crowned Queen of Lentz. We are a small country between Germany and Austria, famous for our cows and chocolate.

"I'm supposed to be on the royal yacht in Portofino, planning my wedding. But I convinced my lady-in-waiting to pretend I was quarantined with the measles and I took the train to Rome. I have six glorious weeks to do anything I want: eat an ice-cream cone, run in the grass with bare feet, shop at the boutiques on the Via Condotti. I bought this dress today, it's vintage Fendi."

"Crown princes, ladies-in-waiting?" Amelia laughed. "You're making this up."

"Small monarchies in Europe are very real." Sophie sipped her wine. "I attended Saint George's Ecole in Geneva, there were twelve princes and princesses in my class. It's a job like anything else: we bless hospitals and name ships and open factories."

Amelia studied Sophie's blue eyes and pink mouth and realized she was perfectly serious.

"How does your fiancé feel about you disappearing?" Amelia wrapped spaghetti around her fork.

"I haven't seen him since I was twelve years old and he was sent to boarding school in America."

"You're having an arranged marriage?" Amelia spluttered.

"The monarchy is dying out, it's my job to produce a suitable heir." Sophie's eyes were serious. "I'm sure Prince Leopold is perfectly nice. He never pulled my hair or put spiders down my dress when we were children and I remember he had beautiful green eyes."

"You can't be serious." Amelia put down her fork. "This is the twenty-first century, arranged marriages went out in the Dark Ages."

"India is the most populated country in the world and arranged marriages are the norm," Sophie argued. "My mother and father played with each other in the royal nursery and didn't meet again until the week before their wedding. They did everything together: skied in the French Alps, sailed around the Greek Islands, hunted in the Black Forest." Sophie's lips wavered. "She died when I was eleven."

"What happened?" Amelia asked.

"A riding accident." Sophie's eyes darkened. "My father never married again, he didn't want me to turn into Cinderella. I had the most wonderful childhood with my own skating rink and stables. Now it's my turn to do something for him. I'm going to be the best ruler Lentz has seen in centuries."

"I don't know what to say." Amelia finished her wine. "I thought it was difficult being an actress. Audrey Hepburn was one of the most-loved actresses in film and the paparazzi are waiting for me to fail. They write articles about whether my waist is too wide or if I have her smile."

"You're gorgeous," Sophie replied. "My father doesn't let photographers near the palace, we take one royal photo at Christmas. People might know my name, but they don't recognize me."

"My boyfriend isn't very happy that I'm an actress." Amelia frowned. "He hates that we live in different cities and only see each other on weekends. And he hates the paparazzi that started following us since I got the lead in *Roman Holiday*. He wishes I went to medical school and was doing my residency in San Francisco."

"Marriage is much more sensible as a business arrangement." Sophie nodded, folding her napkin into precise squares and placing it on her plate.

"I couldn't live without love." Amelia gazed at a young couple sharing a bowl of hazelnut gelato. They fed each other small spoonfuls, laughing and chattering in Italian. Amelia remembered strolling along Union Street with Whit and eating Tutti Frutti frozen yogurt. She pictured Whit taking off his jacket and draping it around her shoulders to protect her from the evening fog.

"I should go." Amelia pushed back her chair. "I'm still on California time and I'm exhausted."

"I'll walk with you. My head is beginning to feel like it's been split open with a hammer."

They left a wad of euros on the table and walked into the street. It was late afternoon and tourists strolled along the sidewalk, licking cones of spumoni. Amelia saw children playing next to the Trevi Fountain and a boy strumming a guitar on the Spanish Steps.


"Here's my room number." Sophie stopped in the lobby and scribbled on a piece of paper. "I owe you dinner for helping me to the clinic, that was very kind of you."

"I'll be working fourteen hours a day, but if I get a moment I'd love to." Amelia slipped the paper into her purse.

Amelia took the elevator to the seventh floor and opened the door to her suite. She put her purse on the pink marble end table and sat on the beige silk sofa. She gazed at the vase of purple irises, the minibar stocked with French champagne, the sketch by Tintoretto hanging over the fireplace.

She pictured Audrey Hepburn sitting in the same spot, and wondered if she ever felt lonely. On the screen she was always perfectly composed but she must have had difficult love affairs, disapproving parents, brushes with the press.

Amelia pictured Whit's curly dark hair and blue eyes. She saw him fastening the diamond teardrop earrings in her ears and suddenly felt cold and tired. She drew a cashmere blanket over her shoulders, curled up on the sofa, and fell asleep.

# chapter three

P hilip opened his laptop and scrolled through his e-mails. He ran
his hands through his hair and poured another cup of black coffee. If he didn't get another freelance job soon he'd have to tell Signora
Griselda he was late with the rent. He gazed at the wooden bedside
table, wondering if she would accept his leather watch or a few
American sport coats.

When he moved to Rome, Adam promised him the title of news
editor and his own corner office. They had been friends at Columbia
Journalism School and Adam started a newspaper in Rome for American expats.

"It won't have the usual baseball scores and Hollywood gossip you
get in foreign newspapers," Adam said, pacing around the living room
of Philip's East Village walk-up. "It will be about Rome: the local poli-
tics, the best restaurants, the latest exhibits. And it won't be written by
Italians trying to promote their favorite tourist traps. I'll hire journalists who have their finger on the pulse of the city."

Philip loved crossing the Piazza di Trevi and climbing four flights of stairs to the newspaper's cramped headquarters. He didn't mind sharing his office with the fax machine and the microwave and the coffee-maker. He enjoyed putting dinners at Alfredo's on his expense account and writing about the Tintoretto exhibit at the National Museum.

But Adam discovered that American expats weren't interested in Rome, they only cared about news from America. The minute they touched down at Rome Airport and rented an apartment in Trastevere, they wanted to know if the Yankees were winning or which actor was entering rehab.

The glossy weekly edition became a two-color bimonthly and Philip became the style editor and the sports columnist. He watched Adam pour over the monthly ledgers, chewing packets of TUMS and drinking bottles of Coca Cola.

Philip started looking for freelance work at *La Repubblica* and *La Messengeria* and *Le Tempo*. But every college kid who spent the summer abroad decided to try their hand at writing. Philip saw them loitering in the reception area in their pressed blue jeans and collared shirts. They were happy to work for the price of a plate of linguini and a glass of Chianti.

Philip skimmed through his e-mails, wishing he could approach the Rome office of the *Wall Street Journal* or the *New York Times*. But after three years he didn't know if his name rang a bell and if the editor in chief knew he had been fired.

He pictured his old cubicle at the *New York Times* with the quote by Edward Morrow above his desk. He remembered the constant smell of cigarette smoke and sweat. He imagined his byline on the financial page and felt like he had been punched in the stomach. He closed his laptop and poured the remains of his coffee in the sink.

"It smells like bacon," a male voice said. "I haven't eaten a thing since breakfast and I'm starving."

"Help yourself." Philip pointed to a plate of half-eaten bacon on the kitchen counter. "The coffee is cold but there's toast and orange juice."

"The countess's chef made egg white omelets with prosciutto and porcini mushrooms." Max pulled out a chair. He had wavy blond hair and blue eyes like a young Robert Redford. He wore blue jeans and a yellow shirt and white sneakers. "We sipped Bellinis on the balcony and listened to Verdi and Puccini."

"No thanks." Philip wiped plates with a cotton cloth. "I'd rather eat dry toast than sleep with an aging countess."

"Mirabella Tozzi is a European woman of a certain age, there's a difference." Max buttered a slice of toast. "I enjoy a lot more about her than her chef's cooking."

"That's because you're young and think happiness lies between the sheets," Philip sighed. "Wait until your heart gets trampled or your wallet is emptied."

"I'm like the Tin Man, I don't have a heart." Max poured a glass of orange juice. "And I don't have enough money to buy a woman a steak dinner."

Max bent down and picked a white silk ribbon off the floor. He glanced at the rumpled bed and whistled.

"It looks like you had company."

"It's not what you think." Philip draped the dishcloth over his shoulder. "I met a girl at the taxi stand, she was sopping wet so I offered to share my cab. She forgot where she left her purse and asked if we could drive around, the next thing I knew she fell asleep on my shoulder."

"So you brought her here?" Max spluttered.

"What was I supposed to do?" Philip demanded. "I let her sleep in my bed and I camped on the sofa. It was the most uncomfortable night I've had in weeks."

"Was she pretty?" Max asked.

"Her wet hair stuck to her head, and her cheeks were smudged with mascara," Philip mused, eating a slice of bacon. "But she had beautiful brown eyes and the sexiest knees I've ever seen."

"You saw her knees?" Max raised his eyebrow.

"Her uniform was soaked so I lent her a shirt," Philip explained. "She's a maid at the Hassler."

Philip tossed the last piece of bacon in the garbage and put the orange juice in the fridge. "Nothing happened and I'll probably never see her again."

"Adam sent me to photograph the press conference at the Hassler. There were fifty female journalists and a buffet of oysters and lobster ravioli and lamb medallions." Max reached for his camera and clicked through the photos. "Look at that ice sculpture and see the woman behind it. She's a reporter for *Paris Match*. Five foot eight inches of blond hair and long legs and pouty lips. I tried to get her phone number but she said something rude in French."

Philip glanced at the photo and saw a familiar figure in the background. She had glossy brown hair and large brown eyes and wore a diamond pendant around her neck.

"Give me that." Philip took the camera and studied it carefully.

"You can't have Francoise," Max replied. "But I met a cute redheaded reporter from London."

"That's her." Philip pointed to the screen. "That's the girl in the taxi."

Max peered at the camera and frowned. "That's Amelia Tate, the star of *Roman Holiday*. She's the new It girl, the press conference was in her honor."

"I'd recognize those eyes anywhere," Philip insisted. "They belong on a young deer."

Max took the camera and grinned. "Maybe you fell harder for the maid than you think but that's definitely not her. She wore a pink satin ball gown and a diamond pendant that cost more than a Fiat."

Philip shrugged and walked to his laptop. He stared at his empty inbox and rubbed his forehead.

"We're having a poker game tonight at Canova." Max stood up. "You should join us."

"I don't have any money." Philip shook his head.

"I'll lend you ten euros." Max reached into his pocket and handed him a ten-euro note.

"Why would you lend me money to play poker?" Philip asked.

"Because you're the only person broker than I am." Max grinned, walking to the door. "It makes me feel better to see you lose."


Philip looked around the lobby of the Grand Hotel, feeling as nervous as a schoolboy. He glanced in the gilt mirror and straightened his tie and smoothed his hair. He crossed the black and white marble and approached a man with gray hair and an angular nose.

"Nice suit, Dad." He held out his hand. "It matches your eyes."

John Hamilton brushed the jacket of his gray herringbone suit. He shook Philip's hand and motioned him to sit in a red velvet chair.

"I stopped in London to see my tailor." John placed his glass on a cocktail napkin. "Will you join me in a dry martini? The Grand makes the best martinis, with just the right amount of vermouth."

"No thanks, I can't afford to drink before six P.M.," Philip gazed at the crystal chandeliers and plush velvet furniture. The walls were covered with ornate tapestries and the ceiling was inlaid with gold mosaic. A harp stood in the corner and crystal vases were filled with white and yellow tulips. "So what brings you to Rome?"

"I came to see you." John scooped a handful of macadamia nuts from the silver dish. He had steel gray hair and gray eyes and a cleft on his chin. He wore a white silk shirt and a yellow tie and black tasseled shoes.

"I thought maybe you were here to add to your Renaissance art collection." Philip shrugged, feeling suddenly hot under his blue blazer.

"I've chosen your secretary," John mused. "Edna is retiring but she recommended her niece. I thought you could have the office on the seventeenth floor. It's not the biggest space but it has the best view of Wall Street."

Philip looked at his father's narrow cheeks and fine mouth and resisted the urge to punch him in the jaw.

"I'm not coming to work for you."

"We made an agreement." John stirred his drink. "And Hamilton men keep their word."

"I don't know anything about being a stockbroker," Philip protested. "Why would you want me to work in the firm?"

"Because the plaque on the building says Hamilton and Sons." John tapped his fingers on the table. "Your mother wants grandchildren, how is she going to get them if you can't afford a cocktail?"

Philip leaned back in his chair and loosened his tie. He remembered the week before his graduation from Yale when he told his father he wasn't joining the family firm. He paced around the foyer of his parents' Central Park duplex, trying to stop his heart from racing. Finally he crossed the pink and white marble floor and knocked on the door of his father's study.

"Come in," John beamed. He wore a white silk shirt and gray slacks. A gold Patek Philippe dangled at his wrist and he wore black Ferragamo shoes.

Philip entered the room and gazed at the Titian on the wall. There was a Rembrandt sketch above the marble fireplace and a Botticelli painting of a young woman holding a vase.

"You've moved things around." Philip glanced at the wide cherry desk and the deep leather chairs. A white wool rug covered the polished wood floor and a round glass table held a crystal decanter and an ivory chess set.

"Your mother loves to redecorate." John smiled. "As long as she doesn't touch my Botticelli she can do what she likes."

"I want to talk to you about my plans after graduation," Philip began. He had arrived from Yale early in the morning and drank three cups of black coffee. Now his hands shook and his shirt collar was drenched with sweat.

"We thought we'd hold a dinner at the Knickerbocker Club," John interrupted. "And then you can take a few weeks' vacation, sit on a sandy beach and drink Bloody Marys and read the latest Clive Cussler. Your mother and I are going to Bermuda for August, you can start the first week of September."

"I got accepted to Columbia Journalism School," Philip blurted out. "Classes begin the last week of August."

John's eyes darkened and he sat very still. He picked up the ivory paper opener and tapped it on the desk.

"You did a great job on the *Yale Daily News,* they were lucky to have you. But journalism isn't a career, there are hardly any newspapers left. How are you going to afford a family on a reporter's salary?"

"I don't need a Jaguar and a house in East Hampton and a month every summer in Bermuda," Philip replied. "But I need to do what I love and I've wanted to be a journalist since I was twelve years old."

"Have you talked to Daphne about this?" John asked.

Philip flinched and his cheeks turned red. He pictured Daphne with her silky blond hair and graceful neck and long French nails.

"Daphne is going to Columbia to get her MBA."

John stood up and gazed at the Botticelli. He studied the girl's glossy brown hair and hazel eyes and alabaster cheeks.

"Then you owe me two hundred thousand dollars."

"I beg your pardon," Philip spluttered.

"I sent you to Yale so you could take over your grandfather's business," John replied. "I'll give you ten years to make it as a journalist, then you have to pay me back."

"How am I supposed to do that?" Philip demanded.

"You can make fifty-thousand-dollar installments, starting in the summer of 2015." John turned and looked at Philip. "If you default you have to join Hamilton and Sons."

Philip gazed at his father's graying hair and felt sweat trickle down his spine. He knew he was crazy; there was little chance he would make that kind of money. But he pictured a crowded newspaper office, the flashing computer screens, the surfaces littered with soda cans and crumpled sheets of paper and knew he had no choice.

He stood up and extended his hand. "It's a deal."

John smiled and shook his son's hand. "Did you bring Daphne? Your mother would love to see her. Shall we say seven o'clock at the Four Seasons? I'll book our usual table."


Philip gazed at his father's martini, wishing he had accepted a cocktail. He leaned forward and rubbed his forehead. "You know I was unfairly fired, I was on my way up."

John saw the anguish in his son's eyes and fiddled with his straw.

"I'm a fair man; you can pay me twenty-five thousand in August and twenty-five thousand at Christmas."

"I don't have that kind of money." Philip slumped in his chair.

John drained his glass and placed it on the napkin. He took a wad of euros out of his pocket and put it on the table.

"I'll have Edna book your flight. You can stay at the house until you get settled; your mother redid your room. We'll have a welcome home dinner at Gramercy Tavern and invite the old crowd." John stood up and smoothed his slacks. "Your mother ran into Daphne at Barneys, she said she looked wonderful. Did you know she just made associate partner?"

Philip watched his father cross the thick Oriental rug to the elevator and felt his pulse race. He remembered the last time he saw Daphne when she packed her Krups espresso maker and her Louis Vuitton cosmetics case and her closet of Donna Karan suits and moved to a brownstone on the Upper West Side. He remembered lying on the sofa and gazing at the leak in the ceiling and feeling like he'd been run over by a truck. He remembered long hours of tapping on his computer and running laps around Washington Square.

Philip reached into his pocket and took out Max's ten-euro note. He scooped up a handful of macadamia nuts and signaled the bartender.

"A dry martini please." He handed him the note. "Straight up, no ice."

# chapter four

A melia perused the platters of roast beef and sliced ham and bread rolls. She saw bowls of M&M'S and plates of chocolate chip cookies and baskets of bananas and green apples. She saw cartons of cold cereal and cans of soda and smiled. No matter where one was on location, the food always looked like the contents of a high school cafeteria.

Amelia grabbed an apple and rubbed it against her sweater. They had been reading through the script all morning and she was hungry and tired. But the jet lag and loneliness had been replaced by a feeling of anticipation and excitement. When she looked in the mirror she saw Princess Ann in her white ball gown and long white gloves and diamond tiara.

"You were perfect," a male voice said behind her. "I knew you were my Princess Ann, your delivery is sublime."

Amelia turned and saw Sheldon Rose filling a plate with cheddar cheese and stone wheat crackers. He added a bunch of green grapes and a peanut butter cookie.

"I want to apologize again for yesterday," Amelia explained. "It was the champagne and the jet lag, I'll never miss a call again."

"When I made *Picasso's Mistress* with Natalie Portman, she missed the first two days of production. I finally tracked her down to an artist's studio on a cliff in Majorca. She was splattered in paint and staring at an empty canvas." Sheldon smiled. He was in his early sixties with thick white hair and horn-rimmed glasses. He wore a beige sweater over a collared shirt and khakis. "I can allow my lead actress some leeway if she delivers a great performance. Audrey Hepburn won an Oscar for her Princess Ann, I think you can do the same."

Amelia watched Sheldon cross the room to talk to the director and pictured Sophie's large blue eyes and upturned nose and creamy white skin. Even before she told Amelia she was a princess there had been something regal about her. She thought about her stories of arranged marriages and ladies-in-waiting and suddenly had an idea. There was no better way to capture the essence of Princess Ann than spend time with a real princess.

Amelia took the elevator to the sixth floor and walked down the hallway. She was still floating from Sheldon's praise and from reading the script. She felt like Princess Ann was slipping under her skin, the way she raised her eyebrows when she talked, her shy smile, the way she wore her hair.

Amelia knocked on the door and waited.

Sophie flung open the door. "I'm so glad you're here." She wore a white crepe dress and flat gold sandals. Her hair was knotted in a low bun and she wore a gold belt around her waist. "I've been shopping all day and I'm exhausted."

Amelia entered Sophie's suite and saw bags scattered over the marble floor. Silk dresses and cotton blouses covered the gold velvet bedspread. There was a stack of shoeboxes on the glass coffee table and a pink ostrich Hermès bag on the Regency desk.

"Where did you get all this?" Amelia fingered a silver evening gown and a floral sundress and a pink angora sweater. There was a pile of silk scarves and several pair of sunglasses.

"The Via Condotti has Prada and Gucci and Armani boutiques." Sophie wrapped a red silk scarf around her neck and stood in front of the full-length mirror. "I've always had a dressmaker who comes to the palace. Do you know what it's like to walk into a shop and try on anything you like?"

"What about when you were at boarding school?" Amelia asked.

"My father sent me with six suitcases of clothes." Sophie tried on round white sunglasses. "He didn't want me becoming Eurotrash in halter tops and miniskirts. Lentz is very conservative; all my dresses had high collars and lots of buttons."

"This must have cost a fortune." Amelia gazed at the ostrich-skin bag and soft Prada pumps.

"I pawned a tiara." Sophie shrugged.

"You pawned a tiara!" Amelia spluttered.

"It was only a small tiara, nothing my father would miss. I didn't have any money, my lady-in-waiting takes care of my expenses."

"I keep thinking you're making this up," Amelia mused, walking to the window. The red rooftops were bathed in the afternoon sun. Amelia could hear cars honking and the low rumble of buses. She peered down at the street and saw uniformed crossing guards and bicycle messengers with brown leather satchels.

"Monarchy is about tradition." Sophie took off the sunglasses and sat on a blue silk sofa. She crossed her long legs and tapped her fingers on the coffee table. "Do you know why Catholics revere the Pope? It's because no matter what terrible things happen in their lives—losing a job or finding out their husband is unfaithful or having a sick child—they can always go to the Pope for comfort. The Pope never changes; he never has his own problems or appears on the balcony of the Vatican in board shorts and flip-flops."

"I never thought about it like that." Amelia nodded.

"For six weeks I get to wear whatever I want and do what I please and no one will know." Sophie's eyes sparkled. "Let's go out, there's somewhere I want to show you."

"You're supposed to keep your foot up." Amelia hesitated, glancing at Sophie's ankle that was still wrapped in a bandage.

"I'll be careful," Sophie persisted. "I only have twenty days left, I don't want to waste them."

"If we're seen together the paparazzi might follow us." Amelia shook her head.

"Not if you wear this." Sophie handed Amelia a large floppy hat and a pair of oversized sunglasses.

"On one condition." Amelia slipped on the sunglasses. "You teach me how to be a princess."

Sophie's face broke into a wide smile and she tied a white scarf around her hair. "I'd be delighted."

"The Villa Borghese was built in 1605 for Pope Paul V's nephew, Cardinal Scipione Borghese, it was the most luxurious residence in Rome," Sophie said, smoothing her hair. "Now it is one of the largest parks in the city, with a museum and galleries and a private lake."

Amelia followed Sophie through the entrance on the Piazza del Popolo and gazed at the leafy trees and colorful gardens and marble statues. She saw couples on bicycles and children clutching pencil boxes and sketch pads. She smelled roses and bougainvilleas and hyacinths.

She walked along the gravel path, remembering Sundays at Golden Gate Park. Whit never worked on Sundays and they often attended outdoor concerts. Amelia loved strolling through the rose garden or flying a kite on the grass. When they got hungry they ate scones and jam in the Japanese Tea Garden.

"It's as if the city didn't exist," Amelia mused, standing in the Flower Garden. The noise and congestion of Rome stopped outside the gates. The only sounds were ducks splashing in the lake and children playing hopscotch on the cement.

"The Romans loved the Borghese family because they opened the park to the public on Sundays and public holidays." Sophie admired the marble arches covered with green trellises. "I want to create a park like this in Lentz, a place where people can come after church and bring their children. I'm going to fill it with roses and oak trees and a coffeehouse and a carrousel."

Amelia gazed at the lake and saw a familiar figure sitting on a stone bench. He held a turkey sandwich and a bag of roasted chestnuts. He had blond hair and wore jeans and a polo shirt.

"You are the patient who didn't write her name on the clipboard," the man said to Sophie, walking toward them.

"How did you recognize me?" Sophie asked. She wore a white tunic dress and flat sandals. Her blond hair was pulled into a ponytail and tucked under her scarf.

"I know my own handiwork." The man grinned, pointing to her bandaged ankle. "My name is Theo."

"Sophie." Sophie gingerly shook his hand. "This is my friend, Ann."

"I told you to keep your foot up." Theo frowned.

"I'm good as new." Sophie waved her hand. "I wanted to show Ann the Borghese Gardens. It's my favorite place in Rome."

"What do you do when you're not falling down staircases or disobeying doctor's orders?" Theo asked, eating a handful of chestnuts.

"Do?" Sophie repeated.

"Do you live in Rome or are you on vacation?" Theo prompted.

Sophie watched a group of schoolchildren throw bread crumbs into the lake and turned to Theo. "We're tour guides, we lead school tours all over the city."

"I volunteer at an orphanage once a week." Theo's eyes lit up. "It's my favorite part of being a doctor."

"We have to go." Sophie tugged Amelia's arm. "It was a pleasure to meet you."

"You should make your friend rest." Theo turned to Amelia. He had smooth brown cheeks and a small cleft on his chin. "She'll heal faster if she follows my orders."


"Why did you say we were tour guides?" Amelia asked, sipping an iced coffee. They had spent an hour in the gallery admiring the paintings by Titian and Raphael and Caravaggio. Now they sat at the outdoor café, drinking iced coffees and sharing a chestnut puree.

"I got flustered." Sophie shrugged, scooping up whipped cream and nuts. "If I told him we were tourists he would have asked where we were from."

"He's very handsome." Amelia looked at Sophie pointedly.

Sophie looked up from her iced coffee and flushed. "I didn't notice."

They finished their coffees and visited the Temple of Diana and the Pincian Hill. Amelia looked down on the Villa Medici and wished

Whit was standing beside her. She wanted to show him the lush gardens and the statues by Bernini and Rubens and Canova.

"My feet are killing me," Amelia said. "Let's go home. I want to take a hot shower."

They walked to the entrance and stood in line for a taxi. Amelia saw Theo striding toward them, his hands jammed into his pockets.

"You should come with me," he said to Sophie when he reached the taxi stand.

"Come with you where?" Sophie peered at him from behind her sunglasses.

"To the orphanage," Theo continued, running his hands through his hair. "I'm driving there tomorrow."

"Why would I go with you?" Sophie asked.

"The children never see any women except the nuns," Theo explained. "It would be lovely for them to meet a beautiful young woman."

Sophie lowered her eyes and studied the pavement. She saw a taxi pull up in front of them and turned to Theo. "All right, I'll come."

"That's wonderful!" Theo beamed. "Where shall I pick you up?"

Sophie climbed into the taxi and leaned out the window. "I'll meet you at ten o'clock at the top of the Spanish Steps."


"What was I thinking? I've never done anything like that before," Sophie groaned, pulling off her scarf. She sat on the blue silk sofa in her suite with her foot propped on an ottoman. The curtains were open and the sun had dropped behind Saint Peter's Basilica. The sky turned purple and a light fog settled over the rooftops.

"He's cute and he liked you," Amelia replied, reclining against the yellow silk cushions.

"I'm engaged!" Sophie exclaimed. "I didn't mean to say yes, it popped out of my mouth."

"Do you really have no contact with your fiancé?" Amelia raised her eyebrow.

"My father thought it was best." Sophie hesitated. "He didn't want us to be tempted before the wedding."

"You must have had boyfriends," Amelia continued.

"We had dances at boarding school." Sophie reached down and massaged her ankle. Her long lashes were coated with thick mascara and she wore light powder and pink lip gloss. "I kissed a lot of boys, but it was as exciting as practicing on a pillow."

"You've never . . . ?" Amelia stopped, trying to find the right words.

"I don't mind waiting until I'm married; I have my whole life ahead of me." Sophie twisted her ponytail. "I should call Theo and tell him I can't come."

"He'll be disappointed," Amelia replied. "He was as excited as an overgrown puppy."

"I want to visit the orphanage but I don't want to give him the wrong impression." Sophie's eyes were wide and she bit her lower lip.

"Welcome to the world of dating." Amelia laughed. "It's like a Shakespeare play. No one says what they mean and someone's heart is bound to get broken."

Amelia took the elevator to the lobby and crossed the marble floor to the gift shop. It was early evening and the space was filled with men in dark silk suits and women in glittering cocktail dresses and narrow stilettos. Amelia glanced at the striped velvet sofas and mirrored walls and ornate ceilings and caught her breath. Even the fragrance from the huge vases of yellow roses was intoxicating.

She purchased *Vanity Fair* and *Variety* and a packet of Life Savers. She was tired from spending all morning on the set and the afternoon at the Villa Borghese. She wanted to curl up in bed with a room service tray of insalata mista and gnocchi pomodoro and tiramisu.

She walked toward the elevator and saw a man standing at the reception desk. He had dark curly hair and wore a blue blazer with beige slacks. He had a leather backpack slung over his shoulder and clutched a bouquet of pink roses.

Amelia froze, her heart hammering in her chest. Whit couldn't possibly be here. He wasn't the kind of person who jumped on a plane and flew over the Atlantic to surprise her. She ran toward the desk and tripped on the Oriental rug. Her package went flying and her magazines spilled on the floor.

She scrambled to collect the magazines and felt a hand on her arm. She looked up and saw Whit's blue eyes and white smile.

"What are you doing here?" she stammered.

Whit found her hair clip and fastened it in her hair. He gathered the magazines and slipped them in his backpack. He leaned down and kissed her on the mouth. "I came to take you to dinner."

"You didn't fly to Rome to take me to dinner," Amelia said, standing on the balcony of the Villa Medici Suite.

Whit stood beside her, gazing at the outdoor bar and marble fireplace. The balcony had a polished travertine floor and a glass dining room table and leather chairs. Music played on hidden speakers and twinkling lights bathed the space in a yellow glow.

"Evan has been trying to hire Alex Tomaselli, the top designer at Maserati, for months." Whit turned his eyes to the skyline. "I volunteered to fly over and close the deal."

"That was noble of you." Amelia giggled, breathing in his Hugo Boss cologne.

"I have heard Rome has delicious food," Whit mused, pulling her toward him. "Apparently the pizza is better than in America."

"I was going to order room service," Amelia murmured, pressing herself against his chest.

"I'd like to take you somewhere where we can talk." Whit's eyes suddenly clouded over. "Somewhere quiet where we can eat pasta and drink a bottle of Italian wine."

"That sounds lovely." Amelia felt a pinprick of uneasiness. She turned and gazed at the bright lights of the Colosseum and the wide dome of Saint Peter's Basilica.

"The restaurants in Rome stay open late," Whit continued. "Most people don't eat dinner until ten P.M."

"Is that true?" Amelia whispered, standing on tiptoes. She kissed Whit on the mouth, running her palm over his shirt.

"That gives us plenty of time to take a nap." Whit kissed her harder. He grabbed her hand and pulled her into the master bedroom. He took off his blazer and folded it over a velvet chair. He turned to Amelia and unzipped her linen dress.

"Suddenly I don't feel tired." Amelia fumbled with his belt and unzipped his slacks. She slipped off her sandals and turned down the cotton sheets.

Amelia wrapped her arms around him, pulling him on top of her. She wanted to feel his slick thighs against hers, his mouth biting her lips, his hands in her hair. She wanted him to carry her with him, fill her up, take her over the edge.

Whit paused and looked in her eyes. He stroked her hair and kissed her on the mouth. He opened her legs and pushed inside her. Amelia felt the delicious sensation of letting go, of not thinking of anything except the warmth between her legs. She felt Whit pick up speed, pushing harder until they came together in one long, dizzying thrust.

"I'm still not tired," she whispered, tucking herself against his chest. "But I'm suddenly starving."

# chapter five

Amelia took Whit's hand and skipped along the cobblestones. She wore a red silk dress and gold sandals. Her hair was fastened with a gold clip and she wore Whit's diamond teardrop earrings.

They had slipped out the revolving doors of the Hassler and run down the Spanish Steps. Now they strode down an alley and approached a yellow building with marble columns. They opened the iron gate and descended the steps to a green door.

"Where are we?" Amelia asked, her eyes adjusting to the dark.

"I asked the concierge to recommend the most intimate restaurant in Rome and they suggested Il Gabriello." Whit stood in the stone entry. "It's in the basement of a seventeenth-century palazzo. The staff is discreet and they serve the best ricotta ravioli and truffled omelets in the city."

Amelia saw a small room with brick arches and a low ceiling. Square tables were set with white tablecloths and sterling silverware. There was a floor-to-ceiling wine rack and a wall filled with murals of heirloom tomatoes and green peppers and purple eggplant.

They sat at a table in the back and ate fresh herb bread dipped in olive oil. The waiter brought prosciutto de Parma and veal scallops cooked in white wine. They shared a plate of bresaola and drank glasses of Chianti.

They talked about her suite at the Hassler and Sheldon and the movie set. Amelia was about to mention the first night's gala but suddenly bit her lip. She didn't want to spoil the evening by talking about escaping from a room full of journalists.

"We met with Sequoia Capital yesterday," Whit said, pushing back his plate. "They want to invest thirty million dollars."

"That's wonderful," Amelia exclaimed. Her cheeks were flushed from the red wine and she felt warm and happy.

"We'll be able to hire more staff and I'll have some time off," Whit continued. "We can buy a condo in Pacific Heights, take cooking classes, go to Hawaii."

Amelia ate a bite of veal and smiled. "I'll buy a swimsuit and a pair of sexy Italian sandals."

Whit put his fork down and fiddled with his napkin. He furrowed his brow and his eyes were suddenly dark.

"I'm serious," he said slowly. "I want you to quit acting and move to San Francisco."

"I can't quit now." Amelia frowned. "I'm at the height of my career, everything is in front of me."

"I don't want to come home to a stale milk carton and an empty bed. I don't want to fold my clothes alone at the Laundromat and spend my nights staring at a computer screen. And I don't want to walk down the street with photographers sticking a camera in my face and asking whether we're breaking up or getting married."

"I'm the flavor of the month," Amelia murmured. "The attention will die down after *Roman Holiday*."

"I'm sorry, I've really tried." Whit sighed, slumping in his chair. "I can't do a long-distance relationship and I can't live with the paparazzi breathing down my neck."

"What are you saying?" Amelia felt a shiver run down her spine.

"I think we should break up," Whit said slowly.

Amelia's cheeks flushed and she felt anger well up inside her. She remembered Whit's mouth on her breasts, his thighs between her legs. She remembered his slick chest and damp hair and warm breath.

"Why did you come all the way to Rome to tell me?" she demanded. "Why did you buy roses and red wine and a delicious dinner?"

"I thought if we got more funding you'd give up acting." Whit looked at his plate. "I thought if we had everything we want, you'd rather be together than make movies."

Amelia glanced at Whit's pale cheeks and white lips and her stomach turned over. She tried to think of something to say but the words stuck in her mouth.

"I'm going to go." Whit threw a wad of euros on the table and pushed back his chair.

"You can't just walk out on four years of being together." Amelia followed him up the stone steps. She felt the cool air on her cheeks and wrapped her arms around her chest.

"I'm not the one walking out." Whit turned to her. "You chose acting over us."

Amelia gazed at his dark hair and blue eyes and felt her heart hammer in her chest. She could demand he give up his company and move to Los Angeles, but what would be the point? They were like a bull and a matador circling in the ring.

"I'll walk you back to the Hassler," Whit suggested.

"You go." Amelia shook her head. "I'm going to stay here."

"It's almost midnight." Whit frowned. "You shouldn't be out alone."

"I'll be fine," Amelia mumbled.

She watched Whit cross the piazza and climb the Spanish Steps. She walked slowly along the cobblestones, listening to her heels click on the pavement. She reached the bottom of the steps and peered up into the dark. Whit was gone; all she saw was a young couple kissing and a man selling roses.

Amelia found an outdoor café in the Piazza di Venezia and ordered a glass of Barolo. She pictured Whit disappearing across the piazza and her stomach heaved. She ordered another glass of wine and tried to stop the feeling of losing everything important to her.

She sat next to an English couple who insisted on buying her a glass of champagne. She listened to them praise her acting, a smile plastered to her face. She drained her glass, scribbled her autograph on a napkin, and stumbled into the street.

Amelia entered the Piazza di Trevi and gazed up at the Trevi Fountain. She saw the stone Poli Palace and the marble figure of Neptune. She studied the statues of Abundance and Health and the chariot led by two horses. She climbed onto the ledge to get a closer look and lost her footing. She tumbled into the fountain, splashing in the cold water. She felt strong hands lift her up and deposit her on the pavement.

"It's you," a male voice said.

Amelia tried to stop shivering. Her hair was plastered to her head and her silk dress clung to her body. She looked up and saw a man with dark brown hair and an angular nose.

"I recognize you," she said numbly. "You're the man who let me share his cab."

"You seem to have an affinity with water." Philip frowned. "What were you doing on the ledge?"

"I wanted to see the animals." Amelia pointed to the fountain. "I read in the guidebook that Bracci carved squirrels and birds. It's hard to see in the dark, I was trying to get closer."

"You did a great job, you're soaking wet."

"I'll dry off." Amelia wrapped her arms around her chest. "It's a beautiful night. Do you see how many stars are in the sky? I've never seen so many stars. They're like a painting by Michelangelo."

Philip looked at her carefully, leaning close to smell her breath. "You're drunk."

Amelia thought about that and broke into a fit of giggles. "I am actually, I haven't been this drunk in ages. I was drinking a glass of wine when this lovely English couple insisted on buying me champagne to thank me for my hard work. It would have been rude to refuse."

"You must be an excellent maid if guests buy you champagne." Philip stuck his hands in his pockets. "You're going to catch cold. Let me take you home."

"I don't want to go home, I want to keep exploring." Amelia shook her head. "There's so much in Rome to see, the aqueducts and the catacombs and the Appian Way."

"It's after midnight and you're soaked," Philip replied. "The Italian police don't like tourists disturbing the peace, you'll be arrested."

"I couldn't get arrested, I'm special."

"I'm sure you're special." Philip smiled. "But that won't get you out of a Roman jail."

"Don't be silly, everyone loves me. Let's ask those nice people over there." Amelia waved at a couple strolling along the piazza. "They'll tell you."

Philip ran his hands through his hair. "If you won't go home, we'll go to my place and get you some dry clothes and a cup of coffee."

"Coffee sounds nice, with lots of milk and sugar." Amelia sighed, suddenly sleepy. "Do you have any profiteroles? They served them at the café and they're delicious."

"I think I can rummage up a profiterole." Philip nodded. "Come with me."

Amelia put the coffee cup on the chipped white saucer and smoothed her hair. Philip had given her a flannel robe and a pair of tube socks. He set the glass table with a pitcher of cream and a bowl of sugar and a plate of digestive biscuits.

"No profiteroles." He walked over from the counter and sat opposite her. "But Signora Griselda's cousin buys these biscuits in London and they're delicious."

"I'm not hungry," Amelia groaned, sipping the hot coffee. The wonderful feeling of light-headedness had been replaced by a throbbing headache. Her throat was parched and her stomach felt like it was coated in lead. "I don't understand what happened. One minute I was drinking a glass of champagne, the next I was swimming in the Trevi Fountain."

"Hardly swimming." Philip grinned, pouring cream into his coffee. "If I were you, I'd stay away from the champagne; it doesn't agree with you."

"I hardly ever get drunk." Amelia hesitated. She pictured Whit in his navy blazer and crisp white shirt and tears sprung to her eyes. "It was just . . ."

"A bad date?" Philip asked.

"You could say that." Amelia nodded.

"I gave up dating when I left New York." Philip shrugged. "The pain-to-happiness ratio isn't worth the effort. Now I have Sophia Loren."

"Sophia Loren?" Amelia raised her eyebrow.

"My parrot." Philip pointed to a striped bird in an iron birdcage. It had green feathers and a sharp black beak.

"I didn't notice her before," Amelia replied.

"She's shy around strangers but she's quite friendly when you get to know her. She can quote Elizabeth Browning and Shakespeare."

"She sounds wonderful." Amelia grinned. She scanned the room and saw a wooden desk with a silver laptop. There was a mug filled with pens and a pile of notepads. "I remember, you're a writer. What do you write?"

"This and that." Philip stirred his coffee. "These days with all the free online content, it's hard to make a living. Newspapers think you should be happy to see your name in print but that doesn't pay the rent. How about you, do you enjoy being a maid?"

Amelia blushed, remembering her lie. She wanted to tell him the truth but she was too embarrassed.

"I love what I do," she said bleakly. "But sometimes things get complicated."

"I always wanted to be a writer," Philip mused. "When I was twelve I wrote an investigative report on the rigging of the Franklin Middle School spelling bee. It made page five of the *Greenwich Gazette*. I went to Columbia Journalism School and got my first job at the *New York Post*. I hate not having enough money to buy a thick steak but I can't breathe if I'm not writing."

"I know the feeling!" Amelia exclaimed. "When you think going to work is the most exciting thing in the world."

"Maybe I'm in the wrong profession." Philip laughed. "I should apply at the Hassler as a bellboy or a valet."

"You know what I mean," Amelia insisted. "It can be being with the person you love or having a fulfilling career. That feeling when you wake up in the morning that you're the luckiest person on earth and you can't wait to start your day."

Philip gazed at Amelia and his eyes were serious. "I lost that feeling a few years ago; now I'm happy to start my day with a cup of coffee and a bowl of cereal."

"You made me a wonderful breakfast," Amelia mused. "Eggs and bacon and muesli and fresh fruit."

"That was a good day," Philip said slowly, dunking his biscuit into his coffee. "One of the best I've had in weeks."

Amelia flushed and glanced around the room. She saw the rumpled bed and the brown sofa. She saw the bookshelf crammed with books and the sink filled with dishes. Suddenly she realized she was in a strange man's apartment in the middle of the night. She pulled the robe tightly around her chest and jumped up.

"I'm late, I have to go."

"It's one o'clock in the morning," Philip protested.

"I'm on the midnight shift," Amelia spluttered. "I'll change into my dress and catch a taxi."

"The taxis don't run this late." Philip shook his head. "I'll walk with you."

"I'll be fine, just point me in the right direction."

"I can't risk you falling into another fountain or standing under a rain cloud." Philip stood up. "I'll grab my coat."

Philip retrieved her dress from the dryer and Amelia changed in the bathroom. She smoothed her hair and reapplied her lip gloss.

"No wonder you can't stay awake if you work all night," Philip said as they approached the Hassler Hotel. The moon had slipped behind a cloud and a light mist settled on the street.

"I don't always have the night shift," Amelia said uncomfortably. "It rotates."

"That's one of the benefits of being a writer, I make my own hours." Philip nodded. "Are you sure you're all right? You could call in sick and get a good night's sleep."

"I'm perfectly fine," Amelia replied as they reached the kitchen door. "You've been very kind."

"It's been a pleasure." Philip held out his hand. "Try to stay dry, you're prettier when you aren't shivering and your lips aren't blue."

Amelia slipped inside and ran up the stairs. She walked quickly through the lobby, covering her face with her purse. She entered the elevator and pressed the button for the seventh floor.

Amelia opened the door of the suite and inhaled the scent of furniture polish and roses. The living room was dark and the lights on the balcony were dimmed. She walked to the bedroom and slipped off her sandals. She unzipped her dress and climbed into bed.

She touched the silk sheets and remembered the bed was empty. She turned off the Tiffany lamp and slipped under the velvet bedspread. She let the tears stream down her cheeks and felt her heart breaking. She closed her eyes and fell asleep.

# chapter six

Philip stood on the corner of the Piazza del Popolo and gazed at the crowded cafés and elegant boutiques. He saw children playing hopscotch next to the marble fountain and a vendor selling sunflowers under the Egyptian Obelisk. He spied a man wearing a yellow collared shirt and blue jeans and white sneakers. He had a newspaper open in front of him and wore dark sunglasses.

"If you sit here any longer, they'll charge you rent," Philip mused, approaching the square table.

"Canova has the best people watching in Rome." Max folded his newspaper. "After a few hours the waitress takes pity on me and brings me free Napolitanos."

"Why the sunglasses?" Philip sat opposite him. He wore a white shirt with the sleeves rolled up and tan slacks. He had scuffed loafers on his feet and a black leather watch around his wrist. "You look like a spy in a James Bond movie."

"The countess and I were having some fun with whipped cream in the kitchen," Max replied. "Her daughter came home and found us.

Alessandria is twenty-two with long black hair and more curves than the Appian Way. Mirabella told her I was the pastry chef." Max took off his sunglasses and squinted in the sun. "It turns out Alessandria and I played footsie at Alpha's last week and she still has the hots for me. I spent the morning hiding in the pantry."

"I can't say you don't deserve it." Philip laughed, gazing longingly at Max's plate of lemon sea bass fillet and Parmesan cheese ravioli. "Don't you ever feel guilty for taking the countess's money?"

"Adam is the one who should feel guilty." Max cut a slice of fillet. "I have a fine arts degree from Parsons and he pays me less than the woman who mops the office floor."

"You'll never guess who I fished out of the Trevi Fountain last night, the maid from the Hassler. She was high as a kite on champagne and soaking wet. I took her to my apartment to dry off." Philip handed his phone to Max. "Does she look familiar?"

Max grabbed the phone and studied the photo of Amelia. Her eyes were huge and her damp hair was plastered to her head. She wore Philip's flannel robe and sipped a cup of coffee.

"That's Amelia Tate, the star of *Roman Holiday*." Max whistled.

"I told you." Philip grinned, eating a bite of Max's ravioli. "She was embarrassed when she sobered up but she still didn't tell me who she was."

"Why would one of the hottest actresses in Hollywood be running around Rome masquerading as a hotel maid?" Max leaned back in his chair.

"I would love to know," Philip mused, dipping a baguette in olive oil.

Max drummed his fingers on the white linen tablecloth and studied the photo. "You're not the only one. I bet the readers of *Inside Rome* would love to know, too."

"What are you saying?" Philip frowned.

"Adam is always complaining his readers only want to read about who George Clooney is married and who got kicked off *The Bachelor*," Max continued. "But what if you got an exclusive on Amelia Tate— the rising movie star with a dark secret?"

"We don't know she has a dark secret," Philip protested.

"She's lying about who she is, she has to have a reason," Max insisted. "We can follow her for a week, I'll take the photos. We're bound to uncover something juicy."

Philip pictured Amelia's sparkling eyes and wide smile. He saw her devouring a plate of scrambled eggs and bacon. "She's an actress, she'd know if she was being followed."

"I have a better idea!" Max exclaimed. "You can ask her out, see how long she'll date you without telling the truth."

"We're not the *Enquirer*, we don't make up stories." Philip shook his head. "I don't want to do anything to hurt her."

"Any publicity is good publicity," Max replied. "You'll be getting her name in front of thousands of readers who will flock to see her movie."

"What if I ask her out and she says no?" Philip wavered.

"You're not that hard to look at. Come on." Max ate a last bite of sea bass and grabbed his sunglasses. "Let's pitch it to Adam before *Inside Rome* goes out of business."


"I like it." Adam nodded, looking up from the tear sheets spread out on his desk. "It has everything my readers want: celebrity, secrets, scandal, all in beautiful Roma."

Adam was only a year older than Philip but he had thinning brown hair and a slight paunch. He wore a blue shirt and khakis and had an unlit cigarette behind his ear.

Philip glanced around the small office and tugged at his collar. The ceiling was made of plaster and the floor was peeling linoleum. A metal garbage can held a pile of cigarettes and candy wrappers. There was a framed *Sports Illustrated* cover on the wall and a signed photograph of Angelina Jolie.

"God she's beautiful." Max stared at the photo. "I don't believe Angelina Jolie really gave you her autograph."

"That was two years ago at the Venice Film Festival." Adam sighed. "She was about to promise me an interview when Brad Pitt whisked her away on a gondola."

"But it needs to be big." Adam turned to Philip. "You have to go all the way."

"I beg your pardon," Philip spluttered.

"You get Amelia Tate to agree to marry you without revealing her true identity and I'll pay you ten thousand dollars." Adam aimed carefully and flicked the cigarette into the trash can.

"Ten thousand dollars!" Philip gasped, leaning forward in his chair. He pictured his father in his gray herringbone suit and black tasseled shoes. He pictured the brick headquarters of Hamilton & Sons with the gold plaque on the building. "We just met, how am I going to propose?"

Adam walked to a metal safe and took out a wad of euros. "I'll give you three weeks. Take her to Il Pagliaccio and Imàgo's and Aroma. Show her the Villa Medici and the Castel Sant'Angelo. I want pictures and lots of juicy details." He peeled off ten notes and placed them on the table. "If you fail, you owe me six hundred euros."

"Do you ever smoke these things?" Max tapped a cigarette from the box of Lucky Strikes on the desk.

"Are you kidding?" Adam stuck another cigarette behind his ear. "Cigarettes will kill you."

"Take her to Agata e Romeo, it has a drop-dead view of the Colosseum," Max mused. "The veal terrine with artichoke is delicious and the chocolate soufflé with Tahiti vanilla ice cream is perfection."

"How do you afford to eat at fancy restaurants?" Philip asked, gazing at the wad of euros on his desk.

He swiveled in his chair and glanced at the view from his narrow window. He saw schoolchildren tossing coins in the Trevi Fountain and couples eating gelato. He saw women in silk dresses and large straw hats and men in summer suits carrying leather briefcases.

"I didn't say I pay for them." Max shrugged, sniffing the coffee in Philip's coffeepot.

"I hate doing something underhanded." Philip frowned. He remembered her easy laugh and a knot formed in his stomach. "I don't want to ruin Amelia's career."

"She's the one who lifted a maid's uniform from the Hassler." Max inspected a tin of biscuits. "And what about your career? Or do you want to become a stockbroker with a temperature-controlled office and a secretary who schedules your dentist appointments."

Philip pictured his father's Wall Street office with its rich maple floors and dark paneled walls. He saw his secretary with her pearl necklace and the cubicles full of young men wearing dark suits and red ties.

He could pay his father a first installment and beg him for an extension. He could get a studio apartment on the Lower East Side and pound the streets until a newspaper hired him. He could go back to reporting about the credit crunch and low-interest mortgages and the stock market in China.

"How would I ask her out?" Philip rubbed his forehead. "I don't even have her phone number."

"You're the Yale graduate, you'll figure it out." Max took a note from the pile of euros. "I saw a pair of earrings that match Alessandria's eyes. They're the most beautiful shade of blue, like two sapphires."

"What about the countess?" Philip raised his eyebrow.

"You're right." Max grabbed another note. "I'll buy her a pair, too."

Philip leaned back in his chair, picturing Amelia waiting at the taxi stand. He saw her sitting in his bed with the sheets pulled around her shoulders. He saw her standing next to the Trevi Fountain, her red dress clinging to her thighs.

He pulled a sheet of paper from his desk and grabbed a pen. He scribbled his signature and sealed the envelope. He stuffed the wad of euros in his pocket and ran down the steps.

# chapter seven

Amelia sat on the balcony, sipping a cup of English breakfast tea and nibbling a scone with strawberry jam. It was Saturday morning and all of Rome seemed to be in a good mood. The traffic guard blew kisses to pedestrians and the street vendors offered free sunflowers to tourists. The businessmen carrying leather briefcases were replaced by young men wearing blue jeans and women in floral sundresses and leather sandals.

Amelia glanced at her newspaper and wondered how to fill her day. She spent almost every minute of the last week on the set. She loved putting on Princess Ann's straw hat and dark sunglasses. She loved riding around Rome on the back of a Vespa. She loved crowding around the video screen and watching the dailies.

It was only when she returned to her suite and glanced at the silver tray of caprese and veal cutlets that she felt a twinge of loneliness. She slipped on a silk robe and took out her script. She read her lines out loud, practicing the lilt in Princess Ann's voice. By the time she closed the script and climbed into bed, her eyes were heavy and she quickly fell asleep.

The doorbell rang and she crossed the marble floor to the entry.

"It's the most beautiful day!" Sophie exclaimed. "I went to the patisserie to buy croissants and the baker gave me an extra pain au chocolat."

Sophie entered the living room and perched on a gold silk armchair. She wore tan cigarette pants and a white cotton shirt tied at the waist. Her hair was pulled into a sleek bun and she wore suede loafers.

"Why did you go out for breakfast?" Amelia asked. "Room service delivered fresh scones and fruit and strawberry jam. I won't be hungry until dinnertime."

"At the palace I always received my breakfast on a tray. Two poached eggs with toast and a sliced orange." Sophie sighed. "Do you know how much fun it is to go to the shops and buy anything I like? I had a chocolate croissant and a latte with extra foam."

"If I ate that for breakfast, my costume designer would faint." Amelia giggled.

"I have my mother's metabolism; she could eat cake every night and never gain an ounce." Sophie's face clouded over. She walked to the balcony and hugged her arms around her chest. "We're going to the orphanage, you have to come."

"Come where?" Amelia asked.

"Theo calls me every day," Sophie replied. "I keep telling him I'm working but he says no one works that much in Italy. The orphanage is in a village named Toffia an hour from Rome. It has an olive tree that is more than two thousand years old."

Amelia pictured driving through the Italian countryside, stopping to drink a cold limoncello. She saw walled towns and abandoned castles and rows of vineyards.

"I should stay and practice my lines." Amelia hesitated.

"You can't sit inside on such a beautiful day," Sophie insisted. "Theo says the nuns grow their own vegetables. We're going to eat pizza with porcini mushrooms and sliced heirloom tomatoes."

Amelia joined Sophie at the window and gazed down at the streets of Rome. Everyone seemed to be going somewhere, to a cozy restaurant or a museum or a lush green park. She saw couples walking hand in hand and mothers pushing strollers. She walked into the bedroom and opened her closet.

She turned to Sophie and smiled. "What does one wear to visit a convent?"

Amelia sat in the back of Theo's green Fiat and held her scarf against her head. She wore white capris and a red cotton sweater and dark sunglasses. She gazed at the sweeping vistas of vineyards and olive trees and felt her chest expand. It was so beautiful: the red and yellow villages perched on hilltops, the castles wrapped in stone walls, the little towns that were nothing more than a post office and a butcher and a souvenir shop filled with postcards and bottles of olive oil.

"Most of the castles date back to the eleventh century," Theo said as they wound up a steep incline. "All the inhabitants lived within the castle walls and spent their days working in the fields. They could spy intruders from miles away."

"I love castles." Sophie sighed, pressing her face against the window. "My favorite is Neuschwanstein Castle in Bavaria. It was built for

Prince Ludwig II and it's the inspiration for the castle in *Sleeping Beauty*."

"You've been to Neuschwanstein Castle?" Theo turned to Sophie. He wore a yellow button-up shirt and blue jeans and leather sandals. His arms were covered with blond hair and he wore a silver watch on his wrist.

"I led a few tours there." Sophie blushed. "They get a million visitors a year."

Theo drove down a gravel drive and stopped in front of a stone building with small lead windows. There was a vegetable garden and a chicken coop and a goat. A wooden door opened and a dozen little girls tumbled into the driveway. They wrapped their arms around Theo's legs, laughing and shrieking.

"Americano Medico!" a girl with brown pigtails exclaimed. "Where is my chocolate? I fed a piece to Palo last week and he threw up. Sister Lea got so angry she took away the whole chocolate bar."

"I told you not to feed chocolate to the goat." Theo laughed, picking the girl up and spinning her around.

"I want to spin, I want to spin," a small girl with blond curls pleaded. She wore a plain cotton smock and woven sandals.

"We will have chocolate and play games but first we have to complete our work." Theo took his leather bag out of the car and opened Sophie and Amelia's door.

Amelia stepped out of the car and breathed lilacs and lemons. She bent down and shook hands with the blond girl. "My name is Ann, it is a great pleasure to meet you."

Sister Lea ushered them into a small parlor with stained glass windows. There was a brown sofa and a threadbare rug over a wood floor. A sideboard held a metal cross and a vase filled with daisies and violets.

Theo placed a cloth on the sideboard and set it with a selection of needles and a box of Band-Aids. He rolled up his sleeves and looked expectantly at the little girls. "Who's my first customer?"

"Anastasia has a stomachache and a fever." A thin redhead approached Theo, handing him a doll with pigtails. "I told her she must be brave and take her medicine."

Theo carefully took the doll and stuck the needle in its arm. He covered the spot with a Band-Aid and solemnly handed it back to the redhead.

"What is he doing?" Amelia whispered to Sophie.

"The children are terrified of getting their shots," Sophie explained. "He vaccinates their dolls and they're not afraid when it's their turn."

Theo put away his leather bag and they moved into the dining hall for lunch. The nuns served butter lettuce with red peppers and baby peas and sliced cucumber. There was a flat pizza topped with tomato sauce and mushrooms and salami. They ate fresh peaches and ripe plums for dessert and Theo handed out pieces of milk chocolate.

"They're lucky to have you," Amelia said as they walked into the garden to watch the children play games.

"I'm the lucky one." Theo held the end of a jump rope. "I help erase their fears."

"Their fears?" Amelia asked.

"Orphans don't know where they are from or who their parents are so they're afraid of everything. If I can help conquer their fears— this pill will make your fever go away, this one will fix your sore throat—they'll have more confidence."

"I never thought about medicine that way," Amelia mused.

"Anyone can fix broken bones; it's like building Legos." Theo shrugged. "The real joy of being a doctor is making a difference in their hearts."

Amelia was about to reply when a little girl ran onto the playground. Her eyes were wide and her mouth quivered.

"Americano Medico, come quickly! The pretty lady fainted."

Amelia glanced around and saw Sophie wasn't in the garden. She raced after Theo through the kitchen and into the pantry. She saw Sophie lying crumpled on the stone floor. Her lips were blue and her breathing was loud and jagged.

Theo bent down and gathered Sophie in his arms. He pressed his lips against hers and blew softly into her mouth. He kept blowing until her cheeks turned pink and the air flowed easily through her lungs.

Sophie's eyes flickered and she made a faint mewing sound. She tried to sit up but she slipped back onto the floor. Theo crouched beside her and gently squeezed her hand. She leaned against him, taking slow, deep breaths.

"What happened?" Theo asked, helping her to her feet.

"Gloria wanted to play hide-and-seek so I hid in the pantry," Sophie explained, smoothing her hair. "I'm sorry I gave you a scare. It's my asthma, it acts up when I'm in small spaces."

"Let's go outside where I can keep an eye on you." Theo grinned, taking Sophie's hand. "You can do something safe like choose the winner of the jump rope contest."

"When I get married I want six children." Sophie sighed, sipping a glass of red wine. "I'm going to be like Julie Andrews in the *Sound of Music*."

They sat at an outdoor café in Casperia, eating ravioli with ricotta and spinach. It was early evening and the sun set behind the Sabine Hills. Amelia watched the fields turn purple and the hilltop villages disappear into the mist.

"You'll need a big house and garden." Theo smiled, pouring olive oil onto a plate. "When I was growing up, we weren't allowed inside during the summer until sunset."

Amelia toyed with her ravioli and gazed at Theo and Sophie. Ever since they left the convent, Sophie had been more animated. She listened closely when Theo talked, laughing and waving her hand. Theo's arm brushed Sophie's sleeve and Sophie's cheeks turned pink.

She saw Sophie smile at something Theo said and suddenly felt lonely. She pictured the master bedroom of the Villa Medici Suite with its king-sized four-poster bed. She saw Whit standing on the balcony and gazing at the bright lights of the Colosseum. She remembered him pulling her toward him and kissing her on the lips.

"You haven't tried the ravioli." Sophie turned to Amelia. "It's a local specialty."

Amelia pushed away the plate and gulped her glass of wine. She had to stop thinking about Whit. She took a deep breath and pictured Sheldon and the movie set and the pink Balenciaga ball gown.

"It's delicious, I'm just not hungry."

Theo dropped them off at the Hassler and Sophie suggested they go to Harry's Bar or the rooftop restaurant at the St. Regis. Amelia mumbled that she had an early call and had to go to bed. She crossed the lobby and saw a man standing at the reception desk. He had dark brown hair and dark eyes and a slightly crooked nose. He wore a white collared shirt with the sleeves rolled up and carried a black leather briefcase.

Amelia darted behind a column and watched the man hand the concierge a letter. The concierge shook his head and shrugged his shoulders. The man pressed a gold coin in his hand and turned to leave. Amelia watched him stride across the marble floor and disappear into the street.

"Excuse me." Amelia approached the concierge.

"Miss Tate!" the concierge beamed. "It is a pleasure to see you, how can I help you?"

"That man." Amelia frowned. "What was he doing here?"

"He is not a guest, he wanted me to deliver a letter."

"A letter," Amelia repeated. "To whom?"

"It is no concern of Miss Tate's," the concierge replied. "Can I get you a magazine or a cup of our excellent espresso? Would you like more roses delivered to your room or a selection of soaps and lotions?"

"I don't need any of those things, Ernesto." Amelia glanced at the concierge's name tag. "But I would love to know who the letter was for."

"I cannot divulge that." Ernesto shook his head, studying his computer screen.

Amelia's face broke into a small smile. "Please, I won't tell a soul."

The concierge fiddled with the envelope, breathing in Amelia's perfume. "He said it was for a maid, but we don't have a maid named Ann Prentiss."

"Could I borrow it for a little while? I promise I'll bring it back."

"Signor Black would not be happy with me." Ernesto hesitated.

"It will be our secret." Amelia leaned forward. "I'm good at keeping secrets, aren't you?"

"Very good," the concierge relented. He pressed the envelope into Amelia's hand and turned back to his computer.

"You are so kind," Amelia beamed, slipping the envelope in her purse.

She entered the elevator and pressed the button. What if Philip knew she was really Amelia Tate and was going to expose her? What if he wrote an article saying she got drunk and went to his apartment? Amelia imagined the newspaper headline and her cheeks turned pale. She fumbled with her room key and opened the door.

Amelia entered the living room and glanced at the oval dining room table. She saw the crystal vase of yellow roses and the silver tray of tea and scones and pots of strawberry jam. She glanced at the neat pile of newspapers and shuddered.

She perched on a blue satin love seat and opened the envelope. She unfolded the white paper and read out loud.

*Dear Miss Prentiss,*

*I hope you are well and have not run into any rain showers or fallen into any national monuments. I thought of you this morning while I was making breakfast. I haven't met anyone in Rome who enjoys bacon as much as you do.*

*I have two tickets to an outdoor concert at Hadrian's Villa and wondered if you might like to take a friend. I received them as payment for an article I wrote and I will be out of town on the date.*

*I'm sure the Hassler pays you handsomely and I know the guests like to tip you with vintage champagne, but honestly, I can't think of anyone else to give them to.*

*There are no strings attached and you don't need to reply. I just don't like to picture you working so hard, without enjoying yourself. After all you are in Rome, and the Italians believe strongly in la dolce vita.*

*Yours Truly,*
*Philip Hamilton*

Amelia gazed at his scrawled signature and thought it would be lovely to sit on a cashmere blanket under the stars. It would be lovely to listen to classical music and eat baguettes and salami and Camembert. But she couldn't risk having any contact with Philip. If he discovered she was Amelia Tate he'd plaster her name across the front page of *Le Repubblica*.

She walked into the bedroom and placed the letter on the Regency desk. She would write him a polite note thanking him but saying she couldn't take time off work. She opened the drawer and took out a piece of ivory writing paper. She put her hand in farther, searching for a pen.

She heard a click and the back of the desk seemed to fall away. She reached in and suddenly felt a stack of papers. She carefully removed them and walked over to the Tiffany lamp.

She peered closely and saw yellowed writing paper covered with flowery cursive. They were tied with a white ribbon and covered with dust. She gently untied the ribbon and glanced at the date. Her eyes grew wide and she sucked in her breath. She sat on the velvet chair and read out loud.

*Dear Kitty,*                                         *June 1, 1952*

*We finished our first day on the set and it was a disaster! How could I possibly think I could be a movie star? The cameras are huge and the set is so crowded I couldn't breathe. Everywhere you turn there is someone wanting to smooth your dress or fix your hair or reapply your makeup. I felt like one of poor Madame Rambert's dogs when it returned from the beauty parlor.*

*I wish we were still together in Madame Rambert's ballet school. It was so easy to concentrate on my pas de deux and arabesques and jettes. I know Mr. Wyler thinks my accent is terrible, I can tell when he crosses his arms and yells: "Cut, let's try that again."*

*Oh, Kitty! I must be mad. It was all right doing* Gigi *on Broadway, that was like performing in Baroness Ella's living room. In the theater you can hear your audience breathe, it's like being part of a club. But to picture my face on a screen in front of thousands of people makes me feel faint.*

*You'll never believe what I did, it was so embarrassing. After lunch (The food is awful. One would think in Rome they would serve gnocchi and veal cutlets and chestnut puree but I got a plate of dry chicken and canned peas and white bread), I sat on a chair waiting for my cue. I shielded my face with a newspaper; the Italian sun is so hot it's like being in Africa.*

*A tall man in a gray suit approached me. He had smooth black hair and dark eyes and an angular nose.*

*"Pardon my late arrival. My plane was delayed in London and I just got in." He held out his hand. "You must be Miss Hepburn."*

*"It's a pleasure to meet you, Mr. . . ." I hesitated.*

*"You don't know who I am?" he asked, his eyes sparkling.*

*"Please forgive me." I blushed. "I'm terrible with faces."*

*"Well you might recognize my name," the man smiled. "It's written on your chair."*

*I turned around and saw* Gregory Peck *written in gold letters. I was talking to one of the most famous movie stars in the world and I hadn't recognized him!*

*"I'm so sorry, Mr. Peck." I shook his hand so vigorously I thought it might break. "I'm honored to be working together. Please let me know if there is anything I can do for you."*

*"The first thing you could do"—he grinned—"is give me back my chair."*

*"Of course, how silly of me." I jumped up. "I didn't know chairs had names."*

"We'll have to get you one of your own." He turned to a production assistant. "Jimmy, can you write Miss Hepburn's name on a chair?"

"I don't want my name on a chair." I shook my head.

"Why not?" He raised his eyebrow.

"I'm quite shy, I'd rather everyone didn't know who I am," I mumbled.

He looked at me carefully and his face broke into a smile.

"Miss Hepburn, after this movie comes out everyone from Athens to Beijing will know your name."

Oh, Kitty, what if I'm the biggest failure since Charlie Chaplin tried to do a talkie? I must go. Mr. Wyler knocks on the door at ten P.M. to make sure I'm asleep. He gave a long lecture on the importance of rest and exercise. As if I'm going to get time to exercise when he works us around the clock!

Hugs to Mimi and Ondine. I'll write more soon.


Amelia held the letter up to the light. The paper was so old she was afraid it would crumble in her hand. She glanced at the signature and her heart hammered in her chest. It was signed with one word.

*Audrey*

# chapter eight

P hilip hung his shirt on the clothesline on the balcony and gazed down at the alley. It was mid-morning and the sun streamed onto the cobblestones. He saw the butcher's door hung with sausages and garlic. He saw the greengrocer's window full of ripe strawberries and peaches. He watched a man climb the stairs to his apartment. He wore a yellow T-shirt and blue jeans and sneakers.

"What are you doing up so early?" Philip asked when Max opened the door. "You don't usually rise from your beauty sleep until lunchtime."

"I need a cup of coffee and a raw piece of meat," Max groaned, sitting on a wooden chair.

"What happened to your face?" Philip peered at the purple welt on Max's cheek. "You look like you got into a street fight."

"I was fastening Alessandria's earrings in her ears and my hair got stuck in her collar. It was perfectly innocent but the countess walked in and saw us." Max rubbed his cheek. "She threw her Prada clutch at me, luckily she wasn't carrying her Hermès bag. That thing has more hardware than a Brink's truck."

"I'm surprised she didn't tear you apart limb from limb." Philip raised his eyebrow. "She invested more money in you than a college education."

"It was time I left anyway, the dolce pears in brandy sauce were making me fat." Max sighed. "I will miss the private art gallery and indoor swimming pool. The countess looked exceptionally good in a bathing suit."

"I'm going to the outdoor market in the Campo de Fiori." Philip stuffed his wallet in his pocket. "You can help me choose a picnic."

"Do you have a date with Amelia?" Max asked.

"Something like that." Philip rubbed his brow. "I got tickets to a concert at Hadrian's Villa."

"Romantic music, a soft breeze, dinner under the stars." Max nodded, eating a banana. "We'll stop at Café Eustachio. Their espresso is so strong it could turn Clark Kent into Superman."

Philip stood in the Campo de Fiori and gazed at the baskets of white truffles and porcini mushrooms and radicchios. There were stands filled with thick sausages and prosciutto and artichokes. He walked through the aisles and saw a dozen kinds of cheese and bottles of olive oil and dried pasta.

"Do you think you're in junior high, preparing an after-school snack for the cute girl in algebra?" Max glanced at the head of lettuce and slices of bacon and red onions in Philip's shopping basket. "You need to buy sexy food—plump red cherries, a jar of caviar, miniature vanilla custards."

"How is food sexy?" Philip frowned, studying the rows of purple asparagus and romanesco broccoli and Japanese eggplant.

"Vegetables aren't sexy unless they're sautéed in butter. Fruit is sexy." Max took a bite of a plum. "If she gets any on her fingers, you can put them in your mouth."

"I'm not sucking the fingers of a woman I just met," Philip protested.

"You have three weeks to ask her to marry you." Max shrugged. "You at least want food you can feed each other—a crusty baguette, some soft cheese, a bunch of green grapes."

Philip picked out ricotta cheese and a rind of Gouda. He bought baskets of raspberries and apricots. He selected a warm baguette and thinly sliced salami and a jar of black olives.

"Salami is okay as long as you both eat it." Max trailed behind him, popping olives in his mouth. "Haven't you ever been on a picnic?"

"Daphne was more interested in dining at Per Se or Tribecca Grill, she didn't like getting grass stains on her skirt," Philip replied.

"You've been in Rome for three years," Max persisted. "Haven't you ever taken a girl to the Borghese Gardens and spent the afternoon making daisy chains in the grass?"

Philip added a bunch of white tulips to his basket. "There haven't been any girls, except the KLM flight attendant. She was always in too much of a hurry to eat."

"No women?" Max gaped.

"I've been trying to earn a living." Philip frowned. "We can't all trade on our blue eyes and blond hair."

"You need a vintage Bordeaux to start the conversation, a chocolate torte to whet her appetite, and a jar of whipped cream."

"Whipped cream?" Philip repeated.

Max tossed the jar in the basket. "If you're with a woman, you can always use whipped cream."

\* \* \*

Philip stood in his kitchen, gazing at the bottle of French wine and pancetta and soft cheeses. He took out his wallet and counted out notes. He had spent almost forty euros and didn't know if Amelia would show up.

He poured a glass of orange juice and pictured Amelia wearing his white shirt. He saw her eating muesli and sliced bananas and washing it down with milk. It was bad enough he was lying about his intentions; he didn't want to pack a fancy picnic of foods he'd never tasted.

He opened the fridge and took out a loaf of wheat bread. He sliced red tomatoes and thick strips of bacon. He rinsed a head of lettuce and opened a jar of mustard. He rolled up his sleeves and started to make a sandwich.

# chapter nine

Amelia poured a cup of English breakfast tea and added milk and honey. She had never been a tea drinker but she loved the way the Hassler served it: on a sterling silver tray with a fresh lemon rind and a selection of scones and biscuits. She put the cup on the white Limoges plate and walked to the window.

It had been raining for two days and Sheldon had to cancel production. Sophie asked Amelia to accompany her to the Vatican but she didn't want to spend the day wrapped in a scarf and sunglasses, hiding behind a program. She decided to stay in the Villa Medici Suite, drinking milky tea and reading Audrey Hepburn's letters.

She sat on the ivory silk sofa and gazed at the stack of yellowed paper. She knew she should tell someone about the letters, a museum or Audrey's family. But she couldn't stop turning the pages. She picked up the top letter and read out loud.

*Dear Kitty,*                                         *June 10, 1952*

*Oh, Kitty! Today I was sure I would be fired; I was ready to call Gil and tell him I'd arrive in New York early. I could start rehearsing* Gigi *in August instead of waiting for the end of September. I pictured New York City in the summer, the heat rising from the sidewalk, the rehearsal room without air-conditioning, and I burst out crying.*

*The last few days had been going so well. I was terrified of Gregory Peck at first, he is so tall and when his brow knots together I think I've done something wrong. But he is a gentleman, going over my lines and bringing me cheese Danishes.*

*Even Mr. Wyler has been kind, complimenting me on my European accent. He said he didn't know how Princess Ann should talk until I opened my mouth, and then he couldn't imagine her sounding like anything else. I took his praise and wrapped myself in it like a blanket.*

*But today something terrible happened. We were rehearsing the final scene where I say good-bye to Joe at the Roman Forum. I imagined the most terrible things, but I couldn't shed a tear.*

*After nine takes, Mr. Wyler paced around the set like an injured lion. "Paramount wanted Elizabeth Taylor to play Princess Ann. Did you see her in* National Velvet? *She was fourteen years old and wept over a horse! I can't get you to cry when you're about to lose the man you love."*

*"I'm so sorry, Mr. Wyler," I replied, biting my lip. "I don't know what's wrong, I've tried everything."*

*"There's one thing you might try." His black eyes flashed. "It's called acting."*

*I was so humiliated, I ran to my dressing room. Suddenly there was a knock on the door and Gregory Peck entered. He wore a* white dress shirt and gray slacks and black loafers. He is so tall his head touched the ceiling.

"Drink this." He handed me a flask.

I took a sip and handed it back to him. "That tastes terrible!"

"It's vodka." He screwed the top on the flask. "One sip works wonders on the nerves, it's a necessity on a movie set."

"The last thing I need is to get drunk, it will give Mr. Wyler an excuse to fire me." I sighed.

"My first director was a French fellow named Jacques Tourneur. After a week of filming, Jacques said he could as easily believe I was a Russian spy as his grandmother was Marie Antoinette. He gave me three days to get rid of my American accent and grow a beard."

"I saw Days of Glory, you were wonderful," I murmured.

"How old are you?" he asked, passing me the flask.

I shook my head and handed it back. "Twenty-four."

"And you're engaged to some British lord," he mused, leaning back in his chair.

"James isn't an aristocrat, his family is in shipping." I blushed. "How did you know?"

"I read the newspapers." He waved his hand. "Have you ever . . ."

"How dare you!" I jumped up. "That's none of your business."

"I was going to ask if you ever waited for a phone call that didn't come or wrote a love letter that didn't receive a reply." His eyes sparkled.

"There was a boy in Amsterdam, Hans." I nodded. "His parents fled to Switzerland in 1944, I thought my heart would break."

"When you look into the camera I want you to be that sixteen-year-old girl in love for the first time." He stood up and grabbed my shoulders. "Full of hope and fear and misery."

*He stood so close I could hear his heart beating. I held my breath, waiting to see what would happen next.*

*"That's the trick, Miss Hepburn." He released me. "Your audience doesn't care what you say or how you wear your hair, they just want to see you make love to the camera."*

*"I don't think Roman Holiday is that kind of movie," I said stiffly, adjusting my skirt.*

*He smiled and ran his hands through his hair. "Every movie is that kind of movie."*

*I'd like to say I walked onto the set and performed my scene but by the time I reapplied my makeup, everyone had gone home. But I know I can do it and I'm glad I have a friend on the set. I'm afraid I'm going to need one.*

*Audrey*

Amelia glanced at the rain falling in sheets outside the window. She poured another cup of English breakfast tea and picked up the next letter.

*Dear Kitty,*                                                      *June 17, 1952*

*Oh, Kitty! The weekend has been such a whirlwind. James arrived from London on Friday evening. It's only been a month since I'd seen him, but my stomach was full of butterflies. I couldn't remember what music he liked or what books he read or what we talked about.*

*The minute he arrived at the door, I remembered why I'm in love with him. He has floppy blond hair and green eyes and a dimple on his chin. I know you think he's too eager to be a member of the Commonwealth Club, but he treats me like a princess.*

*He insisted we go to dinner at the Grand Hotel. I was so exhausted; I wanted to curl up with a glass of warm milk and a copy of* Vogue. *But it would have been childish to say no when he flew over to see me.*

*I wore my black Chanel cocktail dress and diamond earrings and the mink stole James gave me for Christmas. I glanced in the mirror and wanted to giggle. How can I be a movie star who dines in furs and diamonds when I feel like a struggling dancer without enough money to buy a hair ribbon?*

*The dining room of the Grand Hotel has crystal chandeliers and red velvet carpet and a wide marble staircase. It was like being in the first-class salon of a cruise ship, but with a view of the Roman Forum and the Colosseum. James ordered fettuccine Alfredo and rack of lamb and some terribly expensive French wine.*

*"Mother spoke to Father Percy and Saint Stephen's is available on September twenty-first. We'll have a six P.M. ceremony followed by a reception in the garden," James said, buttering a baguette. "It will be tented of course, with a ten-piece orchestra. There'll be a sit-down dinner for five hundred."*

*"Five hundred people?" I dropped my fork so loudly I was afraid the maître d' would ask us to leave.*

*"My parents have lived in Yorkshire for forty years," James replied. "We can't afford to offend anyone."*

*"But filming doesn't end until September eighteenth and rehearsals for* Gigi *start on October first." I bit my lip. "That doesn't leave time to plan the wedding or have a honeymoon."*

*"We'll steal a few days in Cannes and have a proper honeymoon in the New Year." James squeezed my hand. "You don't need to worry about the planning. Mother has it under control. I always say she missed her calling, she should have been a general."*

*I spent a long time cutting my leg of lamb so I didn't say the wrong thing.*

*"I don't want to wedge my wedding into the only free week of the year," I fumed. "Let's get married at Christmas or next spring."*

*"Saint Stephen's is booked until next October." James frowned.*

*"Then we'll get married in London and have a reception at the Savoy. Or we can wait till we get to New York and get married in a registrar's office and have dinner at the Four Seasons."*

*"You know we have to get married at Saint Stephen's," James replied, looking like a schoolboy deprived of his pudding.*

*I stared at the Dresden white china plate and wanted to burst into tears. I dreamed of getting married in a tiny stone church surrounded by my dearest friends. I'd wear a short white dress and we'd have a simple luncheon of steak and roasted potatoes.*

*But, Kitty, isn't marriage all about compromise? James doesn't say a word about my acting and I'd be lost without it. I can spend one day wearing a Givenchy lace gown and shaking hands if it makes him happy.*

*The rest of the evening was wonderful. We danced and laughed and drank a bottle of Veuve Clicquot. I've never been good at having fun. I worry about staying up too late or eating an extra bite of chocolate cake. With James I forget all that and feel young and happy.*

*On Saturday he decided to call a press conference. Apparently I've become quite popular in England and he thought it would be good for business to announce he was engaged to a movie star.*

*I protested I'd rather spend the day strolling through the Borghese Gardens or having a picnic in Tuscany but Mr. Wyler agreed it would be good publicity so I could hardly say no. I wore my red Yves Saint Laurent dress and Ferragamo pumps and a diamond* brooch. James looked so handsome in a navy sport jacket and striped tie and beige silk slacks.

"Mr. Hanson, isn't the engagement sudden? You've only known each other six months."

"When you meet the right person there's no reason to wait." James squeezed my hand. "If you see the perfect Jaguar you don't wait till next season to buy it, you snap it up right away."

"Are you comparing Miss Hepburn to a car?" a female reporter cut in.

"What's wrong with that?" James's eyes sparkled. "Everyone knows men love their cars more than their wives."

"When's the wedding date?" another reporter asked when everyone stopped laughing.

"If we told you that, all you nice folks would attend." James smiled. "Don't worry, we'll give you a full report."

"Miss Hepburn, there are rumors that you've become intimate with your costar on the set."

I sucked in my breath and glowered at the journalist with red hair and freckles. "There was the time Mr. Peck gathered me in his arms and kissed me hard on the mouth." I paused. "Then the director yelled cut and everyone clapped."

"I think he means off camera," another reporter interrupted.

"I know what he meant," I replied. "And I assure you off camera Mr. Peck and I are not even on a first-name basis."

"And what does Lady Carrow think of your engagement? You were spotted having lunch with her at Claridge's last Wednesday."

James went very quiet and his cheeks were pale. I waited for him to answer, a lump forming in my throat.

"I've been lunching with Lady Carrow since we shared bread-and-butter sandwiches in the nursery," James replied. "But I don't know what she thinks of my engagement because I didn't ask her. The only person's opinion I value is the one standing beside me. I think I may speak for my fiancée, we are both delighted."

The rest of the day we spent traipsing around the Roman Forum but James was very quiet. I finally asked him what was wrong and he said he thought it was odd I hadn't introduced him to Gregory Peck. Oh, Kitty, he was jealous! I assured him Mr. Peck was married and almost old enough to be my father. But James wouldn't stop until I promised I'd arrange dinner.

I wanted to ask him about Amanda Carrow but I know it's just those horrid journalists creating a story. James and Amanda have been friends since they were children. The next time someone asks me to speak to the press, I'm going to claim I have laryngitis!

Audrey

Dear Kitty,                                        June 11, 1952

Oh, Kitty, I had the most tiresome day. James arrived at my suite this morning to say good-bye and we were both quite irritable. I know he was smarting about Gregory Peck and all night I kept picturing Amanda Carrow. I'm sure she's one of those horsey English beauties with blond hair and long legs and lavender eyes.

I spent the morning rehearsing a difficult scene and by lunchtime I was starving. I stood at the food service table making a sandwich when a beautiful young woman approached me.

I knew she was French before she opened her mouth, she had brown eyes and thick eyelashes and full pink lips. She wore a perfectly cut blue Dior dress and soft leather pumps. Her auburn hair fell to her shoulders and she wore a silver Cartier watch.

"Miss Hepburn, it's a pleasure to see you."

"Have we met?" I asked, trying to swallow a mouthful of American cheese.

"Veronique Passani," she held out her hand. "I'm a reporter for Paris Soir."

"Excuse me but Mr. Wyler only gives us fifteen minutes for lunch and if I don't eat I get a headache," I replied.

"I don't mind if you eat while we talk." Veronique smiled. She gazed at the selection of processed ham and yellow cheese and wilted lettuce and made a face. "If I was you I'd insist Mr. Wyler order pizza margherita and fresh peaches and apricots."

"That would be heavenly but the unions won't allow it." I put the sandwich on a plate. "What do we have to talk about?"

"Paramount wants Paris Soir to run interviews of the principal actors." Veronique sat on a folding chair and crossed her legs. She had beautiful legs with slender ankles like a dancer.

"I'm not very interesting." I waved my hand. "Interview Gregory Peck, he's a real movie star."

"I interviewed him last winter in Paris." Veronique took a pen and pad of paper from her purse. "It must be difficult to have a career and plan a wedding at the same time. Don't you worry about your fiancé being on the other side of the English Channel?"

"Worry about him?" I asked, feeling a lump form in my throat.

"James Hanson is a very eligible bachelor." Veronique peeled a green grape. "Aren't you concerned he'll get lonely and take up with an old flame?"

"If you're talking about his lunch with Amanda Carrow, they've been neighbors since they were in jumpers. James wouldn't wait until he was engaged to have a fling with her."

*I looked at Veronique scribbling furiously and realized what I'd done. My cheeks turned pink and my stomach turned.*

*"She's quite beautiful in a Katharine Hepburn kind of a way,"* Veronique *mused. "I read they had five courses and a bottle of Dom Pérignon."*

*"Where did you read that?" I asked, trying to stop my hands from shaking.*

*"It was on page three of the* Daily Sun.*" Veronique popped the grape in her mouth. "I suppose you don't get the British papers in Rome."*

*"Miss Passani, as a journalist I'm sure you know reporters make up things to sell newspapers."*

*"On the contrary." Veronique raised her eyebrow. "In my experience, journalists only tell the truth. If they didn't, they'd be fired."*

*I stood up and smoothed my skirt. I took a deep breath and smiled. "If you'll excuse me, I have a job to do."*

*She flipped the page of her notepad and started writing. "So do I."*

*Oh, Kitty, I'm going to call the concierge and cancel my newspapers. I'm going to run a bath and soak in lavender bubbles. Then I'm going to slip on a silk Hassler robe and climb into bed and eat two delicious chocolate truffles.*

*Audrey*


Amelia put the letters on the glass coffee table and walked to the window. The rain had stopped and a rainbow spread across the sky. Amelia stepped onto the balcony and inhaled the scent of roses and chrysanthemums. She gazed down at the street and saw businessmen folding umbrellas and children shedding raincoats.

She walked back inside and saw Philip's letter on the desk. She picked up the concert tickets and examined the date. She thought about Audrey Hepburn trying to appease the press and frowned.

She was tired of sitting in her suite, sipping tea with honey. She would go to the concert with Sophie and they'd eat pizza margherita and drink bottles of limoncello. She flashed on Philip thinking she was a hotel maid and flinched. Philip was away and he said she didn't have to thank him. He would never have to know.

# chapter ten

Amelia stood in front of her closet and selected tan cigarette pants and a beige cashmere sweater. She fastened her hair with a gold clip and put on Whit's diamond teardrop earrings. She slipped on suede loafers and grabbed a light wool jacket.

Sophie was meeting her in the lobby and they were going to the concert at Hadrian's Villa. The concierge had warned her it got chilly at night when the fog rolled in from the Sabine Hills. Amelia was excited to get out of the city, to breathe fresh clean air and see fields of white and purple daisies.

Her phone rang and she picked it up.

"There's been an accident and we're stuck in Casperia," Sophie's voice came over the line. "The road is closed in both directions."

"I didn't know you went to the orphanage." Amelia glanced at her watch. Hadrian's Villa was forty minutes away and the concert started in an hour.

"Theo had to deliver some aspirin and he asked me to come,"

Sophie explained. "I thought it would only take a minute and I could stop and get a picnic."

"If you can't make it, we can do it another time." Amelia felt her shoulders deflate.

"I'll have Theo drop me off at the concert," Sophie replied. "I already bought sausages and feta cheese and green olives. We're going to have a feast."

Amelia hung up and took the elevator to the lobby. She crossed the marble floor and walked through the revolving glass doors. She glanced at the sky and saw thick clouds hanging over the rooftops.

"I need a taxi to Tivoli please," she said to the valet.

"Miss Tate looks very beautiful tonight, are you meeting some lucky man?"

"Thank you, Marco." Amelia blushed, glancing at his name tag. "I'm going to a concert with a friend."

"I will ask it not to rain." Marco grinned, flagging a yellow taxi. "We can't have our favorite movie star getting wet."

Amelia sat in the back of the taxi and watched the lights of Rome disappear. It was almost sunset and the fields were gray and pink and purple. She saw green hills and clusters of clay-colored villages. She opened the window and breathed cut grass and peonies and geraniums.

The taxi pulled down a long gravel drive and Amelia sucked in her breath. Hadrian's Villa was a patchwork of fields scattered with crumbling ruins. Amelia saw stone arches and marble statues and a lake surrounded by olive trees. She saw marble fountains and the remains of ancient buildings.

"The Emperor Hadrian built the villa in A.D. 133; he borrowed the architecture style from the Greeks and Egyptians. It had a theater and libraries and banquet halls." The taxi driver pulled up on the side of the road. "He invited friends from all over the Roman Empire and they played games and had feasts and went swimming."

"How do you know so much history?" Amelia asked.

"Romans are proud of their ancestors, plus the tourists tip well." The taxi driver grinned. "If you like, I can give you a tour of the ruins."

"That's very kind but I'm meeting a friend." Amelia leaned forward and handed him a wad of euros.

"Thank you, signorita." The taxi driver jumped out and opened her door. "Have a wonderful evening."

Amelia stepped out of the taxi and saw a stage draped with gold velvet curtains. It was strung with silver and gold lights and filled with glittering instruments. She saw musicians in black tuxedos and heard the sounds of violins and cellos.

"Wait, signorita," the taxi driver called. "Do you have an umbrella?"

Amelia turned around and smiled. "I don't need one. It couldn't possibly rain, the night is too perfect."

Amelia watched couples spread out wool blankets and unpack baskets of fresh fruit and sliced cheeses. She pictured Sophie's picnic of sausage and green olives and crusty baguettes and realized she was starving.

She glanced at her watch and hoped Sophie would arrive quickly. Soon the lights would dim and it would be impossible for Sophie to find her. She turned around and saw a man standing beneath an arch. He wore navy slacks and a white button-up shirt and carried a wicker picnic basket.

"What are you doing here?" she asked as he walked toward her.

"I was supposed to write an article about a winery in Tuscany but it got canceled because of the rain." Philip spread out a checkered blanket. "I had a sudden urge to hear classical music, so I bought a ticket."

"I'm meeting a friend." Amelia explained. "She got stuck in traffic; there was an accident in Casperia and the road is closed in both directions."

"She won't get here until midnight." Philip frowned. "The Italian police don't work during dinnertime, they're home eating gnocchi and lime spumoni."

"I should go." Amelia gathered her purse.

"Don't be silly," Philip insisted. He unpacked containers of thick sandwiches and sliced pickles and cut peaches. He took out a bottle of Chianti and two plastic glasses. "I made BLTs with heirloom tomatoes and extra bacon. There are fresh raspberries and a chocolate torte, I can't eat it all myself."

Amelia smelled bacon and avocado and her shoulders tightened. She didn't want to go back to her hotel suite and stare at the twinkling lights of the city. She didn't want to spend another night nibbling room service pesto ravioli and wondering if she made the right decision. She suddenly pictured Whit sipping a glass of Chianti at Il Gabriello and felt like she couldn't breathe.

"I suppose I should stay." Amelia hesitated. "Sophie could arrive any minute."

"While you wait you can pour two glasses of wine." Philip handed her the bottle. "And try the peaches, they're from Signora Griselda's garden."

They listened to Puccini and Vivaldi and ate pancetta and figs wrapped in prosciutto. The BLTs were delicious, with crisp lettuce leaves and sweet tomatoes and olive oil and sea salt. During intermission they talked about Rome's torrential rain and crowded streets and expensive restaurants.

"Living in Rome is like falling in love with the wrong woman." Philip sipped his wine. "You think it's all priceless art and delicious pastas and then you discover the streets are dirty and the fountains overflow and it costs ten euros for a packet of potato chips."

"Why don't you go back to America?" Amelia asked.

"Because when you let yourself be seduced by Michelangelo's paintings and Puccini's operas and Bellini's architecture there's no place like it," Philip mused. "That's the thing about love, it rarely makes you happy."

Amelia ate a sliver of chocolate torte and dabbed her mouth with a napkin. She glanced up and saw Philip staring at her.

"What are you looking at?" she asked.

"Those earrings," Philip said. "They're spectacular."

"My boyfriend gave them to me before I left for Rome," Amelia replied slowly. "We broke up, he didn't like being apart or my choice in careers."

"My girlfriend got an MBA and joined a merchant bank." Philip ate a bite of chocolate torte. "Suddenly she could only buy her coffee at Zabar's and her underwear at Saks. She spent so much time on the Upper West Side she decided to get an apartment."

"I'm sorry," Amelia murmured.

"I still had the neighborhood cats for company." Philip shrugged. "I left a bowl of cat food on my fire escape and they visited every night."

Amelia wanted to tell him when she was on the set she felt like Dorothy in the Emerald City. She loved slipping on Princess Ann's pink satin ball gown and white silk gloves. She loved skipping through the streets of Rome with the cameras trailing behind her. But she realized Philip still thought she was a maid at the Hassler.

She glanced up at the sky and felt a large raindrop fall on her forehead. She saw people open umbrellas and slip on brightly colored raincoats. She watched Philip close their picnic basket and hastily gather their blanket.

They ran across the soaking grass and stood under a stone arch. Amelia watched the musicians scurry off the stage, carrying their instruments. She watched the rain come down in sheets, crushing the beds of daisies. She hugged her arms around her chest, feeling cold and wet and miserable.

"I should have known if I was with you I'd get wet." Philip shook the rain out of his hair. "You're like a lightning rod for water."

"It can't rain." Amelia sighed, gazing at the muddy field. "It was such a beautiful evening."

Suddenly the feeling of elation from the beautiful music and delicious sandwich and fruity wine was replaced by an aching loneliness.

"I was wrong when I said you were prettier when your hair wasn't wet and your lips weren't blue." Philip pulled her toward him. He kissed her softly on the mouth, cupping her chin with his hand. "You're beautiful when you're soaked, like a painting by Botticelli."

Amelia pulled away and felt her legs trembling. She pictured Whit's dark curly hair and blue eyes and her heart pounded in her chest.

"I should go, I'm going to catch a taxi."

"Don't be silly, we'll wait until it stops raining and catch a taxi together."

"It's almost stopped." Amelia turned to Philip and extended her hand. "It's been a pleasure, thank you for inviting me."

"Ann, wait!" Philip called after her. "You're going to catch pneumonia."

Amelia strode through the field, covering her hair with her hands. She ran faster, her shoes sinking into the mud. She reached the gravel driveway and saw a yellow taxi idling at the side of the road.

"Good evening, Miss Tate." The driver grinned, opening the door.

"The concierge told me to wait, they didn't want their favorite movie star to get wet."

Amelia climbed into the taxi and leaned against the cushions. She gazed out the window and saw the ancient ruins and marble statues and stone arches. She remembered the warmth of Philip's mouth on her lips and shivered.

# chapter eleven

Philip tapped on his laptop and leaned back in his chair. He pictured Amelia in her tan slacks and cashmere sweater. He saw her glossy brown hair and the sparkling diamond earrings in her ears.

He hadn't meant to kiss her, but she looked so lovely with the raindrops in her hair and her sweater clinging to her breasts. He hadn't expected her lips to be so soft and her skin to smell like raspberries and some kind of floral perfume. He remembered her running across the field and groaned. He had probably scared her off and ruined his chances.

"Signora Griselda gave me your mail." Max appeared at the door. He wore a blue collared shirt and jeans and sneakers. His hair was freshly washed and his camera was slung over his shoulder. "It looks like you have a female admirer."

Philip took the ivory envelope and recognized his mother's handwriting. She refused to use e-mail and sent her letters in thick envelopes doused in Chanel No. 5.

"I got some great photos last night before it started raining harder than the deluge." Max pulled out a chair. "Amelia is very pretty. If I wasn't the wingman of this operation I'd take a shot at her myself."

Philip grabbed the camera and clicked through the pictures. He saw Amelia leaning back on her elbows, looking up at the stars. He saw her eating a slice of chocolate torte and dabbing her mouth with a napkin. He saw her large brown eyes and her small pink mouth.

He knew what he was doing was wrong, he should have told her the truth. But she was so easy to talk to; he didn't want the evening to end.

"I'm lucky I didn't ruin my camera," Max continued, adding milk and sugar to a mug of coffee. "I met a Belgian nurse who offered to share her umbrella. What happened after it started raining?"

"We ran under a stone arch. I don't know what got into me, but suddenly I pulled her toward me and kissed her," Philip replied. "She just broke up with her boyfriend, I think I scared her off. She ran across the field and got into a taxi."

"A recent breakup is good." Max nodded. "It means she's used to sleeping with a warm body and having middle-of-the-night sex. You have to ask her out again."

"I think I should stop." Philip shook his head. "I feel terrible pretending I don't know who she is."

"You're not the Pope and this isn't the Vatican." Max grabbed an apple and polished it against his sleeve. "You're a journalist writing a story for his boss. Without the countess's contributions I'm not going to be able to afford a plate of spaghetti unless I get paid."

"What if I ask her out again and she says no?"

"She'll say yes." Max took a bite of the apple. "This time pick somewhere dry, preferably with a fireplace."

"I'll think about it," Philip murmured.

"I have to return Dominique's umbrella." Max walked to the door.

"I'm going to ask her to take my temperature, I think I'm coming down with a cold."

Philip walked to the counter and sifted through his mail. He remembered Amelia's innocent smile and felt like he'd swallowed something whole. He would tell Adam she refused to go out with him. He would return the euros and tell him to deduct what he owed from his paycheck.

He picked up his mother's letter and tore open the envelope. He scanned the flowery cursive and read out loud.

*Darling Philip,*

*Your father told me you are coming home in August and I'm so pleased. I'm sure you'll get your own place soon but I stocked the pantry with your favorite muesli and I renewed our subscription to the* New Yorker *and the* Atlantic.

*I'm planning a small dinner party at Gramercy Tavern and inviting Daphne. I ran into her at Barneys, she cut her hair and it looks lovely. I know you had a falling out but you were such a beautiful couple. I'm sure now that you will be in the same line of work you'll have so much in common.*

*Please don't think I'm interfering, but I can't help wanting you to be happy. To me you will always be the little boy sitting at the kitchen table drawing hearts on Missy Smith's Valentine's card. You'll understand when you have children of your own.*

*I'm off to buy your father some clothes for Bermuda. I tell him they have perfectly fine shops, but he won't get on the plane without a selection of linen shorts and leather boat shoes.*

*Mom*

Philip crumpled the letter and threw it on the counter. He couldn't spend his days watching imaginary numbers dance on a computer screen. He couldn't live in a world where success was determined by the size of an engagement ring and the price of a prep school education.

He sat at his desk and took out a sheet of paper. He scribbled a note and stuffed it in an envelope. He grabbed his keys and ran out the door.

# chapter twelve

Amelia stood in front of her closet and selected a turquoise chiffon dress and silver sandals. She tied a white scarf around her hair and put on oversized sunglasses. She rubbed pink lip gloss on her lips and spritzed her wrists with Estée Lauder's Lovely.

She was meeting Sophie to go shopping on the Via Condotti and have lunch at Caffé Greco. Sophie had called that morning and apologized for standing her up at the concert. The road was closed for hours and she didn't get home until midnight.

Amelia pictured the plaid picnic blanket with the platters of sandwiches and fruit and chocolate torte. She saw Philip pouring glasses of red wine. She remembered the kiss under the stone arch and shivered.

She lay awake all night thinking about Whit. She remembered his smooth cheeks and Hugo Boss cologne. She could call him and say they couldn't throw away four years; they should wait until she finished filming *Roman Holiday*. She imagined drinking Bloody Marys at Clock Bar and talking about his new factory and the pile of scripts on her bedside table. She saw Whit kissing her on the mouth and telling her how much he missed her.

But then she remembered Whit running up the Spanish Steps and her stomach clenched. He made it clear he didn't want to be with her if she was an actress. Suddenly she thought about Sheldon and what he would say if Philip learned her true identity and leaked the story. Playing Princess Ann was the most important thing in the world and she couldn't do anything to jeopardize her career.

She grabbed her white leather tote and walked to the door. She was going to spend the afternoon with Sophie browsing in Prada and Fendi. They were going to eat seafood pasta and spumoni in the oldest café in Rome. She was going to forget about Whit and Philip and concentrate on acting.

Amelia took the elevator to the lobby and found Sophie perched on a gold velvet armchair. She wore a white linen skirt and a yellow silk blouse and white leather sandals. Her hair was scooped into a bun and covered with a yellow scarf. She wore oval sunglasses and carried a red leather purse.

"You look gorgeous." Amelia smiled. "Is that purse new?"

"I bought one for my lady-in-waiting but it was so soft I had to buy one for myself." Sophie nodded. "I don't know what the Italians feed their cows, in Lentz the leather is stiff as a board."

"Aren't you afraid someone will see us?" Amelia asked, glancing around the marble lobby. It was midday and the space was filled with women in sleek linen dresses and wide hats and oversized sunglasses. They wore gold sandals and had bright leather totes slung over their shoulders.

"I told you no one knows what I look like." Sophie smiled. "As long as we wear our sunglasses we resemble all the other shoppers."

They stepped into the noon sun and Amelia felt warm and happy. The Via Condotti was flanked by stately palazzos and filled with boutiques with white awnings and tinted windows. They drifted in and out of Valentino and Burberry, admiring silk blouses and geometric scarves and jewel-encrusted sandals.

Amelia had never cared about her wardrobe. She liked her uniform of capris and cotton dresses and flat leather sandals. When she walked the red carpet, the studio sent a stylist and a selection of dresses by Dior and Yves Saint Laurent.

But it was fun to try on sheer cocktail dresses and satin pumps. It was fun to imagine what she would wear to the premiere of *Roman Holiday*—an ivory ball gown or a silver sheath with a plunging back.

"This would be wonderful to wear to the Villa Medici." Sophie held up a white linen dress with gold buttons. "Theo is taking me to the opening of the Donatello exhibit."

Amelia raised her eyebrows. "You've seen him every evening this week."

"It's lovely to have someone to go to galleries with." Sophie blushed, taking the dress into the dressing room. "He's interested in history and he knows all the museums and monuments."

"You're lucky." Amelia sighed, following Sophie into the dressing room. "I go home to a hot bath and an empty bed."

"I adore Rome." Sophie slipped the white linen dress over her shoulders. "I love the boutiques and the cafés and the gardens. But in a few weeks I'll go home and return to my royal duties." Sophie turned to Amelia. "When I slip on the royal tiara and stand next to my father in a receiving line, I'm exactly where I belong. I'm Princess Sophia de Grasse and I could never be anyone else."

"What about Theo?" Amelia asked.

"Theo is like this dress." Sophie sighed, gazing in the mirror. Her eyes were wide and her lips trembled. "It's lovely but I know I can't keep it. It's too short; princesses never wear anything above the knees."


They left the boutique and walked toward Caffè Greco. Suddenly Amelia heard footsteps and turned around. She saw a man striding toward them, a silver camera bouncing against his chest.

Amelia grabbed Sophie's hand and raced across the cobblestones. They ran down the Via del Corso, jostling tourists licking ice-cream cones. They ran through the Piazza del Piccolo, dodging street vendors and musicians. Amelia glanced back and saw the photographer coming closer, his heels thudding on the pavement. She looked around and saw a stone church with tall spires. She pulled Sophie through the iron doors and shut them behind her.

"I took off my sunglasses in the dressing room, one of the salesgirls must have seen me." Amelia sat on a wooden pew, trying to catch her breath. "I'm sorry, I hope no one recognized you."

"I haven't had that much fun since Game Day at St. George's." Sophie grinned. "We almost knocked over that cart of roasted chestnuts."

"It was a bit like a scene in a *Mission Impossible* movie." Amelia giggled.

"And we ended up in a six-hundred-year-old church surrounded by priceless art." Sophie studied a metal plaque. "The Santa Maria del Popolo was built in 1492 and houses paintings by Caravaggio and Raphael."

Sophie smoothed her scarf and opened the tall doors. "Come on, we're going to share a caprese salad and a plate of spaghetti calamari. If we're going to run marathons through the streets of Rome we can't be hungry."

Amelia climbed the steps of the Hassler Hotel and walked through the revolving glass doors. They had a delicious lunch of mozzarella and sliced heirloom tomatoes and spaghetti with clams and porcini mushrooms. They shared a profiterole for dessert and drank glasses of Marsala.

It was lovely sitting with Sophie at Caffé Greco, talking about Raphael and Modigliani. It was lovely gazing at elegant women wearing Bulgari diamond chokers and Gucci belts. It was wonderful not thinking about her lines, just enjoying the afternoon sun and the delicious food and the sweet wine.

"Good afternoon, Miss Tate," the concierge called. "I hope you are having a wonderful day."

"Thank you, Ernesto." Amelia beamed. "I had a delicious lunch and went shopping, I'm enjoying Rome very much."

"That gentleman was here," Ernesto continued. "He may have left something of interest to you."

"What kind of thing?" Amelia asked.

"A letter of some kind." Ernesto shrugged, turning back to his computer screen.

"Perhaps I could borrow it." Amelia opened her purse and took out a ten-euro note. "I promise to return it."

"Miss Tate, I could not take your money." Ernesto shook his head.

"Then why don't I leave the note on the counter and you put the letter beside it?" Amelia approached the desk. "Maybe I'll pick up the wrong one."

Ernesto inhaled Amelia's floral perfume. He took the envelope from his pocket and let it fall on the marble counter.

"Excuse me." He bowed. "I must help another guest."

Amelia glanced at the words "Ann Prentiss" scrawled on the white envelope. She slipped it in her purse and hurried to the elevator. She pressed the button and waited for the doors to open.

Amelia dropped her shopping bags on the glass end table and slipped off her sandals. She sat on an ivory silk sofa and opened the envelope. She unfolded the white paper and read out loud.

> *Dear Ann,*
>
> *I apologize for my boorish behavior at the concert last night. I blame the red wine and the rain. You are not just a danger to yourself when wet, but to anyone who comes in contact with you.*
>
> *I would like to show you I am capable of enjoying clever conversation and fine wine without acting like a character in a D. H. Lawrence novel. I made a reservation at La Pergola for Saturday night. At least five waiters hover around your table at all times, so there is no chance of impropriety.*
>
> *We can finish our conversation about black market truffles and see if you like duck ravioli with foie gras sauce as much as I do. If you leave a note with Ernesto, he can let me know what time and where to pick you up.*
>
> *Warmly,*
> *Philip*

Amelia put the paper on the glass coffee table and giggled. She imagined Philip drinking from a crystal wineglass and eating off gold inlaid china. She saw them sipping demitasses of coffee and sharing a vanilla crepe and hazelnut ice cream.

She walked to the balcony and gazed at the late afternoon sun dropping behind the Colosseum. Suddenly her cheeks were flushed and she felt a slight chill. She walked back inside and slipped the letter in its envelope. She sat on the ivory silk sofa and pulled the cashmere blanket around her shoulders.

# chapter thirteen

Amelia gazed at her pale cheeks in the gilt mirror and frowned. She came down with a fever the evening after the concert and spent two days in bed. Sheldon sent a bouquet of pink roses and baskets of peaches and strawberries. Sophie took her temperature and made sure she drank hot tea with lemon and honey.

She finally felt well enough to sit in the living room and eat a bowl of clear soup. But she missed chatting with the makeup artist while she brushed her hair. She missed slipping on satin evening gowns and diamond tiaras. She missed the glow she felt after a long day on the set.

She ate a slice of peach and glanced at the stack of paper on the glass coffee table. She had spent the last day reading Audrey Hepburn's letters. She loved learning about her relationship with her fiancé and her friendship with Gregory Peck and her excitement about becoming a star. She loved picturing Audrey taking a bath in the white porcelain bathtub or curled up in the four-poster bed with a copy of *Vogue*.

She glanced at Philip's envelope and flinched. She tried to reply but every time she pulled out a piece of paper she froze. He had been so kind, letting her share his cab and rescuing her from the fountain.

She ate another slice of peach and picked up a page in Audrey's sloped handwriting. She still didn't feel well enough to do anything but read.

*Dear Kitty,*                                    *June 27, 1952*

*Something very disturbing happened on the set today. I was sitting in the sun, eating a turkey sandwich and a cup of fruit salad. We spent all morning shooting the scene at the Trevi Fountain and Mr. Wyler still wasn't satisfied.*

*Mr. Peck sat beside me and unwrapped a baguette with salami and provolone cheese and red onions. He bit into a fresh plum and wiped his mouth with a napkin.*

*"You're drooling, Miss Hepburn," he remarked. "Would you like a bite of my sandwich?"*

*"It smells delicious." I sighed. "My lunch tastes like cardboard."*

*"The first trick of being an actor is to become friends with craft services." Mr. Peck handed me half a sandwich. "I paid Palo ten lire to go to the delicatessen and bring me a sandwich and a bottle of limoncello."*

*I bit into the sandwich and dribbled olive oil onto my shirt. Mr. Peck handed me a napkin and gazed at my neck.*

*"That's a stunning necklace. Aren't you afraid someone will steal it?"*

*"It's broad daylight, Romans aren't complete barbarians." I fingered the gold and emerald pendant. "It's a gift from my fiancé. He was supposed to visit this weekend but he had to fly to New York."*

"He sent you an emerald necklace instead?" Mr. Peck whistled. "Sounds like quite a guy."

"James is six foot four, I love tall men," I glanced at Mr. Peck's long legs spread out in front of him and blushed. "He's wonderful, he treats me like a princess."

"How did you meet?" he asked.

"At a Christmas party in London," I replied. "I sat too close to the fire and burned a whole in my skirt. I was hiding in the library and James appeared looking for a cigar.

"He said I couldn't lurk among the dreary volumes of Thackeray and Hardy and offered me his jacket. When I arrived back at the Connaught there was a silver box from Harrods. Inside were six Chanel silk dresses with a note that he couldn't decide which shade complimented my eyes so he bought every color they had."

"Sounds like a charmer," Mr. Peck murmured, letting plum juice drip on the pavement.

"You make it sound like an affliction." I frowned. "The next thing I knew James followed me to New York to see me on Broadway. He took Baroness Ella and me to lunch at the Four Seasons and drove us around Manhattan in his town car."

"Baroness Ella?" Mr. Peck asked.

"My mother." I blushed. "She's Dutch and quite old fashioned. She still has a calling card and pays social visits in the afternoon."

"I take it Baroness Ella approves of your fiancé?"

"Is there anything wrong with that?" I demanded.

For some reason he was making me cross. But the sandwich was so heavenly, I didn't want to be rude.

"It depends on why you're getting married," Mr. Peck mused.

"Why does any girl get married?" I retorted. "James is everything

I dreamed of. We're going to have a flat in Convent Gardens and a country house in Surrey and half a dozen children."

"Then I'm happy for you." Mr. Peck took out his handkerchief and wiped his brow. "I hope I'm invited to the christenings."

Suddenly I remembered James's last visit and how we argued about the wedding and the honeymoon. I pictured Amanda Carrow's white-blond hair and wide blue eyes and started to cry.

"That's not how a bride behaves." Mr. Peck handed me the handkerchief. "Use this."

I told him I dreamed of an intimate wedding luncheon but James insisted on a reception for five hundred people. I told him I longed for two weeks in Capri or Majorca but our honeymoon would be a glass of champagne in the first-class lounge of Heathrow on our way to New York.

Mr. Peck took out a Cadbury Fruit and Nut bar and offered me a square. "The British have the best chocolate, I discovered that on the set of Spellbound," he mused. "Do you really love this guy?"

"I wouldn't be getting married if I didn't." I handed him the handkerchief.

"Then I'd hightail it back to England and let the bishop pronounce you man and wife. I'd have four noisy children and a closet full of Shetland sweaters. I'd get a box at Ascot and a courtside seat at Wimbledon and never make another movie in my life."

"I didn't know you thought I was such a bad actress," I said hotly. "I'm sorry Mr. Wyler hired me, you could be starring with Vivien Leigh or Elizabeth Taylor."

"I think you're the greatest actress I've ever worked with. You're going to be a huge star and make movies all over the world. You'll arrive at Christmas laden with presents and your children won't recognize you. You might have a flirtation on the set because you haven't been home in so long, you forgot the scent of your husband's cologne. Or you'll find a box of Lucky Strikes in the glove box of your car when you only smoke Marlboros."

I didn't know what to say. Finally I turned to him and whispered, "How old are your children?"

"Jonathon is eight and Stephen is six and Carey is three." He showed me the photos in his wallet. "They all have blond hair and blue eyes like their mother. I met Greta when I was twenty-six and doing theater in New York. I was so poor I slept on a park bench and she let me stay in her apartment in Greenwich Village. Now we have a twenty-room hacienda in Beverly Hills with a swimming pool shaped like a kidney."

"What a lovely tableau," a female voice interrupted. "It's like a painting by Seurat."

I squinted into the sun and saw Veronique Passani standing above us. She wore a red Nina Ricci dress with camel-colored pumps. She clutched a sandwich in one hand and a newspaper in the other.

"I thought I was going to have to settle for egg salad on soggy white bread but I smell sausage and onions and baguettes."

"You're welcome to the rest of my sandwich." Gregory Peck jumped up. "Miss Hepburn and I were discussing the merits of marriage over a career."

"What a beautiful necklace," Veronique mused. "Is it a Cartier?"

"It's a present from my fiancé." I touched my neck.

For some reason Veronique makes me nervous. She has long eyelashes and sharp brown eyes like a cat.

"It's quite striking, I saw one just like it." She unfolded her newspaper and pointed to a photograph of a blond woman wearing *a wide-brimmed hat and narrow heels. She had emerald earrings in her ears and an emerald and gold pendant around her neck.*

*I scanned the caption and read: "Lady Amanda Carrow makes an entrance at Convent Gardens in a cream Pierre Balmain dress and Mainbocher hat."*

*"What an interesting coincidence." I held the newspaper closely so they couldn't see my cheeks. "If you'll excuse me, I must go."*

*Oh, Kitty, I ran to my dressing room and slammed the door. I tore the necklace off and tossed it on the desk. I lay on the bed and burst into tears.*

*Audrey*

*Dear Kitty,*  June 30, 1952

*Tonight, I opened the door of my suite and couldn't believe my eyes. There were boxes piled on the glass dining room table and the black and white marble floor. I ripped them open and discovered evening gowns by Balenciaga and Dior and Jacques Fath. There was a black velvet Balmain stole and half a dozen shoes by Roger Vivier.*

*The phone rang and I sifted through tissue paper to answer it.*

*"Did they arrive?" James's voice came down the line.*

*"It must have taken the concierge three trips in the elevator." I laughed. "What have you done?"*

*"I stopped in Paris on the way here. I couldn't resist picking up a few things."*

*"Where will I wear any of it?" I picked up a green silk taffeta dress. "I spend all day on the set."*

*"I'm taking you to dinner at the Hotel Quirinale," James insisted. "Wear the pink Jacques Fath, it will make your skin look like alabaster."*

I spent an hour in the bathtub, soaking in lavender bubbles. I spritzed my wrists with L'air Du Temps and stepped into the pink silk dress. I paired it with gold Vivier pumps and white silk gloves.

I fastened the diamond and emerald pendant around my neck and suddenly felt ill. I told myself it didn't match the dress, but, Kitty, I couldn't wear it. I put it back in my jewelry box and draped a white fur stole around my neck.

The Hotel Quirinale is smaller than the Hassler, almost like a country house in the center of Rome. It has a stone floor and Oriental rugs and yellow plaster walls.

The maître d' led us into the hotel's gardens and I caught my breath. The tables were covered with white linen tablecloths and set among palm trees and bougainvilleas. We ate cold tomato soup and Parmesan ravioli and roasted lamb with wild mushrooms and chestnuts.

"I brought you something." James passed a black velvet box across the table.

I opened it and saw a diamond bracelet with a pearl clasp.

"It's gorgeous, but it must cost a fortune," I gasped, turning it over.

"We signed three new shipping contracts." James smiled, fastening it around my wrist. "I had to celebrate."

I admired the sparkling diamonds but suddenly I couldn't breathe. I pictured Amanda Carrow's silky blond hair and pink mouth and long legs. I saw her cream Balmain dress and the emerald and gold pendant hanging around her neck.

"You're not wearing your pendant." James frowned.

"I saw a photograph in the newspaper of Amanda Carrow wearing the same necklace."

I waited for James to answer and thought my lungs would explode. He put his napkin on his plate and smoothed his hair.

"I know I'm guilty of not being original." He looked at his plate. "Amanda wore it to dinner at the Savoy last week. I thought the emeralds would match your eyes, I went to Cartier and bought the same one."

"You had dinner at the Savoy?" I stammered.

"It was Amanda's engagement party," James explained. "She and Graham are getting married next July."

"I didn't know she was engaged," I replied, tearing a baguette.

"It's quite sudden," James agreed. "She's always been impulsive."

We danced under the stars and my feet barely touched the ground. James is handsome and generous and fun. When I'm with him I forget the war years and think life can be about beautiful clothes and delicious food and wonderful music.

I should be happy attending dinner parties and garden weddings and first nights at the ballet. Perhaps Mr. Peck is right and I should quit acting. But, Kitty, we've always been the ones on the stage. Can I really give that up without becoming someone else?

Audrey

Dear Kitty,                                          July 2, 1952

Today was so hot I thought I would melt like the witch in The Wizard of Oz. Even Veronique Passani looked uncomfortable in her Dior jacket and pleated skirt.

I sat in my dressing room, longing for an English summer. I imagined a chilly drawing room and a warm fire and windows *splattered with rain. I pictured a cup of Earl Grey tea and fresh scones with orange marmalade.*

*Mr. Wyler's assistant appeared and said Mr. Wyler wanted to speak to me. I crossed the set to his dressing room and knocked on his door.*

*"Good afternoon, Miss Hepburn, I trust you're keeping cool."*

*"I'm fine, thank you." I smoothed my skirt and tucked my hair behind my ears.*

*"Mr. Peck and I were going over these movie posters from Paramount." He pointed to a poster spread out on the desk. I read* Roman Holiday *in big orange letters and my name at the bottom of the page.*

*"Mr. Peck thinks we're making a mistake by keeping your name here."*

*I looked up and the room started to swim. How could Mr. Peck desert me after he gave me so much praise? I'm sure he wishes we got the scenes done faster so he could go back to his hotel and drink a cold beer and eat a thick steak.*

*Mr. Wyler leaned over the desk and pointed to Mr. Peck's name at the top of the poster.*

*"Mr. Peck thinks after the movie is released you're going to be a big star. He says we're going to have egg on our face unless we put your name under his."*

*I knew he was waiting for me to say something but I couldn't open my mouth.*

*"You look a little pale." Mr. Wyler frowned. "Would you like to sit down?"*

*I watched Mr. Wyler open the fridge and take out a bowl of strawberries and a jar of whipped cream. He tucked a white napkin under his collar and handed me a spoon.*

"I can't eat any of the crap craft services prepares." He wiped his mouth. "Mr. Peck tells me you're engaged; who's the lucky man?"

I ate berries and whipped cream and we talked about Broadway and the West End and Hollywood. After we ate, Mr. Wyler shook my hand and said I was exactly how he imagined Princess Ann.

I rushed out of his dressing room and almost tripped over Gregory Peck. He was sitting in a folding chair, reading a newspaper.

"You look radiant in this heat," he said, loosening his tie.

"I don't know how to thank you," I stammered.

"Thank me for what?" he asked.

"For telling Mr. Wyler my name should go above the movie title." Mr. Peck folded his newspaper and smiled.

"I didn't do anything, Miss Hepburn. You're doing it yourself."

Oh, Kitty, I skipped back to my dressing room like Dorothy following the yellow brick road. I can't wait to call James and tell him I'm going to be a movie star!

*Audrey*

Amelia put the letter on the glass coffee table and glanced at the marble fireplace and the yellow silk curtains and the framed Tintoretto on the wall. Sometimes it still seemed like a dream: the spectacular suite, the glamorous clothes, the starring role in a major motion picture.

She walked to the dining room table and smelled the pink roses. She had worked so hard; she couldn't let anything get in the way. She would meet Philip for dinner and tell him she couldn't see him again. She would say she was leaving Rome and it had been lovely to meet him.

She took a sheet of paper and scribbled a note. She sealed the envelope and picked up the phone.

"Ernesto," she said into the receiver. "I wonder if you could do me a big favor."

# chapter fourteen

Philip flipped through his checkbook and drummed his fingers on the desk. He picked up a freelance assignment on the olive oil festival in Montelibretti and was able to pay this month's rent. But unless he picked up a few more jobs, he'd be living on dry rigatoni and tomatoes from Signora Griselda's garden.

He stood up and walked to the kitchen counter. He sent Amelia the letter three days ago and hadn't received a reply. He told himself he was relieved he didn't have to continue the charade. Just thinking about sitting across from her at La Pergola, cutting a thick steak and buttering a warm baguette, made him nervous.

His mother sent another letter with the menu for his dinner party and his father sent a plane ticket with the note:

> *Philip,*
> *Enclosed is your plane ticket and the address of my tailor in London. Edna routed you through Heathrow so you could choose a*

*new wardrobe. Every young man should own a double-breasted*
*suit and a white dinner jacket from Saville Row.*

*Dad*

Philip opened the fridge and stared at the wilted head of lettuce and the loaf of bread and the single tomato. He was tired of eating soggy sandwiches and drinking cartons of orange juice. He was tired of staring at the clothesline on the balcony and listening to Signora Griselda's singing.

He glanced at the pile of euros on the dining room table and grabbed a handful of notes. He was going to have a proper lunch at a café. Then he was going to the Hassler and pray that Amelia left a reply. She had to have dinner with him at La Pergola; the alternative was too difficult to bear.

"What are you doing here?" Max approached his table. He wore a striped collared shirt and blue jeans and sneakers. His blond hair was freshly washed and his cheeks were smooth with aftershave. "I thought you didn't like watching the beautiful people."

"I'm having lunch," Philip retorted, wiping his mouth with a napkin.

He had taken a table at Caffe Strega and ordered pizza with sweet peppers and buffalo mozzarella and artichoke. He drank a cappuccino in a tall glass and flipped through *Le Tempo*. He gazed at the men and women strolling down the Via Veneto and wondered how they all looked so happy. The women wore white linen dresses and gold sandals and the men wore light-colored suits and leather loafers.

"You don't have lunch on Fridays." Max pulled up a chair.

"Today I do," Philip snapped, shielding his eyes from the sun. "I'm tired of living like a boy scout on a scavenger hunt."

"I saw your movie star the other day." Max ate a slice of pizza. "I was in the Fendi boutique on the Via Condotti. She was with a gorgeous blonde with legs up to her neck and skin like polished alabaster."

"What were you doing in the Fendi boutique?" Philip frowned.

"It's the best place to meet women," Max explained. "I saw this beautiful brunette and pretended I was buying a present for a girlfriend. I asked which scarf she preferred; by the time she chose the red silk scarf we had a date for Saturday night. Her name is Lara and her husband owns a glass factory in Genoa."

Philip stirred his cappuccino and imagined Amelia wearing a light summer dress. He pictured her slender calves and graceful neck. He saw her large brown eyes and her hair smoothed behind her ears. "Did Amelia see you?"

"I followed them to the Piazza del Piccolo but they disappeared into a church." Max shrugged. "I could have gotten some great photos."

"You followed her?" Philip pictured Amelia escaping across the cobblestones and his stomach clenched.

"My job is to take pictures," Max replied. "I wouldn't mind getting a few close-ups of her friend."

"I don't want Amelia to recognize you in case she sees us together," Philip mumbled. "It doesn't really matter. She hasn't replied to my letter, I'm going to return the money and tell Adam I failed."

"Don't you have a fight song at Yale about never giving up?" Max mused. "If you went back to New York, I'd spend my nights in the back of a smoky club, drinking absinthe and losing at cards."

"You can take care of yourself," Philip replied. He gazed at the elegant boutiques on the Via Veneto and frowned.

He'd rather watch Adam flick cigarettes into a trash can than share an office suite with men wearing Tom Ford suits and Alexander McQueen shoes. He'd rather eat spaghetti every night than sit at his parents' walnut dining room table and talk about arbitrage and margins.

"Come on." He pushed back his chair. "We're going to the Hassler to pay a visit to Ernesto."


"Ernesto wasn't there." Philip exited the revolving glass doors and joined Max on the sidewalk.

"Did Amelia leave a note behind the counter?" Max asked.

"Nothing." Philip shook his head. "Let's get out of here."

Philip ran quickly down the Spanish Steps and strode across the Piazza di Spagna. Suddenly the thought of leaving all this—the street vendors whistling at pretty women, the tourists taking pictures of the Vatican, the ancient churches and modern shops and cramped trattorias—made his head throb.

He approached his apartment and saw a man standing on the sidewalk. He wore a white uniform with gold buttons. His dark hair was slicked back and his hands were jammed in his pockets.

"Ernesto," Philip called. "What are you doing here?"

Ernesto nodded and reached into his pocket. "I have a delivery for you."

Philip took the letter and bounded up the steps. He ripped it open and scanned the page. He turned to Max and grinned.

"Get out your white dinner jacket, we're dining at La Pergola."


Amelia stood in front of the closet and selected a floral dress with a wide belt. She slipped on white sandals and tied a yellow scarf around her head. She glanced in the mirror and added pink lip gloss and blush.

She woke up full of energy. She spent the morning exploring the Pantheon and Capitoline Hill. She drank a frothy cappuccino in the Piazza Navona and bought a silk scarf on the Via del Corso. Now she took the elevator and pressed the button for the sixth floor.

Sophie answered the door in a white cotton robe and yellow slippers. Her hair was pulled into a ponytail and her face was free of makeup. There were circles under her eyes and her cheeks were drawn.

Amelia entered the suite and put her purse on the marble end table. The silk curtains were open and the room was bathed in sunlight. Amelia saw a silver tray with a bowl of muesli and sliced bananas and fresh scones. There was a pot of coffee and a pitcher of cream.

"Room service brought breakfast but I'm not hungry." Sophie shrugged, sitting cross-legged on the beige silk sofa.

"It's a gorgeous day," Amelia said. "I thought we could take a picnic to the Borghese Gardens."

"I don't have time to go to the Borghese Gardens." Sophie sighed, pointing to the sketches spread out on the glass dining room table. "My lady-in-waiting sent the designs for my wedding dress; I have to choose my favorite. The wedding is in December and it takes six months to make the gown."

"They're stunning." Amelia picked up a sketch of a gown with an ivory bodice and a full satin skirt. It had a wide silk bow and a fifteen-foot lace train.

"After the wedding it will hang in the museum next to my mother's wedding dress." Sophie bit her lip. "Her gown was made of sixteenth-century Belgium lace. She wore a diamond and ruby tiara and gold satin slippers."

"You look like you're preparing for a funeral instead of a wedding." Amelia gazed at Sophie's pale cheeks and white lips.

"Yesterday Theo and I went to the Caravaggio exhibit at the

Corsini Gallery." Sophie paced around the living room. "I had an asthma attack and by the time Theo found my inhaler I was hysterical. He found a quiet bench and told me a story."

"A story?" Amelia asked.

"When I was a little girl I'd get asthma attacks in bed. It got so bad I was afraid to go to sleep," Sophie continued. "My mother would sit at my bedside and tell me a story. Even if she had a dinner party or a ball she wouldn't leave until I fell asleep."

"She sounds lovely." Amelia smiled.

"No one has ever told me a story since she died." Sophie's eyes grew wide and her lips trembled. "I listened to Theo and the strangest thing happened. Suddenly all I wanted was for him to kiss me."

"You were scared and Theo comforted you," Amelia soothed. "It's perfectly natural."

"There are a team of seamstresses waiting to sew my wedding dress and a kitchen staff planning the wedding breakfast and every rose grower in Lentz creating roses for my bouquet. I can't think about kissing another man."

"You haven't seen Prince Leopold since you were twelve," Amelia mused. "Theo is kind and handsome and you have fun together. Would it be so terrible to have a summer romance?"

"Morals aren't something you can bend to suit your needs," Sophie insisted. "I couldn't stand at the altar knowing I've broken my vows before I recited them."

"What are you going to do?" Amelia asked.

"Theo asked me to dinner tonight, I'm going to tell him I can't see him again." Sophie turned to Amelia. "I don't want to be alone with him, you have to come with me."

"I'm having dinner with Philip," Amelia blurted out. She had been too embarrassed to tell Sophie about the kiss.

"With Philip?" Sophie raised her eyebrow.

"Just as friends." Amelia shrugged. "To thank him for being kind to me."

"That's even better!" Sophie exclaimed. "I'll tell Theo I got a second job and don't have time to go to the orphanage or visit museums. We'll have a lovely dinner and I won't see him again."

Amelia gazed at the sketches of ivory wedding dresses with wide silk bows. She studied the drawings of lace veils and satin pumps. She had been worrying that having dinner with Philip was a mistake. She should have written a polite note saying she was too busy but thanking him for the invitation.

"All right, I'll tell Philip." Amelia nodded.

She pictured his dark eyes and narrow cheeks and thought she didn't want to be alone with him either.

# chapter fifteen

Amelia entered the restaurant and glanced around the wide space. She saw large windows and smooth wood floors. Glass tables were set with white ceramic plates and gleaming silverware.

She realized if they ate at La Pergola someone would recognize her. She hastily sent Philip a note asking if her friends could join them and whether they could change the location. Theo was a struggling doctor and couldn't afford a three-star Michelin restaurant.

Philip wrote back suggesting Glass Hostaria in Trastevere and offered to pick her up. Amelia replied she would get a ride with Theo and Sophie and meet him there. Now she glanced at her floral dress and sandals and wondered if she was underdressed. She had expected a cramped trattoria but the room was all glittering glass and sleek edges.

"Good evening, Miss Prentiss." The maître d' consulted his clipboard. "Your party hasn't arrived, would you like a drink while you wait?"

Amelia followed him to the bar and sat on a leather stool. "That sounds lovely, what would you suggest?"

"A Kir Royal is perfect for a summer night."

"Thank you." Amelia nodded. "I'll have one of those."

"There you are," Philip approached the bar. He wore a white dinner jacket and black slacks. "I'm sorry I'm late. Taxis don't like to go to Trastevere on Friday night, they'd rather stay at the Piazza di Trevi and shuttle tourists to the Roman Forum."

Amelia took a sip of the sweet fizzy drink and her shoulders relaxed. She glanced at his crisp white shirt and black bow tie and giggled.

"Aren't you overdressed for Trastevere?" She smiled.

"I told you I was going to show you I could be a gentleman." Philip grinned. "Besides, I already got my dinner jacket pressed. I didn't want it to go to waste."

Theo and Sophie arrived and everyone shook hands. Sophie wore a shimmering turquoise dress and silver sandals. Her hair was tied in a loose bun and secured with an ivory chopstick. She wore a delicate gold necklace and a diamond bracelet.

"We almost couldn't find a place to park," she explained. "Theo is a magician, he could fit his car into a matchbox."

Amelia watched Sophie gaze at Theo and her heart turned over. She saw Theo pull out Sophie's chair and offer her a baguette. She saw him consult the menu and suggest the tagliatelle with wild asparagus. She saw him fill Sophie's wineglass and wait for her approval.

"This place is lovely." Amelia gazed at glass vases filled with white tulips. She saw waiters carry platters of scallops and risotto and spring vegetables. She glanced at Philip and her heart hammered in her chest. She hadn't dined with a man since Whit walked out of Il Gabriello.

"I reviewed it for *Gourmet* magazine." Philip ate a bite of bruschetta. "Not all restaurants in Rome have pizza ovens and checkered tablecloths."

"I love Italian food." Sophie's blue eyes sparkled. "Theo and I had lunch at Ciampini yesterday; it has the best view in Rome. I could sit for hours gazing at the Vatican and eating veal parmigiana and tiramisu."

"Sophie's Italian is excellent." Theo nodded. He wore a blue cotton shirt and pressed khakis. His blond hair was neatly brushed and his cheeks were smooth. "She can translate the whole menu."

"And what about you?" Philip addressed Amelia. "Does the Hassler feed you well?"

Amelia was about to answer when she realized Philip thought she was a maid at the hotel. She blushed and gulped her drink. She looked at Philip and her eyes were huge. "The Hassler treats the staff very well, there is always ravioli and ice cream."

They talked about Theo's years at Johns Hopkins and Philip's time at Columbia. They discussed American football and Italian soccer. Amelia pushed green tortellini around her plate and let the waiter refresh her drink. She glanced at Philip and wished she was in the Villa Medici Suite. She wanted to be sitting on the balcony, reading her script and concentrating on *Roman Holiday*.

"I think being a doctor is noble." Philip ate smoked potatoes. "I get queasy at the sight of blood. In seventh grade, I let my lab partner dissect the frog and I wrote the report."

"The hardest part is getting the patient to trust you," Theo replied. "If you don't gain their trust, you can't help them."

Amelia stood up to use the ladies' room and her knees buckled and lights flashed before her eyes. She tried to remember how many times the waiter refilled her glass. She had barely eaten since she got sick and suddenly the lack of food and the sweet drink made her light-headed.

"Are you feeling all right?" Philip asked. "Your cheeks are white as a plate."

Amelia covered her face with a menu. She turned to Philip and blushed.

"I'm perfectly fine. All the desserts look wonderful. Should I try the passion fruit ice cream or the tapioca pudding?"

Philip dabbed his mouth with a napkin. He looked at Amelia and his eyes were suddenly serious.

"Trust me, the passion fruit ice cream is delicious."

"It was a lovely dinner, thank you for letting us join you." Sophie shook Philip's hand. "We'll give Ann a ride home."

"But it's such a beautiful night, the moon is as big as a saucer," Amelia declared. "Who wants to go for a walk?"

They stood outside the restaurant inhaling the sweet night air. Amelia glanced up at the sky and saw stars twinkling against black velvet. She smelled pizza and garlic and felt light and happy.

"I'll walk with Ann, don't worry." Philip turned to Sophie. "I'll make sure she gets home safely."

"Are you sure?" Sophie hesitated.

"Of course he's sure." Amelia waved her hand. "I can't sit in a car on such a gorgeous night, I want to walk forever.

"I love Trastevere," Amelia exclaimed, skipping along the pavement.

They strolled down the Viale di Trastevere to the Piazza de Santa Cecilia. They sat on the cobblestones and gazed at the stone basilica with its marble columns and stained glass windows.

"I feel like I'm in the fifteenth century." Amelia sighed. "Any minute Romeo and Juliet will appear and drink vials of poison."

"Your friend Sophie is very nice, they make a lovely couple," Philip mused.

Amelia turned to Philip and giggled. "Sophie is engaged, but she hasn't seen her fiancé since she was twelve years old."

"What do you mean?" Philip frowned.

"It's a secret," she whispered. "Sophie is really Princess Sophia de Grasse of Lentz."

"Is that so?" Philip asked, a smile flickering across his face.

"She has ladies-in-waiting and a royal yacht in Portofino and a diamond and ruby tiara." Amelia leaned close to Philip. "But you have to promise not to tell anyone."

"Scout's honor." Philip crossed his chest. He smelled her floral perfume and asked, "Do you have any other secrets?"

Amelia tried to think but suddenly the lights of the piazza flashed like a million fireflies.

"Only one, I'm afraid of spiders." She rested her head on his shoulder and fell asleep.

# chapter sixteen

Amelia opened her eyes and groaned. She sat up and saw a tile floor covered by a red rug and a plain brown sofa. She saw a glass dining room table and wooden chairs. There was a tall bookshelf and a wooden desk littered with papers.

She glanced at the narrow bed and pressed her hand against her head. She remembered insisting they go for a walk. She remembered the winding alleys of Trastevere and the wide dome of the Basilica de Santa Cecilia. She tried to remember how she ended up in Philip's apartment but her mind was blank.

The room was empty and Philip's keys were missing. She could grab her purse and leave before he returned. She'd write a quick note apologizing for her behavior and saying she was leaving Rome.

She walked into the bathroom and glanced at her creased floral dress. She smoothed her hair and tucked it behind her ears. She rubbed her lips and entered the living room.

"There you are." Philip smiled. He held a mesh shopping bag with a carton of orange juice and a basket of strawberries. "I thought you slipped out the fire escape."

"What happened?" Amelia moaned. She sat on a wooden chair and put her head in her hands.

"At least your clothes didn't get soaked." Philip grinned. He poured tall glasses of orange juice and handed one to Amelia. "What were you drinking last night?"

"Kir Royal." Amelia sipped the orange juice. "The waiter recommended it."

"It's great if you like crème de cassis and champagne." Philip sliced bananas and strawberries. He added sugar and put the bowl on the table. "It can be a lethal combination."

"How could it get me drunk?" Amelia sighed. "It tasted like fizzy grape juice."

"Don't worry, it was Friday night." Philip sat opposite her. "Everyone gets a little tipsy."

Amelia remembered sitting next to Philip on the cobblestones and her heart hammered in her chest. "Did I say anything I shouldn't?"

"Like what?" Philip ate a spoonful of fruit salad.

"I'm not sure," Amelia hesitated. "Anything unusual."

"There was one thing," Philip mused. "You said you were afraid of spiders."

Amelia felt the air escape her lungs. She ate large bites of fruit salad and finished her glass of orange juice. She put her spoon on her plate and smiled. "I insisted my friends join us and then I embarrassed you, I'm sorry."

"I like it when you're drunk." Philip sat back in his chair. "It's the only time I see your shoulders relax."

"Sometimes life is complicated," Amelia mumbled.

"I imagine being a maid is stressful," Philip agreed. "All those beds to make and towels to fold and silk robes to replace."

Amelia glanced at Philip's dark eyes and angular nose. She wanted to tell him she wasn't really a maid, she was an actress starring in *Roman Holiday*. She wanted to apologize for lying and ask if they could start again.

"It can be stressful, but it pays well and the management is nice." She stood up. "I have to go, I'll be late."

"I'll walk with you." Philip followed her to the door.

Amelia shook her head. "I've taken up too much of your time."

"Have dinner with me tomorrow night," Philip suggested. "We'll eat pizza carbonara and licorice gelato and drink ice cold lemonade."

"I'm leaving Rome," Amelia replied. "I'm going to Florence and Venice."

"But I thought you loved Rome." Philip frowned. "You like the food and the art and the architecture."

"Sometimes you have to leave behind things you like." Amelia opened the door. "It's important to try new places."

"Are you sure you won't change your mind?" Philip asked. "The Hassler will be sorry to lose you."

Amelia hurried down the stairs. She stopped at the bottom and turned around. She saw Philip leaning against the railing and smiled.

"I won't forget it," she called. "Rome has been lovely."


Philip entered his apartment and glanced at the half-empty bowl of fruit and glass of orange juice. He sat on the rumpled bed and saw a tube of lipstick on the floor. He picked it up and stuffed it in his pocket.

He walked to the desk and flipped open his computer. He typed "Princess Sophia of Lentz" into the search engine and pressed enter. He scrolled down and saw a grainy photo of a man in a royal blue and white uniform wearing a gold crown. His arms were around a young girl with white-blond hair and blue eyes. She wore a satin dress and had a diamond tiara in her hair.

Philip drummed his fingers on the desk and shut the computer. He grabbed his wallet and hurried down the stairs.


"Here you are, I've been looking for you all over Rome." Philip entered the shop and glanced around the small space. Glass cases were filled with dark chocolate truffles and mini éclairs. There were trays of profiteroles and fruit tarts and vanilla custards. The center of the room had a round marble table piled with silver boxes and velvet bows.

"What do you think Lara would like?" Max looked up from a selection of mini cheesecakes and jam tarts. "A box of éclairs or some of these crostate—the hazelnut filling is delicious."

"Cioccolateria is the most expensive chocolate store in Rome." Philip frowned.

"I have one chance to make a good impression." Max handed a box of opera cakes to the salesgirl. "I miss the countess. Her pastry chef made the finest cannoli with fresh ricotta and pistachio. We both recognized his genius."

They walked into the street and crossed the Piazza del Popolo. They sat at an outdoor table at Canova and ordered two iced coffees. Philip ran his hands through his hair and squinted into the sun.

"You were so obvious last night, I was terrified Amelia would see you."

"You're the one who picked a restaurant where everything is made of glass." Max sprinkled nutmeg onto whipped cream. He wore a yellow collared shirt and jeans and sneakers. His blond hair touched his collar and he had a shaving nick on his chin. "I couldn't even hide behind a potted plant."

"I thought the night was going well." Philip rubbed his forehead. "The moon was bright and the sky was full of stars and we strolled through Trastevere. But then Amelia passed out on my shoulder."

"What happened after that?" Max raised his eyebrow.

"I took her to my apartment and put her to sleep in my bed." Philip stretched his legs in front of him. "This morning, I made fruit salad and we talked about this and that. I asked her to dinner tomorrow night but she said she's leaving Rome."

Max sipped his iced coffee and tapped his fingers against the glass. "Don't they teach you anything about women at Yale? If she didn't want to see you, she would say so."

"What do you mean?" Philip asked.

"See this box of chocolates." Max pointed to the silver box with the gold bow. "Some people can't resist the temptation, they have to hide the box or throw it away. She didn't have to make an excuse, unless she couldn't trust herself to say no."

Philip felt a weight lift from his shoulders. He gazed at the piazza and saw couples eating cones of pink gelato. He watched a boy and a girl jump rope and a waiter carry a silver tray of tartufo.

"Look at her photo." Max picked up his camera. "When she looks at you her eyes sparkle."

Philip grabbed the camera and studied the picture of Amelia. Her eyes were wide and her mouth was open in a smile. Her head was cocked to one side as if she was listening to something.

Philip wanted to race across the piazza to the Hassler. He wanted to run through the revolving glass doors to the elevator. He wanted to knock on the door of the Villa Medici Suite and tell Amelia to stop the charade.

"Her friend is like a character in a Disney movie." Max clicked through the photos. "I've never seen eyes that blue or hair the color of flax. She could make a man swear off brunettes."

Philip glanced at Sophie's large blue eyes and thick dark lashes. He studied her pale cheeks and slender shoulders. He thought about the picture of the girl wearing the diamond tiara and his heart raced.

If Amelia was telling the truth, this could be a bigger story than Amelia Tate pretending to be a maid. He pictured Adam's face when he told him the princess of a small European country was hiding in Rome. He saw his byline on the front page of *Inside Rome*.

But what if Sophie wasn't a princess? Amelia would know he betrayed her and wouldn't speak to him again. He clicked through the photos and handed the camera to Max. He sipped his iced coffee and leaned back in his chair.

"What did you do!" Max exclaimed. "You erased the photos."

"I'm such a klutz." Philip shrugged, shielding his eyes from the sun. "You'll just have to take some more."


Philip closed the door and tossed his keys on the dining room table. He sat at his desk and flipped through the mail. He opened the bill from the butcher and the gas company and the electricity. He sighed and walked to the kitchen counter.

His phone rang and he picked it up.

"I haven't heard from you or Max," Adam's voice came over the line. "I'm afraid I'm throwing my euros into the Tiber River."

"It's going wonderfully." Philip held the phone against his ear. "Last night we had a romantic dinner in Trastevere, followed by a moonlight stroll to the Piazza de Santa Cecilia. We touched shoulders and talked about poetry and art and literature. Max got some wonderful photos."

"I was beginning to think I should have taken my money to the racetrack," Adam replied. "So what happens next?"

"I have tickets to *Cinderella* at Opera Roma. I planned a day trip to Orvieto and wine tasting in Montepulciano."

"I knew when I hired you I did the right thing," Adam beamed. "I'm going out tonight to celebrate."

Philip hung up the phone and sat at his desk. How was he going to get Amelia to go out with him again when she was leaving Rome? And if she did, could he really keep lying to her? He flashed on Max who was counting on him and Adam who was trying to save the newspaper. He pictured Amelia's sparkling brown eyes and knew no matter what he had to see her. He opened the computer and stared at the blank screen. He was a writer, he would think of something.

Amelia entered the Villa Medici Suite and placed her purse on the marble end table. She walked to the balcony and gazed at the Spanish Steps and the Via Condotti. Suddenly the sun was too bright and the cars were too noisy and the smells made her nauseous. She closed the curtains and sunk onto the ivory silk sofa.

She remembered waking up in Philip's bed and never felt so humiliated. She was like a child who kept failing a spelling test. She leaned against the silk pillows and resolved to never drink champagne again.

She gazed at the pile of letters on the glass coffee table and wondered if Audrey Hepburn had ever gotten drunk or done something foolish. She picked up the top page and began to read.

*Dear Kitty,*                                    *July 2, 1952*

*James arrived this morning, he has meetings in Rome and came a day early. The Hassler prepared a picnic of baguettes and salami and Edam cheese and we took it to the Pantheon. The sky was so blue, I felt like I was on a Greek island.*

*The sun was shining and there was a soft breeze and he wrapped his arms around me. I realized how lonely I've been eating room service insalata mista and cream of tomato soup. We strolled back to the Hassler and he said he had a present.*

*Oh, Kitty, you can't guess what the surprise was; it was the most beautiful wedding dress I've ever seen! I was terrified his mother would insist I wear a satin gown with a huge bow and a twelve-foot train. But I unwrapped the tissue paper and discovered a white crepe dress that stopped just below my knees.*

*"Is this for me?" I gasped.*

*"My mother knew you were too busy for fittings." James smiled.*

*He wore a dark suit and white shirt and narrow tie. His blond hair flopped over his forehead and he smelled of Clive Christian cologne.*

*"How did she know my style?" I asked, holding it against my chest.*

*"She invited Baroness Ella to stay at Huddersfield," James replied. "They designed it together."*

*"It's perfect." I admired the cinched waist and flared skirt. "I couldn't imagine anything better."*

*"And perhaps you can look over this." He drew a piece of paper from his suit pocket. "Mother suggested we have a noon ceremony followed by a luncheon. Very small, just one long table in the dining room."*

I took the paper and glanced at the names of my dearest friends. I looked up at his sparkling eyes and my heart hammered in my chest.

"I thought you wanted a reception for five hundred people," I stammered.

"That will be in the evening." James nodded. "But it's impossible to talk when the orchestra is playing and half the night is spent in a receiving line."

"We'll serve Cornish hens and summer vegetables." I clapped my hands. "Maybe we can pick blueberries and have a blueberry pie for dessert."

"And there's one more thing." James handed me a cream envelope.

I opened the envelope and read an invitation to a private viewing at Coco Chanel's atelier on September 27.

"But we're not going to be in Paris." I frowned.

"If we honeymoon in Cannes we'll spend most of our time driving to the South of France," James mused. "I booked four nights in the presidential suite at the Crillon. We can fly to New York directly so you'll have plenty of time to shop and . . ."

I flung myself into his arms before he could finish. Four days in Paris with nothing to do but sit at the outdoor cafés on the Champs-Élysées and visit the boutiques on the Rue Saint-Honoré. Gil will be furious if I arrive in New York five pounds heavier but I don't care. I'm going to eat pain au chocolat and escargots and soufflé.

I looked at James's green eyes and narrow cheeks and knew that marrying him is the best decision I ever made. We are going to be so happy!

Audrey

*Dear Kitty,* *July 3, 1952*

*I woke up this morning with a craving for English sausages. I know sausages are fattening but Mr. Wyler works us so hard, sometimes we don't stop until dinner. I called room service and ordered sausages and toast and scrambled eggs.*

*I opened the* Observer *and saw a picture of James in the Style section. He was wearing white tie and tails and dancing with a slim brunette. She wore a white satin gown and long silk gloves. His arm was around her waist and he was kissing her on the side of her mouth.*

*I was about to call James's room when the doorbell rang.*

*"I thought I'd join you for a cup of tea before my meetings." He entered the suite.*

*"What's this?" I handed him the newspaper.*

*He studied it closely and smiled. "That was at Henrietta Fleming's debutante ball. Don't you remember Gordon Fleming's little sister? Henrietta used to invite us to her dolls' tea parties when we came home from Eton."*

*"You are kissing her," I said stubbornly.*

*"Hardly a kiss." James shrugged.*

*He turned the page and pointed to a photo of him with an older woman in a blue silk gown.*

*"Here's one of me kissing Lady Fleming, do you think we're having a tryst?"*

*I sat at the dining room table and sprinkled pepper on scrambled eggs. But suddenly the eggs were stiff and the toast was dry and the sausages were cold.*

*"Surely you're not going to worry about some silly photos in the* Observer," *James insisted. "I wish you had been at the debutante ball, I spent most of the night dancing with women over seventy."*

I imagined James gliding across the ballroom with dowagers in silk ball gowns and giggled.

"That's better." He put his hand under my chin. "You know there's no one in the world except you."

The morning seemed to drag on forever. We were filming at the outdoor market in the Campo de Fiori and the sun was so hot I felt like I was in the jungle.

I was refreshing my makeup when I saw James approach the piazza. He wore a red blazer and navy slacks and clutched a bouquet of tulips.

"What are you doing here?" I ran over to him.

"I brought you these." James handed me the flowers. "I thought I'd take you to lunch at Alfredo's."

"They're lovely," I replied. "But we might not break for lunch for hours."

James gazed at the huge cameras and the bright lights and the row of canvas chairs.

"I'll wait," he said, hopping onto a chair.

We were shooting the scene where I drop a basket of apples and they roll on the pavement. Joe helps me collect them and we end up kissing. It's a tiny kiss but suddenly I was nervous. I saw James consult his watch and stride over to Mr. Wyler.

"You should have stopped for lunch hours ago," he fumed. "It's three o'clock in the afternoon."

"This is a major motion picture." Mr. Wyler glared at him. "I don't stop until it's perfect."

"I run an international transportation business." James knotted his brow. "There's nothing more important than delivering on time."

"Let's behave, gentlemen." Mr. Peck approached them. He had a light sheen on his cheeks. "I'm sure Mr. Hanson is only concerned for Miss Hepburn's well-being."

"I don't think we've been introduced." James held out his hand. "I'm James Hanson, Audrey's fiancé."

"Gregory Peck." He shook his hand. "It's a pleasure to meet you."

"You're in an odd line of business," James said slowly. "Kissing other women for a living."

Mr. Peck dropped his hand. "At least when I kiss another woman, I'm only acting."

I glanced at Mr. Peck's chair and saw a copy of the Observer. I ran to my dressing room and shut the door. I laid my head on the desk and burst into tears.

Oh, Kitty, I kept picturing James whirling around the dance floor with a debutante in a white satin gown. I heard a knock on the door and got up to answer it.

"You're going to give Willy a heart attack if you don't finish the scene." Mr. Peck entered the dressing room.

"I'm sorry for the way James behaved," I mumbled.

"If I was your fiancé and saw you kissing another man, I'd punch him in the jaw."

"You would?" I raised my eyebrow.

"Of course." He shrugged. "What man wouldn't?"

"But we were acting, it's my job," I protested.

He drew a newspaper from under his arm and opened it on the desk. "I'm guessing Mr. Hanson's job includes attending debutante balls and rubbing elbows with dukes and duchesses."

"It is important that he maintains the right connections," I conceded.

"Then neither of you have anything to worry about." He

*walked to the door. "Let's finish the scene, I'm dying for a plate of spaghetti and a cold beer."*

*"How can I thank you?" I asked. "I feel like such a nuisance."*

*He turned to me and stood very close.*

*"There's one thing you can do," he said.*

*"There is?" I replied.*

*"You can call me Greg."*

*Oh, Kitty, sometimes I feel like I'm not a good actress or a good fiancée. But every now and then, when Mr. Wyler smiles or Gregory Peck says a kind word, I think I have the best job in the world.*

*Audrey*

*Dear Kitty,*                                        *July 4, 1952*

*This evening I was changing out of Princess Ann's pink satin ball gown when there was a knock on the dressing room door.*

*Gregory Peck poked his head in. "We're going to Harry's Bar for a drink. You should join us."*

*"No, thank you." I shook my head. "I'm going home to study my lines."*

*"An old friend of mine wants to meet you," he insisted. "He's directing a movie and thinks you'd be perfect for the lead."*

*"You said I should retire to Yorkshire and wear wide hats and learn to play croquet." I raised my eyebrow.*

*"I've changed my mind." He shrugged. "My friend saw you on Broadway and thinks you are the finest actress of your generation."*

*"I've nothing to wear." I flushed.*

*"What you have on will do," he replied. "It's just a small group of friends."*

*"This is a four-hundred-dollar Dior couture gown," I protested. "Mr. Wyler would kill me."*

"If anything happens I'll tell him it was my fault." He took my arm and propelled me toward the door. "Come on, I'm dying of thirst."

We entered Harry's Bar and I could barely breathe from the cigarette smoke. The walls were covered with gold velvet and the floors were dark wood. I saw waiters in white jackets carry silver trays of chilled prawns and caviar and melba toast.

"There you are." Veronique Passani crossed the room. "We've ordered a round of Negronis and a platter of oysters. I just got off the plane and I'm starving."

I hadn't seen Veronique in a week and I'd hoped she finished her interviews. She makes me nervous, as if she's going to write down everything I say.

"I didn't know you were away," I said, following them to a table in the back.

She wore a red crepe Dior dress and ivory pumps. Her auburn hair fell to her shoulders and she carried a Chanel clutch. I glanced down at my pink satin ball gown and felt hopelessly overdressed.

"I was in London doing a story on Queen Elizabeth." Veronique dipped oysters in cocktail sauce. "I ruined three pairs of shoes in the rain and drank endless cups of tea. I couldn't live in a city where you can't get a decent cup of coffee."

"You've brought Audrey Hepburn." A man approached the table. He had thick brown hair and gray eyes. He wore a white dinner jacket and tan slacks. "It's a pleasure to meet you."

"This is Mel Ferrer," Greg introduced us. "We acted in some plays in New York, now he's an up-and-coming director in Hollywood."

"That's a nice way of saying 'struggling.'" Mel laughed. "I do have my eye on a project, and you would be perfect for the lead."

"What is it called?" I asked.

"War and Peace," he replied, popping an olive in his mouth.

"War and Peace," I spluttered.

"Do you think I haven't read it?" Mel asked, looking amused.

"Mel went to Princeton," Greg explained. He wore a black dinner jacket and gray slacks. "He's trying to elevate the movie business."

"Princeton?" I raised my eyebrow.

"You don't believe me?" Mel asked.

"I can't say, I've never met anyone who went to Princeton."

He squeezed into the table beside me. His cheeks were smooth and he smelled of peppermint aftershave. "Well, Miss Hepburn, now you have."

Greg and Mel walked to the bar to order another round of drinks and Veronique tapped her long red fingernails on the marble counter.

"Mel Ferrer is very handsome," she mused.

"I wouldn't know, I'm engaged," I bristled.

"I admire you, you're such a progressive fiancée."

"Progressive?" I repeated, feeling a prickle on the back of my neck.

"Allowing your fiancé to dance with fashionable young women," she replied, scooping up a handful of cashews.

"If you're talking about Henrietta Fleming's debutante ball, Henrietta is the little sister of one of James's oldest friends."

"I was talking about them dancing at the Flamingo Club in Soho the other night," Veronique continued.

"I'm sure they were with a group," I said icily. "The Observer prints all sorts of gossip without telling the whole story."

Veronique swallowed the cashews and looked at me. "I didn't read about it in the paper, I saw them together."

*We drank Bloody Marys and Mel asked me to dance. He is a wonderful dancer, I could barely keep up. But I listened to Cole Porter and pictured James in a smoky London nightclub.*

*Oh, Kitty, I can't expect James to sit at home while I make a movie in Rome. But sometimes I picture his sparkling eyes and white smile and think I want too much.*

*Audrey*

Amelia put the letters on the glass coffee table. She leaned against the silk cushions and tucked her feet under her. She closed her eyes and fell asleep.

# chapter seventeen

Philip poured another cup of coffee and studied the photo on the dining room table. It was the only picture that hadn't been erased from Max's camera. He picked it up and looked at Amelia's wide brown eyes and white smile. She was gazing at Philip and her hand rested on his sleeve.

He tossed it on the table and walked to the fire escape. For three days he had been trying to come up with a plan to see Amelia. He imagined running into her in the Hassler lobby or at a café in the Piazza di Trevi. But what if she was with her producer or on her way to the set? If she were forced to reveal her identity the charade would be over.

He heard a knock on the door and went to open it. He saw an older woman with auburn hair and slender cheekbones. She wore a beige linen dress with a cropped jacket. She carried a white leather Gucci purse and wore large white sunglasses.

"Mom!" Philip exclaimed. "What are you doing here?"

"I'm glad I found you." She entered the room. "Your father said I should wait at the hotel, but I love exploring the streets of Rome. Every woman should be whistled at, it makes me feel ten years younger."

Philip studied his mother's large blue eyes and wide red mouth. She was almost sixty but she was still a beautiful woman. She had been a model in New York before she married his father. She spent the last thirty years being a society hostess but she still looked lovely in a designer dress and pumps.

"I mean, what are you doing in Rome? I thought you were on your way to Bermuda."

"It's a quick trip." She moved around the living room, running her fingers over the wooden bookshelf and glass dining room table. "We arrived late last night and we're leaving for Paris tonight. Your father had business and I decided to join him."

"Can I get you something?" Philip waved his hand. "A cup of coffee, a slice of toast."

"A glass of water would be nice. I already drank more coffee than Dr. Burns allows me in a week. Everything in Rome is irresistible, the espresso, the fashion, the pasta. I can see why you're here, but I'm glad you're coming home. We've missed you so much."

Philip collected cups and saucers and put them in the sink. He poured a glass of water and handed it to his mother.

"What a pretty girl." She examined the photo of Amelia. "Is she someone special?"

Philip grabbed the photo and put it on his desk. "She's just a friend."

"She reminds me of a young Audrey Hepburn," she mused. "She's always been my favorite movie star. When your father and I got married I had a little black dress I wore every Saturday night. John used to call me Holly Golightly. If only I still had a twenty-four-inch waist and natural eyelashes."

The front door opened and Max walked in. He wore a yellow shirt and jeans and sneakers. His camera was slung over his shoulder and he was eating an almond croissant.

"I didn't mean to interrupt," he stumbled. "I can come back later."

"This is my mother, Lily Hamilton," Philip introduced them. "She and my father made a surprise visit."

"It's a pleasure to meet you, Mrs. Hamilton." Max took her hand. "It's a shame you just had this ugly guy, you would have created some beautiful girls."

"All this flattery is going to my head." Lily laughed. "I should go back to the hotel and have a beauty rest. Perhaps we can have an early dinner before we leave. We're staying at the Hassler."

"The Hassler," Philip spluttered, spilling coffee on the dining room table.

"Your father prefers the Grand Hotel but I insisted." Lily shrugged. "I love the location, all of Rome is at my feet."

Philip glanced at the photo of Amelia and his heart raced. If his mother bumped into Amelia in the lobby she might recognize her and say something. He tugged at his collar and glanced at Max.

"Max and I are going to Umbria," Philip improvised. "I'm writing an article on the truffle industry and Max is taking photos. You should come with us, it's a beautiful drive."

"Your father has meetings and I do love the countryside." Lily hesitated. "I'll run back to the Hassler and change my clothes."

"No!" Philip interrupted. "We don't have time, we want to get some photos while the light is good. Why don't you take off your jacket and splash water on your face?"

Lily opened the door to the bathroom and beamed. "How can I refuse such a wonderful invitation? I'll just be a minute."

Philip dragged Max onto the landing and shut the door. "My

mother saw the photo of Amelia. If she runs into her at the Hassler, she could ruin the whole thing. We have to keep her busy until her flight."

"How are we going to get to Umbria?" Max frowned. "We don't have a car."

Philip reached into his pocket and took out a wad of euros. He flashed on Adam saying he was throwing his money in the Tiber River and shuddered. "Here, take this and go rent one."

They drove in a red Fiat through the outskirts of Rome into the winding hills of Umbria. Philip glanced out the window at the deep valleys and green fields and wished he explored the countryside more often. But it cost money to rent a car or take a train and he felt nervous if he wasn't drumming up assignments.

His mother sat in the backseat exclaiming over the medieval castles and ancient churches and tiny villages. They took photos at Lake Trasimene and sampled sheep cheese in Norcia. They ate a picnic lunch of sausages and ham and unsalted bread and washed it down with sparkling water.

They visited the Ducal Palace in Gubbio and the fourteenth-century cathedral in Orieto. They admired the Renaissance architecture in Spoleto and the chapel in Assisi. Philip gazed at the portrait of Saint Francis and remembered childhood trips to the Met and the Guggenheim. He and his mother spent many Saturday mornings studying paintings by Rembrandt and Picasso. Afterward they would share a cheeseburger and shake at Sardi's.

"I haven't done anything like this in years." Lily sighed, eating spinach salad with goat's cheese. "When I travel with your father, our itinerary includes three-star Michelin restaurants. I love Tour d'Argent in

Paris and the Connaught in London but it's nice to eat at a simple trattoria."

Philip glanced around the piazza in Perugia and almost forgot the money in his pocket was Adam's. Tourists sat under striped umbrellas, sipping limoncellos. There were elegant boutiques and shop windows filled with colorful bottles of olive oil.

"You should come here with Daphne," Lily mused, tearing apart a baguette. "She would love the chapel in Assisi."

Philip put down his fork and pushed back his plate. "I haven't seen Daphne in three years."

"She was very warm when I ran into her and I don't think she's seeing anyone seriously." Lily sipped a glass of water.

"I don't want to date Daphne and I don't want to drink Bloody Marys at the Knickerbocker club," he snapped. "I'm a journalist."

"You may think you know what you want, but you don't know what you'll miss," Lily said quietly. "You can't spend your life in a bedsit in Rome."

"I'm a grown man, I can make my own decisions," Philip bristled.

"Some people find their passion in work and others have hobbies that fulfill them," she replied. "You can write in the evenings, perhaps start a novel."

"If you flew to Rome to convince me to join Hamilton and Sons you're wasting your time." He threw his napkin on the table. "I know I don't have a choice but that doesn't mean I like it."

Lily drizzled olive oil on spinach leaves and added salt and ground pepper. She looked at Philip and her eyes were dark.

"There are worse things for a father than expecting his son to keep his word."

"I had to sample every chocolate in the store." Max approached the table. He carried two silver and blue boxes tied with silver ribbons.

"Baci chocolate is the most famous chocolate in Italy, each piece is wrapped in a love letter."

"Why do you have two boxes?" Philip asked.

"I bought one for Lena and one for the countess." Max shrugged, dipping a baguette in olive oil. "She loves hazelnut cream filling."

They drove back to the Hassler and Philip walked his mother up the stone steps.

"I just have time for a quick bath before our flight." She glanced at her watch. "I can't arrive in Paris with grass stains on my skirt."

"It was great to see you." Philip stuffed his hands in his pockets.

"Do you want to come up and say hello to your father?" Lily asked.

"I don't have anything new to say to him." Philip shook his head.

Lily leaned forward and kissed him on the cheek. "I had a wonderful afternoon, you and Max are terrific tour guides."

Philip ran down the steps and poked his head in the Fiat.

"You can return the car, I'm going for a walk."

"Do you mind if I make a couple of deliveries?" Max pointed to the silver boxes on the passenger seat.

Philip nodded. "Be my guest."

Philip strode down the Spanish Steps and through the Piazza di Spagna. It was early evening and the sun slipped behind the Colosseum. He watched elegant couples consult menus and enter intimate restaurants. He saw men and women sitting at outdoor cafés, holding hands and sipping Bellinis.

He pictured his mother in her white sunglasses and his father in his wingtip shoes and felt a pain in his chest. He didn't mean to disappoint them, but he couldn't put on a Calvin Klein suit because his name was on the building. If he didn't write his skin itched and his heart pounded.

He passed a café with yellow awnings and plate glass windows. He peered inside and saw a young woman with a silk scarf tied around her head. She wore dark sunglasses and was reading a paperback book. She wore a red cotton dress and silver sandals.

Philip opened the door and walked inside. He sat at a table in the front and drummed his fingers on the white linen tablecloth.

"Good evening, how can I help you?" a waiter asked.

Philip glanced at Amelia's table and saw a slice of raspberry cheese-cake and a frothy cappuccino.

"I'll have what she's having." He waved his hand.

The waiter looked in Amelia's direction and shrugged. "I'm sorry, sir, that's the last piece of cheesecake. Would you like to make another selection?"

"No, thank you." Philip rubbed his forehead.

He strode to Amelia's table and waited for her to look up. Finally she put her book down and gazed at Philip. "Can I help you?"

"You took the last piece of cheesecake."

Amelia smiled and closed her book. "I've heard ReCafé has the best cheesecake in Rome."

"Are you sure your source is reliable?" Philip pulled out a chair.

"I heard it from a well-known local writer." Amelia nodded.

"I have to sample it to make sure." Philip picked up a fork. "Some-times reviewers are paid for their reviews."

"How scandalous!" Amelia exclaimed. "This writer is the most honest person I've ever met."

Philip took a bite of cheesecake and wiped his mouth with a napkin. "The raspberry is a little tangy and the cheese is very creamy, but overall it's delicious."

"I'm glad to hear it." Amelia grinned and picked up her book. "If you'll excuse me, I'm reading."

Philip sat back in his chair. He sipped a glass of water and felt his heart racing.

"I thought you left Rome."

"I had a few things to wrap up," she mumbled, turning the page.

"Then you can help me, I need your advice."

"My advice?" Amelia looked up.

"I'm writing a feature on Rome's most famous fountains, I don't know which ones to include."

"Include all of them," Amelia suggested.

"There are dozens, I don't want to bore my readers." Philip's eyes sparkled and his face broke into a smile. "Come with me, help me choose my favorites."

"Now?" Amelia raised her eyebrow.

"The feature is due tomorrow," Philip pleaded. "It'll just take an hour."

Amelia gazed out the window at the pink sun streaming on the cobblestones. She turned to Philip and shrugged. "I have to finish my cheesecake."

He picked up a fork. "I'll help you."

They crossed the Piazza di Trevi and saw the silver lights of the Trevi Fountain. They studied the Fountain of Nymphs with its naked nymphs and the Fountain of Turtles with its marble turtles. They entered the Piazza Navona and saw the Fountain of Four Rivers.

"The Fountain of Four Rivers is the most complex fountain in Rome," Philip began. "Pope Innocent X held a contest to choose the designer and Bernini won. It was completed in 1651 and it was so expensive he had to raise the bread tax to pay for it."

Amelia looked up and saw a tall Egyptian obelisk flanked by huge marble figures. There were thick snakes and birds and palm trees surrounded by rushing water.

"It's impressive but it's not my favorite," Amelia mused. "I like the Trevi Fountain, it's like an underwater palace."

"If you turn your back to the Trevi Fountain and toss in a coin, you are promised to return to Rome," Philip explained. "But if you make a wish and throw a coin into the Fountain of Four Rivers, your wish will come true."

"Any wish?" Amelia raised her eyebrow.

Philip fished two coins out of his pocket and handed one to Amelia. "Let's try it."

Amelia glanced at the gold coin and giggled. She closed her eyes and tossed it into the fountain.

Philip threw a coin into the fountain and turned to Amelia. "What did you wish?"

"I'm not telling." She smiled, watching the stars twinkle in the night sky.

"I'll tell you mine," Philip whispered, pulling her close and tipping her head up to his. "I wished I could kiss you."

Philip covered her mouth with his and ran his hands down her back. She kissed him back, wrapping her arms around his waist.

"Now tell me your wish," he pulled away.

Amelia rubbed her lips and giggled. "I wished for another slice of cheesecake."

They sat at an outdoor table and shared raspberry cheesecake and iced coffee with nutmeg and cinnamon. They talked about books and magazines and movies. Philip tucked a loose hair behind Amelia's ear and curled his hand around her fingers.

"Do you miss New York?" Amelia asked. "Don't you get lonely living where everyone speaks another language?"

"You can be lonely anywhere, even in the place where you grew up, especially if the people you love don't understand you," Philip said slowly. "Sometimes it helps to go somewhere new and realize what's important to you."

"I think I know what you mean." Amelia pictured Sheldon and the huge silver cameras on the set. She remembered Whit saying acting was a phase and she'd get over it. She thought about all the glorious hours she'd spent curled up on an ivory sofa in the Villa Medici Suite rehearsing her lines.

"If you look hard enough you can find things in the new place that make you happy: a café that serves pesto spagettini, a used bookstore that carries old Archie comic books." Philip traced a circle around her palm. "Someone who's beautiful and smart and has a wonderful smile."

Amelia pulled her hand away and glanced at her watch. "I have to go, I had a lovely time."

"I'll walk you home," Philip replied.

Amelia shook her head. "I have some errands to run before I go to work."

She strolled along the cobblestones and then stopped and turned around. "I've decided not to go to Florence and Venice."

"The Hassler will be happy to hear that." Philip slipped his hands in his pockets. "And so am I."

# chapter eighteen

Amelia sat at her dressing table and gazed in the mirror. She dusted her cheeks with sparking blush and coated her eyelashes with Lancôme mascara. She rubbed shimmering lip gloss on her lips and dabbed her wrists with Estée Lauder's Lovely.

She pinned her hair with a ceramic clip and glanced at her watch. She had an early morning call and didn't want to be late. They were filming the scene at the Mouth of Truth and she couldn't wait to ride through Rome on a shiny red Vespa.

She grabbed her purse and remembered Philip's kiss at the Fountain of Four Rivers. She shouldn't have kissed him when she still thought about Whit and should be concentrating on *Roman Holiday*. Then she flashed on sharing raspberry cheesecake and talking about love and books and movies. There was something about Philip that made her feel secure and happy.

She heard a knock on the door and wondered whether maid service arrived early. She opened the door and saw a man wearing a navy blazer and beige twill slacks. His dark curly hair touched his collar and his chin had a faint stubble.

"Whit!" she exclaimed, dropping her purse on the marble floor. "What are you doing here?"

"I had one more meeting with Alex Tomaselli," he replied. "And I wanted to see you."

Amelia picked up her purse and tried to stop trembling. She remembered him crossing the Piazza di Spagna and disappearing up the Spanish Steps. She remembered lying in bed and thinking her heart was breaking.

"I can't be late for the set." She hesitated. "Can we talk this evening?"

"It will just take a minute." He entered the living room and glanced at the gold silk curtains and glass dining room table and vases of yellow and white roses. He saw the maple sideboard set with a silver coffeepot and Limoges cups and saucers. He saw a tray of fresh scones and strawberry jam and whipped butter. "I see they are treating you well."

"Sheldon is a stickler for punctuality." Amelia glanced at her watch.

"I didn't want to come to Rome, but Evan insisted I take the meeting with Alex." Whit slipped his hands in his pockets. "On the plane I watched *Hannah's Secret,* I hadn't seen it in years. You were very good. I realized I might have been hasty."

"Hasty?" Amelia repeated.

"Insisting that you quit acting," Whit replied. "A lot of actors move away from Los Angeles and make a movie every couple of years. You could still be an actress and we could be together."

"But they already have established careers." Amelia frowned. "And what about the paparazzi?"

"If you only made a movie every two or three years they wouldn't hound you when you stood in line at Peet's," Whit continued. "We could lead a normal life but you could still do what you loved."

Amelia glanced at Whit's blue eyes and tan cheeks. She smoothed her hair and slipped on white leather sandals.

"I have to go; can we talk after I finish shooting?"

Whit caught her hand and held it tightly. He tucked a loose hair behind her ear and kissed her on the lips.

"I'll be waiting in the lobby."

Amelia glanced at the platters of turkey and Swiss cheese sandwiches. She saw wooden bowls of red apples and purple grapes and overripe peaches. She saw hard-boiled eggs and cinnamon Danishes and soft chocolate chip cookies.

She nibbled a grape and realized she wasn't hungry. The crew had filmed outside all day and she felt like she had a layer of gasoline and sweat stuck to her blue crepe dress. She tucked her hair behind her ears and thought about Whit's arrival at the Villa Medici Suite.

She remembered his proposition and wondered if she could really have an acting career if she left Hollywood. She wasn't Nicole Kidman who could live in Tennessee and get any role or Katie Holmes who performed in an occasional Broadway play while raising Suri. She was starring in her first major role, and there were plenty of young actresses who would take her parts if she moved to San Francisco.

Suddenly she pictured Philip standing in his tiny kitchen making a bacon and lettuce sandwich and shivered. He had been very kind but their relationship was nothing more than an on-set romance. He was a struggling writer living in Rome who thought she was a maid at the Hassler. She couldn't consider him when she was making a decision.

"There you are." A man approached her. "I was afraid we left you sweltering on the Via dei Cerchi."

"I wouldn't mind a limoncello," Amelia admitted. "But I think the scene went well."

"The scene was good." Sheldon nodded. He wore a checkered shirt and khakis. His thick white hair was brushed over his forehead and he wore round glasses. "If I can only get craft services to provide chilled soft drinks, my crew wouldn't keep threatening to quit."

"The grapes are delicious." Amelia popped one in her mouth.

"I need to talk to you." Sheldon frowned. "Can I see you in my trailer?"

Amelia put her plate on the table and took a deep breath. She wondered if Sheldon noticed she was preoccupied and had to repeat her lines. She followed him across the piazza and climbed the steps to his trailer.

"Have a seat." He gestured to a blue plastic chair. There was a white metal desk and a wooden bookshelf and a potted plant. "Every movie I ask for an air-conditioned trailer with a refrigerator and a leather desk chair. I have a bad back; if I sit in this crap chair I look like the Hunchback of Notre Dame."

"I want to show you something." He rummaged through the drawer and brought out a manila envelope. He slit it open and dropped the contents on the desk.

Amelia looked at the papers on the desk and saw glossy color photos. She picked up a picture of herself wearing the pink Balenciaga gown and diamond tiara. There were close-ups of her wearing thick mascara and bright red lipstick, and a picture of her in a polka dot dress and wide straw hat.

"These are publicity shots for *Roman Holiday*," Sheldon explained. "I want you to choose your favorites."

"What are they for?" Amelia asked.

"*People, Vanity Fair, Us, E!*" Sheldon adjusted his glasses. "The publicity department gets a dozen requests a day and it's only going to increase. You're the talk of Hollywood."

"I am?" Amelia raised her eyebrow.

"I may have sent some of the dailies to Warner Brothers and they may have leaked one or two to the press." He grinned. "When *Roman Holiday* comes out, you're going to be the biggest star since Julia Roberts."

Amelia glanced at the photos again and felt her shoulders relax. She looked at Sheldon and her eyes were bright.

"How can I possibly choose? I love all of them."


Amelia hurried across the Piazza di Spagna and ran up the Spanish Steps. By the time she removed her makeup it was almost seven o'clock. She had brushed her hair and reapplied her pink lip gloss. She changed into a red linen dress and gold sandals.

She ran up the last step and heard footsteps behind her. She turned and saw two men carrying silver cameras. They wore black jeans and white T-shirts and leather jackets.

"Bella Amelia," one called. "*Uno foto per favore.*"

"I can't." Amelia kept walking. "I'm late."

"It will take no time at all," the other man insisted. "Such a beautiful smile."

Amelia felt the bulb flash and tripped on the pavement. She stood up and strode toward the Hassler. She entered the revolving glass doors and looked around the lobby.

She saw bellboys in gold uniforms carrying Louis Vuitton trunks and Dior garment bags. She glanced at the Hassler Bar and saw Whit sitting in a high-backed leather chair. He wore a navy blazer and tan slacks and held a shot glass in one hand.

"I'm sorry I'm late." She approached the mahogany table.

"Are you all right?" Whit asked. "You look like you've been running."

"I'm fine." Amelia smoothed her hair. "I'd love a gin and tonic over ice."

Whit walked to the bar and Amelia perched on the leather chair. She suddenly saw a familiar figure standing across the room. He wore a white collared shirt and beige slacks. He had dark wavy hair and wore a leather watch.

The man turned around and Amelia realized it wasn't Philip. She felt her cheeks flush and something inside her shifted.

"I'm starving." Whit placed the shot glass on the table. "Maybe we can go upstairs and order veal Parmigiana and scalloped potatoes and strawberry gelato."

Amelia sipped her drink and thought about the glossy photos on Sheldon's desk. She pictured long days on the set and the feeling of having done something wonderful. She remembered sitting at ReCafé with Philip and sipping tall iced coffees.

"I don't think so," she said slowly, setting her glass on the table. "I don't want to make a movie every couple of years and I don't want to avoid photographers. I want to wake up every morning grateful that I do what I love, and I want to thank every person who buys a magazine or movie ticket. I might grow to hate the paparazzi or get tired of craft service sandwiches but I love acting and I don't want to give it up."

"I didn't say you should give it up. . . ." Whit interrupted.

"Doing something you love every two years is worse, I'll watch other actresses get the best roles while I learn hatha yoga." Amelia bit her lip. "If you'll excuse me, I'm going upstairs to take a cool bath."

"Amelia, wait." Whit jumped up.

"You left because you knew it wouldn't work." Amelia blinked away sudden tears. "Nothing has changed, I think it's best if we say good-bye."

She strode across the gold and black lobby and pressed the button on the elevator. She entered the Villa Medici Suite and went into the marble bathroom. She unzipped her dress and turned on the gold faucet. She stepped into the deep bathtub and realized Whit never said he loved her. She closed her eyes and inhaled the scent of lavender bubbles.

# chapter nineteen

Amelia put down her script and sipped a cup of English breakfast tea. She tore apart a scone and covered it with honey. She glanced out the window and saw the morning light reflected on the red rooftops. She breathed the scent of roses and felt light and happy.

Sheldon had left a message saying she wasn't needed on the set until the afternoon. She sent Philip a note and asked him to join her for lunch. Afterward they would walk to the Castel Sant'Angelo or up to the Capitoline Hill. Amelia imagined leaning against the stone wall with Philip's arm around her waist.

Since the night Whit left they had been almost inseparable. Every evening Philip met her at the Piazza di Trevi or in a café on the Via Condotti. She always had some excuse why he couldn't pick her up. He stopped asking where she lived and she didn't tell him.

No matter how many times she told herself she couldn't see him again, something inside her protested. She knew she had to tell him the truth but the words got stuck in her throat. She couldn't bear to lose him when they were having so much fun.

There was a knock at the door and she ran to the entry to answer it.

"I hope it's not too early." Sophie entered the marble foyer.

She wore white slacks and a white silk blouse knotted at the waist. Her blond hair was pulled into in a low ponytail and tied with a red ribbon.

"I went to the market and bought plums and berries and melon." She handed Amelia a basket of fruit. "I bought too much, but it all looked delicious."

"You've already been to the market?" Amelia asked.

"I couldn't sleep. I walked around the Roman Forum and ran up and down the steps of the Colosseum." Sophie perched on a blue velvet armchair. "Then I had a croissant in the Piazza del Popolo and bought a silk scarf on the Via Condotti."

"But it's only nine in the morning." Amelia frowned.

"I saw the scarf in Gucci and had to have it." Sophie blushed. "The salesgirl opened early."

"Why are you up so early?" Amelia asked, eating a juicy strawberry.

"I hadn't seen Theo since we had dinner in Trastevere," Sophie began, tucking her feet under her. "Last night I was buying olive oil at the Campo de Fiori and I ran into him at the flower stall. He asked if I would join him for dinner and I agreed. I knew it was a mistake, but he wore jeans and a light blue shirt and he looked so handsome.

"After dinner we strolled to the Piazza Santa Maria and sat on the steps of the fountain. It's the oldest fountain in Rome, built in the eighth century." Sophie twisted her hands. "I don't know what got into me, suddenly I turned to Theo and kissed him."

"What did he do?" Amelia gasped.

"He pulled away and strode across the piazza," Sophie replied. "I was mortified, I searched for a taxi to go home. Then I heard footsteps and I saw him walking toward me. He took my head in his hands and kissed me on the mouth."

"What are you going to do?" Amelia asked.

"In two weeks I'm going back to the Royal yacht." Sophie's cheeks turned red. "Nothing has changed but I've ruined everything."

"You haven't done anything any normal twenty-five-year-old girl wouldn't do," Amelia soothed.

"In six months I'm getting married in a sixteenth-century cathedral. There'll be a reception for a thousand people and we'll eat raspberry fondant cake and drink Moët & Chandon and it will be the best night of my life."

Sophie sunk against the ivory silk cushions and buried her face in her hands. She gazed at Amelia and her cheeks were streaked with tears. "But how will I survive until then?"


Amelia stood at the mirror and tied a yellow scarf around her head. She thought about Sophie in her white silk blouse and slacks. She pictured her big eyes and pale cheeks.

Amelia gazed at the shopping bag filled with melons and peaches. Suddenly she didn't feel like eating Parmesan ravioli at an outdoor café. She didn't want to sit across from Philip and lie about being a maid.

She selected a shiny apple and entered the bedroom. She climbed on the four-poster bed and sat against the pillows. She picked up a letter and began to read.

*Dear Kitty,*                                    *August 2, 1952*
*Today is James's last day in Rome; we won't see each other again until the wedding. I was supposed to meet him for dinner at the Grand Hotel but shooting lasted forever. Some people think Mr.*

Wyler doesn't care about his actors but it's the reverse. I watch the dailies and can't believe it's me riding on the back of a Vespa or dancing by the river. He has made me into an actress!

By the time I reached the dining room, it was almost nine o'clock. I searched the restaurant but the maître d' said James left earlier. I didn't know how to contact him and knew he would be furious. James's most valued possession is his Patek Philippe watch and he hates that Italians use the sun as a clock.

I entered the gold revolving doors and saw James sitting at the Hassler bar. He wore a navy suit and white shirt and thin black tie. His hair flopped neatly over his forehead and he wore black leather shoes. I tried to slink to the elevator and run up to my suite. I wanted to change into something sexy and douse myself with perfume.

"There's my charming fiancée," he called out. "How kind of you to make an appearance. Have you been at a club with your actor friends?"

I approached the bar and saw James's eyes were glazed and his cheeks had a thin sheen. He held a martini and there was a martini shaker on the table.

"I'm terribly sorry, shooting ran late," I mumbled.

"Did you tell your director you were having dinner with your fiancé on his last night in Rome?" James put down his drink.

I sat opposite him and tried to smile. "I'm here now and there's still time for dinner. Let's go to Ristorante Rinaldi and have spaghetti and mussels."

"I'm tired of spaghetti and I'm tired of the humidity and I'm tired of a country where no one knows how to dress after six P.M.," James protested. "I'll be glad if we don't come back to Rome."

"Well, I'm starving," I replied, suddenly exhausted. "I'm going to order room service veal Parmigiana and a glass of Burgundy."

*James softened and put his hand on mine.*

*"I've had two martinis and a handful of pretzels. Why don't we order a couple of steaks?"*

*We ordered rib eye steak and smoked potatoes and I felt my shoulders relax. We talked about his upcoming trip to Toronto and the newest shows in London and he draped his arm around my chair.*

*"We're meeting Father Percy on September nineteenth and the rehearsal dinner is on the twentieth. Mother rented out the dining room at the Excelsior. We can move it to the garden if the weather is nice but September in Yorkshire is iffy."*

*I cut my steak slowly and dabbed my mouth with a napkin. I put my fork on the plate and looked at James.*

*"We've gotten behind schedule, I don't think shooting will wrap until September twenty-fifth."*

*"Our wedding is on September twenty-first."*

*"We may have to postpone it, I'm under contract." I gulped.*

*"You tell Mr. Wyler that on September twenty-first you're going to be standing at the altar." He stood up and clutched the table. "If I have to come to Rome and carry you off the set."*

*I took the elevator to the Villa Medici Suite and threw myself on the bed. I couldn't possibly leave the set of* Roman Holiday *early. How am I going to appear at a stone church in Huddersfield when I'm shooting a scene in the catacombs? I shouldn't have become an actress; I need to be a magician!*

*Dear Kitty,*                       *August 12, 1952*

*On Thursday night I was drinking a cup of warm milk and honey in bed. I've been going to bed early since James left. After spending all day in the sun, I want nothing more than to step into* a cool bath and soak in the bubbles. Then I sit on the balcony and practice my lines and eat cold tomato soup and crusty baguettes.

I just turned off the light when the phone rang. I reached over the bedside table and picked it up.

"Is this Audrey Hepburn? This is Marjorie, Harry Henigson's secretary."

"My goodness." I sat against the silk pillows. "Aren't you working late?"

"It's nine A.M. in Los Angeles," Marjorie replied. "Mr. Henigson wanted to tell you Paramount would like to give your entire wardrobe as a wedding present."

"My wardrobe?" I frowned, glancing at the antique armoire in the bedroom.

"All the clothes and accessories you wore on Roman Holiday," Marjorie explained. "Four Givenchy evening dresses, two Dior ball gowns, three Chanel suits, a selection of Ferragamo shoes and Manbocher hats, and one evening gown designed by Edith Head herself."

"That's very kind," I replied. "But how did Harry know I was getting married?"

"Mr. Hanson called yesterday and said the ceremony was on September twenty-first in Yorkshire." Marjorie paused as if consulting her notes. "He requested you be let out of your contract if shooting continues past September eighteenth."

"He did what?" I jumped out of bed. My heart was pounding and I could barely breathe. "Let me speak to Harry."

"I'm afraid Mr. Henigson is at his house in Santa Barbara," Marjorie replied. "He won't be in the office until Monday."

I tried calling James but he was on his way to Toronto. I was so angry; I tossed and turned all night. Finally I saw the sun rise behind the Pantheon and slipped on a dress and sandals and ran to the set.

"You're here early." Veronique Passani approached me. It was barely eight o'clock but she looked like she was dressed for a cocktail party. She wore a blue Lanvin dress and beige pumps. Her auburn hair fell smoothly to her shoulders and she wore emerald earrings and a Cartier watch.

"I need to speak to Mr. Wyler," I replied.

"He's not here yet." Veronique extracted a cigarette from a pearl cigarette case and looked at me curiously. "You look like you just rolled out of bed."

"James told Harry Henigson that the wedding is on September twenty-first," I blurted out. "He said if shooting is delayed I want to be released from my contract."

"He didn't just tell Harry." Veronique blew a thin line of smoke. "Let's go somewhere private."

We walked to my dressing room and she handed me a copy of the Observer. I flipped to the front page of the Style section and read out loud:

"International shipping scion James Hanson announced his upcoming nuptials to Audrey Hepburn. Miss Hepburn is a stage actress and the star of the much anticipated American film, Roman Holiday.

"The press conference was held in the Savoy and Mr. Hanson told reporters the ceremony will take place on September twenty-first in Yorkshire, followed by a sit-down dinner at the family home.

"When asked if the date was scheduled so soon as a result of the recent photos of Mr. Hanson squiring various models around London, he bristled and replied:

" 'Audrey and I are getting married because we love each other *and want to spend our lives together. Any other hypothesis is invented purely to sell newspapers.'*

"One reporter asked about the rumor that shooting of Roman Holiday *was behind schedule and would not be completed by the wedding date. Mr. Hanson reflected:*

" *'That doesn't surprise me, I visited the set and it is run with the discipline of a kindergarten class room. Paramount is aware of the date and is prepared to release her from her contract. If I can speak for Miss Hepburn, acting is wonderful fun, but there is no greater role than being my wife.'*

"I would never break my contract." I crumpled the newspaper. "How could he say such things without asking me?"

"Men don't change from the time they are babies and latch onto their mother's breast," Veronique mused. "They always want to come first."

"But he's been so supportive of my acting," I protested. "He bought me wonderful presents and took me to dinner and told everyone I'm going to be a big star."

"It's one thing to have a glamorous fiancée." She stubbed her cigarette in the glass ashtray. "It's another to be dating a girl who'd rather be on a movie set than walking down the aisle of the parish church."

"What am I going to do?" I collapsed into the chair.

"Why don't you take the day off?" Veronique suggested. "I'll tell Willy you have feminine problems and you can go home and take a bath."

"I can't disappoint him." I shook my head. "I'm going to sit here for a while."

*I waited until Veronique left and then I threw myself on the sofa. I thought about Greg making sure my name was above the title and Mr. Wyler applauding my acting and the endless bottles of*

*Coca Cola. I remembered learning how to ride a Vespa and getting soaked in the Trevi Fountain and not being able to cry on cue.*

*I brushed my hair and powdered my cheeks and smoothed my dress. Then I walked onto the set and found Veronique drinking a cup of espresso. I said:*

*"You need to do something for me."*

*On Monday I woke up and had a slice of toast and a glass of orange juice. I put on my favorite Chanel dress and white gloves and a wide straw hat. I slipped on Ferragamo pumps and hurried to the set.*

*The minute I arrived everyone grew quiet. Oh, Kitty, they looked at me as if someone died. I glanced at my canvas chair and saw the* Sunday Times *with my picture in the Style section. I picked it up and read:*

Audrey Hepburn announced that her engagement to British shipping magnate James Hanson has ended. Miss Hepburn, daughter of Baroness Ella Van Heemstra and a rising star in Hollywood, was scheduled to wed Mr. Hanson in an elaborate ceremony in Yorkshire in September.

"When I get married, I want to be the best wife in the world," she commented. "At this time, my commitments in film and on the stage make that impossible. James and I have the utmost respect for each other and will remain dear friends for life."

*I put the paper down and saw Gregory Peck looking at me. He walked over and put his hand on my arm. "Are you feeling all right?"*

*"I'm wonderful, though it's much too hot for these gloves." I*

*stripped off my gloves and tossed them on the chair. I took off my*
*sunglasses and gave him my most dazzling smile.*

*I glanced up and saw Veronique standing on the edge of the*
*piazza. She had a cup of coffee in one hand and a cigarette in the*
*other. She wore a two-piece red linen suit and white pumps.*

*"How did I do?" she asked.*

*"It's worded perfectly." I nodded, putting on my sunglasses so she*
*couldn't see the tears in my eyes.*

*Everyone was so kind and Mr. Wyler even broke for lunch be-*
*fore six o'clock. But I picture James's blue eyes and floppy blond*
*hair and don't feel very brave. I have to be a good actress because*
*now that's all I am, and that's all I may ever be.*

*Audrey*

*Dear Kitty,*                                      *August 17, 1952*

*Today I slept until noon and stayed in a silk robe all day. It was*
*glorious to have nothing to do except read* Vogue *and* Bazaar *and*
Paris Match. *I even swore I wouldn't practice my lines; I wanted*
*one lazy Saturday of sitting on the balcony, enjoying the view and*
*eating white chocolate truffles.*

*The phone rang and I ran inside to pick it up.*

*"A gentleman is here to see you," the concierge said.*

*"Did he give his name?" I asked.*

*"No, Miss Hepburn, but he said you would be happy to see him."*

*I quickly put on a floral dress and smoothed my hair. I rubbed*
*my lips with lipstick and coated my eyes with mascara. For a mo-*
*ment I thought it was James, I hadn't heard from him except for a*
*terse note to return his grandmother's diamond ring. I did see his*
*picture in the* Sunday Times. *He was entering Convent Garden*
*with a blonde in a silver Dior gown.*

There was a knock at the door and I crossed the marble entry to open it.

"I wasn't sure if you'd be in on a Saturday afternoon." Gregory Peck stood at the door. He wore a white shirt and tan slacks. His hair was brushed over his forehead and his cheeks glistened with aftershave. "I was downstairs at the barber and thought I'd look you up."

"Why didn't you give your name to the concierge?" I asked, ushering him into the living room.

"And have the newspapers report 'Gregory Peck visited Audrey Hepburn's suite'?" He chuckled.

He gazed at the plush silk sofas and ivory damask curtains and crystal vases filled with pink and white roses and whistled. "Harry is treating you well."

"James paid for the suite." I blushed, sinking onto a blue satin love seat. "I'll probably have to move to a room next to the laundry."

"I'll fix it up with Harry." He glanced at the photo of James in the Sunday Times. "I see James hasn't been wasting any time."

"He probably had tickets to Swan Lake he didn't want to waste." I picked up the newspaper and tossed it in the garbage.

"I feel a bit responsible." Greg slipped his hands in his pockets. "I don't think your fiancé liked me."

"He didn't like me either," I mused. "He loved the fashionable actress in kitten heels and pearls, but he didn't like the girl who sleeps with an eye mask and would rather eat sausages for dinner."

"Do you really sleep with an eye mask?" Greg raised his eyebrow.

"I'm very sensitive to light," I murmured.

"One day you'll meet the man who makes you want to give all

this up," Greg said slowly. "Until then acting is a better gig than accounting."

"I could never be an accountant, I'm terrible with numbers," I replied.

"I've got a horse and buggy downstairs, would you like to come for a ride?"

"Horse and buggies are for tourists," I teased.

"Publicity sent it over this morning for a few stills," he explained. "It's such a lovely afternoon I thought I'd keep it and explore the city."

"Why not?" I grabbed my purse. "I've read every page of French *Vogue* and I'm not that interested in the new collections."

We took the elevator to the lobby and walked through the gold revolving doors. I saw a red buggy and two magnificent black horses.

"There you are. Gregory said you'd be home." Veronique Passani sat in the backseat. She wore a lime green Chanel suit and beige leather pumps. She wore a green felt hat and had a crocodile bag tucked under her arm.

"It's wonderful to see you." I stumbled, looking at the pavement so she didn't see me blush.

"Mel is joining us, too." Greg pointed to a man standing at the corner, smoking a cigarette.

I glanced up and saw Mel Ferrer walking toward me. He wore a gray suit and a white shirt and a narrow black tie. He tossed his cigarette onto the road and took my hand.

"I asked your agent how to convince you to do War and Peace and he said I must use my charm." He smiled.

We climbed into the buggy and the driver set off down the street. Oh, Kitty, how silly I was to imagine that Gregory Peck

*wanted to take me on a horse and buggy ride through Rome! He's*
*married and is a decade older but he does have the kindest eyes and*
*when he dropped me off he held my hand just a little too long.*

*Audrey*

Amelia put the letters on the bedside table and heard the bells chime twelve o'clock. She pictured Audrey Hepburn with her pixie smile and large brown eyes ending her engagement. She imagined her sitting next to Gregory Peck in a carriage, slowly falling in love.

She remembered when Whit left and she told Sophie she couldn't live without love. She pictured Philip's dark eyes and the way his face lit up when he smiled. She tied a silk scarf around her head and slipped on her sunglasses. She was meeting Philip for lunch and didn't want to keep him waiting.

# chapter twenty

A melia sat at an outdoor table at Rosati and stirred sugar into creamy espresso. She nibbled a piece of biscotti and searched the piazza for Philip.

Rosati had become their favorite place; they loved the wooden tables and the glass cases filled with profiteroles and chocolate tortes.

Amelia usually arrived first and got a table next to the door. She loved having a few moments to herself after a long day on the set. She finally understood how Italians could sit at cafés all morning and return for a glass of Chianti at night. The whole world seemed to pass in front of her.

After they shared plates of grilled scampi and risotto they sauntered along the Via Veneto. Sometimes they climbed to the top of the Colosseum and kissed against a stone wall. Amelia felt Philip's hand creep up her skirt and longed for his fingers to slide inside her. She wanted him to stroke her breasts and take her over the edge.

But if they made love she'd have to tell him the truth and the relationship would be over. He asked her to come to his apartment but she laughed and said she'd slept there enough. He begged her to let him take her home but she insisted it was out of his way.

Sometimes she pretended she had to work late and let him walk with her to the Hassler. They stood at the kitchen entrance and she wished she could bring him to her suite. She wanted to sleep together in the four-poster bed and eat scrambled eggs and bacon at the glass dining table.

She opened a copy of *Inside Rome* and read Philip's feature on the Pope's summer residence at Castel Gandolfo. She turned the page and saw a photo of a blond woman wearing a wide straw hat and white sunglasses. She was standing in the Campo de Fiori clutching a basket of strawberries. She wore a white lace dress and leather sandals.

Amelia studied the picture and her heart raced. She scanned the headline and felt like she couldn't breathe. She read:

European Princess Hiding in Rome.

An anonymous source revealed that Princess Sophia de Grasse of Lentz has been masquerading as a tour guide in Rome. Princess Sophia is the heir apparent to one of Europe's oldest monarchies. The twenty-five-year-old princess is set to marry Prince Leopold of Bulgaria later this year at an elaborate ceremony in Lentz's eight-hundred-year-old Cathedral.

A spokesman for the palace vehemently denied the report and insisted Princess Sophia is recovering from a bout of measles on the royal yacht in Portofino. The beautiful blond princess graduated from St. George's Ecole in Switzerland and has led a scandal-free life. But like many young royals, she may have found her schedule confining. Perhaps she is sowing her wild oats before she takes the throne.

Amelia put the newspaper down and looked wildly around the piazza. She remembered Sophie telling Philip at the restaurant in Trastevere she was a tour guide. She pictured strolling through the alley after dinner and ending up in the Piazza de Santa Cecilia. She remembered sitting on the cobblestones and falling asleep on Philip's shoulder.

Philip assured her she hadn't said anything unusual but maybe he was lying. Would he really betray her confidence and print the story without telling her?

She threw a wad of euros on the table and grabbed her purse. She ran across the piazza to the Via del Corso. She raced up the stairs to Philip's apartment and knocked on the door.

"This is a lovely surprise." Philip opened the door. He wore a yellow collared shirt and tan slacks. He held a cup of coffee in one hand and a pencil in the other. "I was just proofing this article and coming to join you."

"How could you do this to Sophie?" Amelia demanded, spreading the newspaper on the glass dining room table.

"What are you talking about?" Philip asked.

"The night we had dinner in Trastevere with Sophie and Theo." Amelia's cheeks were white. "I got drunk and didn't remember anything I said."

"You were very beautiful with your sparkling eyes and flushed cheeks." Philip grinned. "But you didn't say anything embarrassing."

"How else would it end up in *Inside Rome*?" Amelia exclaimed. "Nobody knows that Sophie is a princess."

Philip picked up the newspaper. He read it quickly and looked at Amelia.

"I don't know anything about this." Philip frowned. "Maybe Theo discovered the truth."

"Theo knew nothing about Sophie's true identity." Amelia shook her head. "He is a doctor, he's hardly going to spend his time writing exposés."

"There's no byline or photo credit," Philip mused.

"I don't care if you didn't put your name on it." Amelia started shaking. "You're the only person who could have written it."

"You may have mumbled something about Sophie being a princess but I thought you were drunk." Philip shrugged. "I gave it as much thought as if you were telling me the story of the Little Mermaid."

"I don't believe you." Amelia's eyes filled with tears.

"Why don't you splash water on your face and I'll get some biscuits from Signora Griselda," Philip said softly. "We'll solve this together."

Amelia walked into the bathroom and gazed in the mirror. Her lips were white and her cheeks were smudged with mascara. She thought about Philip sharing his taxi and bringing her to his apartment. She pictured him drying her clothes and feeding her scrambled eggs and bacon. She remembered the concert at Hadrian's Villa and their first kiss in the Piazza Navona.

There had to be another explanation. She splashed water on her cheeks and tucked her hair behind her ears. She entered the living room and saw the room was empty. She walked to the desk and glanced at a photo. It was a picture of Amelia and Sophie sitting outside Caffè Greco. They were drinking iced coffees and sharing a bowl of gelato.

Amelia heard Philip climb the stairs and felt her heart pound. She ran out the door and hurried down the steps.

"Where are you going?" Philip leaned over the railing.

She raced through the Piazza di Spagna and up the Spanish Steps. She strode through the gold revolving doors and pressed the button on the elevator. She entered the Villa Medici Suite and collapsed on a royal blue love seat. She put her head in her hands and burst into tears.

Amelia stood in front of her closet and selected a floral cotton dress. She brushed her hair and slipped on silver Gucci sandals. She spritzed her wrists with Estée Lauder's Lovely and walked to the marble entry.

She stayed awake all night thinking about the article in *Inside Rome*. She pictured Sophie in her white lace dress and felt her stomach turn. She couldn't believe she broke Sophie's trust and wondered if Sophie would ever forgive her.

She remembered the photo on Philip's desk and frowned. If Philip discovered Amelia was an actress, he would have printed her photo in the newspaper. He must think she met Sophie when she was cleaning her room at the Hassler.

She knocked on Sophie's door last night but there was no answer. She called the suite in the morning but the line kept ringing. Now she took the elevator to the lobby and approached the concierge desk.

"Good morning, Ernesto," she called. "Isn't it a lovely day?"

"Miss Tate, it is wonderful to see you." Ernesto nodded. "Can I get you a bottle of limoncello?"

"No thank you," Amelia replied. "I tried calling suite 607 and got no answer."

"Let me try for you." Ernesto picked up the phone. He waited while it rang and placed it on the receiver. "I am sorry, Signorita Sophie is not in."

"I wonder if you could lend me the key." Amelia bit her lip. "I want to make sure she's all right."

"I cannot allow a guest to enter another guest's room." Ernesto shook his head. "I will have one of the housekeepers check the suite."

"I'm afraid the maid might miss something." Amelia leaned over the marble counter. "Have you ever heard of Nancy Drew, Ernesto?"

"I have not, Miss Tate."

"She is the most famous detective in American literature," Amelia mused. "Nancy Drew never missed a clue."

"I don't understand." Ernesto frowned.

"If I could borrow the key for a few minutes, I promise to return it," Amelia suggested.

"That is out of the question," Ernesto insisted.

"It would be our secret, you know I'm very good at keeping secrets."

Ernesto inhaled Amelia's perfume and glanced around the lobby. He took a gold key from the desk and handed it to Amelia.

"You are the best." She smiled, clutching the key to her chest.

Amelia took the elevator to the sixth floor and slipped the key in the door. She entered the living room and gazed at the oriental rugs and the crystal vases and the Rembrandt sketch over the fireplace. She saw a stack of magazines on the glass coffee table and a pitcher of lemonade. There was a silk scarf draped over an armchair and a pair of Prada loafers tucked under the sofa.

She walked into the bedroom and opened the closet. She saw silk dresses by Armani and Fendi. There were boxes of Bottega Veneta pumps and a quilted Chanel purse. She thought about how much Sophie loved the boutiques on the Via Condotti and smiled.

She glanced around the bedroom and saw the canopied bed with its gold brocade bedspread. The pillows were plumped and there was a silver tray of Baci chocolates. She wondered if Sophie spent the night at Theo's but she remembered how upset Sophie had been about their kiss.

She looked in the corner and noticed a set of Louis Vuitton luggage. She remembered when Sophie bought them and Amelia asked if she really needed two steamer trunks and a couple of carry-ons.

Sophie laughed and said how else was she going to carry her new clothes to Portofino.

She studied the luggage and realized the Louis Vuitton duffel bag was missing. She ran out of the suite and pressed the button on the elevator. She crossed the lobby and approached the concierge desk.

"You are back, Miss Tate." Ernesto sighed. "I have good news. Marco saw Signorita Sophie leave the hotel last night."

"Did he say where she was going?" Amelia asked.

"He is in front of the hotel." Ernesto shrugged. "You can ask him."

Amelia walked through the glass revolving doors and saw a valet in a white uniform with gold buttons.

"Good morning, Marco, it's lovely to see you."

"Good morning, Miss Tate," Marco beamed. "Today you won't need an umbrella, there is nothing but blue sky and sunshine."

"Ernesto said you saw Sophie leaving last night," Amelia continued.

"Signorita Sophie is an admirer of Renaissance art." Marco nodded. "We discussed Donatello and Raphael."

"Did she say where she was going?" Amelia asked.

"We stood for a while waiting for a taxi," Marco replied. "Then she changed her mind."

"Changed her mind?" she raised her eyebrow.

"She decided to walk." Marco slipped his hands in his pockets.

"She walked through Rome in the middle of the night carrying a Louis Vuitton duffel bag?" Amelia felt her heart pound.

"It is my fault." Marco lowered his head. "I tell Mr. Black we must always have a line of taxis. One must not keep guests of the Hassler waiting."

"Thank you, Marco." She said, striding along the cobblestones.

"Wait, Miss Tate," Marco called. "Would you like me to call a taxi?"

*  *  *

Amelia squeezed through the afternoon crowds on the Via Condotti. She had checked Hermès and Armani and Dolce & Gabbana. She looked inside Caffé Greco and asked the salesgirls at Prada and Burberry. She thought about asking Theo, but if he hadn't seen the article in *Inside Rome* she didn't want to tell him Sophie was a princess.

She stood in front of the Gucci boutique and gazed at the window display. The mannequin wore a two-piece metallic bathing suit and a visor that said Portofino. There was a quilted beach towel and gold sandals.

Amelia flashed on Sophie's lady-in-waiting and the royal yacht in Portofino. She was the only other person who knew Sophie was in Rome. Amelia hurried back to the Hassler and strode through the glass revolving doors. She took the elevator to the Villa Medici Suite and entered the living room. She picked up the phone and called the front desk.

# chapter twenty-one

P hilip shielded his eyes from the sun and glanced around the Piazza del Popolo. He saw a man with blond hair sitting outside Canova. He wore blue jeans and white sneakers and was eating a chocolate croissant.

Philip clutched his newspaper and hurried across the piazza. He stayed up all night, hoping Amelia would return. This morning he scribbled a note and delivered it to Ernesto. He had to find Amelia and make her believe he was telling the truth.

"Where were you last night?" Philip approached the wrought iron table. "I called you for hours."

"The countess and I attended a cooking class." Max added sugar to a cup of espresso.

"You and the countess?" Philip raised his eyebrow.

"I gave her the box of Baci chocolates and we realized how much we missed each other," Max replied. "We're going to learn how to make ricotta cheesecake."

"How could you print this without telling me?" Philip flung the newspaper on the table.

"And I thought Sophie was just Amelia's friend." Max whistled, studying the photo. "No wonder she has eyes like cornflowers and skin like alabaster. She's European royalty."

"Amelia is furious." Philip sunk into a chair. "You ruined everything."

"If I discovered Sophie was Princess Sophia de Grasse of Lentz I would have sold it to *People* and *Us*." Max folded the newspaper.

"You didn't do this?" Philip asked.

"I snapped a few photos of Amelia and Sophie together." Max shrugged. "I thought we'd use them in the articles about Amelia."

"There aren't going to be any articles." Philip sighed. His throat was parched and he realized he was starving. "Amelia ran out of my apartment, I don't know where she is."

"You better find her." Max sipped his coffee. "I paid for six cooking classes in advance."

"I thought the countess paid for everything." Philip ate a piece of Max's croissant.

"I'm turning over a new leaf," Max said. "I don't want to be a kept man."

Philip crossed the Piazza di Trevi and ran up four flights of stairs. He entered the tiny reception area and opened the door of Adam's office.

"Just because I can't afford a secretary doesn't mean you don't knock." Adam looked up from a stack of tear sheets. He wore a creased blue shirt and khakis and had a cigarette stuck behind his ear.

"Where did you get this story?" Philip tossed the newspaper on the desk.

Adam glanced at the picture of Sophie and grinned. "Largest circulation we've ever had. The paper has already gone back to press three times and it hit newsstands yesterday. If this keeps up I might redecorate the office, get rid of the linoleum and put in an oak floor."

"Who told you Sophie was a princess?" Philip demanded.

"It says 'Anonymous' for a reason." Adam flicked a cigarette into the metal garbage can. "I don't reveal my sources."

"You tell me where you got this or I'll light the damn cigarette and make you smoke it," Philip seethed.

Adam stood up and walked to the window. He turned and looked at Philip.

"I promised I wouldn't tell anyone."

"Amelia and I are becoming so close, I think she's falling in love with me," Philip persisted. "Now she accused me of planting the article and disappeared."

"You really think you can get her to marry you?" Adam hesitated.

"I'll bet you a new espresso maker." Philip nodded.

Adam sat at his desk and leaned back in his chair. He looked at Philip and ran his hands through his hair.

"She gave it to me."

"Who?" Philip asked.

"She walked in wearing a white crepe dress and silver sandals. I haven't seen legs like that since I stopped reading my father's *Playboys*." Adam tapped a cigarette from the box of Lucky Strikes on the desk. "She opened her leather tote and took out a manila envelope. I thought she was a high-priced call girl about to spill dirt on the prime minister."

"Who was she?" Philip leaned forward.

"The girl in the photo."

"Sophie gave you the picture!" Philip sucked in his breath. "Why would she write an exposé about herself?"

"I have no idea." Adam shook his head. "She had the article written and everything."

"Did she want money?" Philip asked.

"I don't have that kind of money." Adam laughed. "She said it was free and gave me an exclusive."

"It doesn't make any sense." Philip paced around the tiny office.

"I gave up trying to understand women years ago." Adam shrugged, flicking the cigarette into the garbage can.

Philip stood at the entrance of the Hassler and glanced around the lobby. He saw black and gold marble floors and thick gold columns. He saw velvet wallpaper covered with paintings by Titian and Botticelli. There were marble statues and crystal vases filled with white and yellow tulips.

"Good afternoon, Ernesto." He approached the concierge desk. "Has anyone picked up my letter?"

"I'm afraid not." Ernesto shook his head.

"I have another one." Philip reached into his shirt pocket.

"The woman interested in your letters is not here," Ernesto said slowly.

"Has she checked out?" Philip asked.

"She took a little trip." Ernesto hesitated. "She will return on Tuesday."

"Where did she go?" Philip felt his heart pound.

"I cannot reveal her destination." Ernesto glanced around the lobby.

"Please, Ernesto." Philip drew forty euros out of his pocket. "It's very important."

"I am not at liberty to say." Ernesto eyed the notes. "But most travel arrangements are made with Signora Rosa."

"Signora Rosa?" Philip repeated.

Ernesto pointed to a woman sitting behind a mahogany desk. "Signora Rosa is our travel concierge; she is the best in Rome."

"Thank you," Philip beamed.

He smoothed his hair and slipped his hands in his pockets. He approached the desk and took a deep breath.

"Hello, I wonder if you could answer a few questions."

Signora Rosa glanced up from a stack of brochures. She had brown eyes and blond hair pulled into a bun. She wore a yellow silk dress and narrow heels. She looked at Philip's rumpled shirt and creased slacks and frowned.

"Are you a hotel guest?" she asked.

Philip hesitated. "Not exactly."

"I am sorry, I only assist guests of the Hassler." She tapped her red fingernails on a ceramic ashtray.

"I'm a journalist and I'm writing a feature on Rome's top travel concierges." Philip sat in a gold velvet chair. "I heard you are one of the best."

"I may have a free moment," Signora Rosa murmured. "How can I help you?"

"What are the most popular trips from Rome?" Philip began. "Where have you booked guests in the last couple of days?"

"Spoleto is always attractive." Signora Rosa flipped through her notes. "And guests love Villa d'Este in Tivoli. Wine tasting in Pienza is popular and I booked a group to visit Monte Oliveto Maggoire; it is one of the oldest Benedictine monasteries."

"Some place farther." Philip rubbed his forehead. "Somewhere they would spend the night."

"A lot of guests visit Pompeii," she mused. "Or in the summer it is nice to travel to Portofino and sail on the Mediterranean."

"Portofino?" Philip sat forward. He pictured Amelia giggling and telling him Sophie was a princess. He remembered her saying she had a diamond tiara and a lady-in-waiting and a royal yacht in Portofino.

"Portofino is only four hours by train and it is the jewel of the Ligurian Riviera," Signora Rosa replied. "It is home to countless movie stars and the harbor is full of quaint wooden fishing boats and sleek yachts. The restaurants are exceptional and the view from Castello Brown is spectacular."

Philip stuck his legs in front of him and let his shoulders relax. "If a guest was going to Portofino, where would she stay?"

"There is only one property comparable to the Hotel Hassler." Signora Rosa smiled. "The Hotel Splendido."


Philip placed two pieces of wheat bread on a plate. He added bacon and sliced heirloom tomato and red onions. He cut a wedge of Edam cheese and sat at the glass dining room table.

He took big bites of the sandwich, sifting through his mail. His mother sent a letter saying she bought tickets to *The Book of Mormon* in September. His father sent the address of the Bruno Magli store in Rome with the note:

> *Could you pick me up a pair of burgundy velvet slippers? My pair*
> *is so worn your mother made me donate them to the Salvation Army.*

Philip glanced at the thin pile of euros on the table and frowned. If he took the train to Portofino he would only have a few euros left. He wasn't sure if Amelia was there but he had no other leads.

Max opened the door and entered the living room. He wore a yellow collared shirt and jeans and sneakers. His camera was slung over his shoulder and he carried a packet of digestive biscuits.

"Signora Griselda told me to give you these." Max handed him the biscuits. "She thinks you haven't been eating."

"Sophie gave Adam the photo. She wrote the exposé herself." Philip wiped his mouth with a napkin.

"Why would she do that?" Max took a green apple from the fruit bowl.

"I don't know." Philip shrugged. "But I think Amelia went to Portofino to see Sophie's lady-in-waiting."

"Ladies-in-waiting, royal yachts." Max bit into the apple. "It sounds like a James Bond movie."

"I have to go to Portofino but the train ticket cost seventy-five euros." Philip pushed away his plate.

"I'd go with you but the countess and I are seeing *Rigoletto* at Opera Roma," Max replied.

"You're going to the opera?" Philip raised his eyebrow.

"We saw *Othello* last night. The countess wore a gold lamé dress and a sapphire and diamond necklace. She looked like Cleopatra," Max mused. "We sat in a red velvet box and she dug her nails into my arm, I've never done anything so erotic."

"I better hurry." Philip pushed back his chair. "The train leaves at four o'clock."

"You can borrow my car." Max drew a car key out of his pocket. "Be careful on the Appian Way, Italians drive like race car drivers."

"Since when do you have a car?" Philip frowned.

"Mirabella gave it to me," Max replied. "It's a beauty, a baby blue Alfa Romeo Spider."

"I thought you weren't going to be a kept man." Philip grinned, fingering the car key.

"I did her a favor." Max tossed the apple in the garbage. "She bought an Aston Martin and didn't have room in the garage."


Philip closed his suitcase and strode down the stairs. He threw the bag in the trunk and climbed into the small blue car. He rolled down the window and started the ignition.

He pictured Amelia's glossy brown hair and large brown eyes. He saw her slender neck and small pink mouth. He turned into the narrow alley and stepped harder on the accelerator.

# chapter twenty-two

Amelia stood on the balcony of her room at the Hotel Splendido and gazed at the harbor. The water was pale blue and dotted with wooden fishing boats. Wide catamarans sailed beside glittering speedboats and huge yachts rested at the dock.

She took the late night train to Rapallo and a taxi dropped her off at the Hotel Splendido. She followed the concierge to her room and fell asleep in her cotton dress and sandals. She woke in the morning and felt the warm breeze waft through the lace curtains.

Now she gazed at the sparkling Mediterranean and had never seen anywhere so beautiful. The Hotel Splendido was perched on a hill, high above the piazza. Amelia saw green inlets and lush tropical gardens.

She walked inside and admired the white marble floor and the lace bedspread scattered with pink and blue satin pillows. Signora Rosa apologized she couldn't secure a suite at short notice but Amelia liked the cozy room.

She glanced at the silver tray of fluffy scrambled eggs and fresh scones and wished she were hungry. She unpacked her suitcase and slipped on a white linen dress and sandals. She tied a yellow silk scarf around her head and put on oversized sunglasses. She rubbed pink lip gloss on her lips and crossed the hall to the elevator.

The lobby had a white marble floor and tall French windows. The walls were covered in raw silk and crystal chandeliers dangled from the ceiling. Floral sofas were scattered over Oriental rugs and ceramic vases held white orchids.

Amelia hurried through the glass doors and walked down the hillside to the piazza. She smelled espresso and fresh bread and longed to have lunch at an outdoor café. She wished Philip were sitting opposite her, sharing a plate of calamari. Then she remembered the photo of her and Sophie outside Caffé Greco and shivered. She strode to the dock and approached a fisherman in a blue sweater.

"Excuse me, do you speak English?"

"Everyone in Portofino speaks English," the man replied. "How else would we talk to beautiful women?"

"Do you know if the Royal Yacht of Lentz is parked in the harbor?" Amelia asked.

The man smiled and pointed to the end of the dock. "Of course, it is the biggest yacht in Portofino."

Amelia walked along the dock and saw a long white yacht with sleek windows. The deck had a round swimming pool and brown leather sofas. There was a marble bar with rows of glittering bottles.

"Excuse me," Amelia called. "Do you have a moment?"

"The princess is confined to bed with the measles." A woman stood at the railing. "There will be no photos."

"I'm not a photographer, I'm a friend of Sophie's." Amelia shielded her eyes from the sun.

"Princess Sophia is not talking to anyone." The woman turned away. "Leave us alone."

"I promise I'm not paparazzi," Amelia insisted. "I'm trying to find her."

"I don't believe you," the woman murmured, glancing at Amelia's silk scarf and white leather sandals.

"I know Sophie has asthma and loves Hans Christian Anderson fairy tales and wants a house full of children," Amelia blurted out.

"Who are you?" The woman hesitated.

"My name is Amelia Tate, I met Sophie in Rome," Amelia replied. "I thought she might be here."

The woman glanced around the dock. She nodded to Amelia and pointed to wooden steps. "Come on board, we will talk in private."

Amelia followed the woman into a long room with a beamed ceiling. The floor was polished wood and the walls were painted ivory. There were white leather sofas and tall mahogany book-shelves.

"I'm Elspeth, Princess Sophia's lady-in-waiting." The woman held out her hand. She had brown hair and slender cheekbones. She wore a cream dress and beige pumps. "It's my fault she's in Rome. I've known Princess Sophia since she was a little girl, and she hardly asks for any-thing. She begged me to let her go, I should have said no."

"She's been having a wonderful time, she loves the boutiques and museums." Amelia perched on a white leather sofa. "This article came out and she disappeared."

"I have to tell his Royal Highness, something might have happened to her."

"Please don't," Amelia protested. "I'm going to find her."

"I assured King Alfred the article is false and Princess Sophia is in bed." Elspeth paced around the room. "If he discovers the truth, I'll lose my position. You have until tomorrow night."

"I'll find her, I promise." Amelia nodded. She gazed at the ceramic fruit bowl filled with peaches and apricots and thought she had no idea where to look.

Amelia sat on the balcony of La Terrazza restaurant and gazed at the view. It was early afternoon and the sun sparkled on the blue water. The harbor was shaped like a horseshoe and everywhere there were green plants and brightly colored flowers.

She glanced at the white linen tablecloth and gleaming silverware. Everything on the menu—the Ligurian ravioli with herb filling, the taglietelle with prawns and artichokes—sounded delicious. But now that the waiter delivered a platter of seafood salad with lemon sauce, Amelia couldn't eat a bite.

She fingered a glass of sparkling water and pictured Sophie with her blond hair and blue eyes. She imagined her seeing her photo in the newspaper and felt her stomach rise to her throat. She remembered Philip denying he had anything to do with it and flinched.

She would take the last train to Rome and wait for Sophie at the Hassler. If Sophie didn't return by morning, she would have to ask Theo for help.

Amelia pushed away her plate and called for the check. She took the elevator to the third floor and opened the door. She slipped off her sandals and felt the cool marble under her feet. She opened her suitcase and drew out a stack of papers.

At the last minute she was afraid the maids would discover Audrey Hepburn's letters and stuffed them in her suitcase. She took the top page and began to read.

*Dear Kitty,*                                        *August 24, 1952*

*Mr. Wyler had to go to Florence so we have the whole day off! I woke up early and strolled through the Roman Forum. It's wonderful to explore the city before the streets are full of cars and the sidewalks are crammed with tourists. Sometimes I'm so busy looking at the camera, I forget that I'm in Rome.*

*I came back to the Villa Medici Suite and ran a bath. I thought it would be a perfect day to wash my hair and mail these letters. Oh, Kitty, don't be angry when you get a stack of mail. I love sitting at the antique desk and writing my thoughts, but I never have time to address the envelopes.*

*I was about to step into the marble bathtub when the telephone rang. I wrapped myself in a fluffy white towel and answered it.*

*"We're going to take a picnic to the Villa d'Este," a female voice said. "You must join us."*

*"Veronique?" I hesitated. She never called before but I don't know anyone else with a French accent.*

*"Gregory and Mel and I are in a car downstairs," Veronique replied. "Don't take too long, we want to beat the traffic."*

*"I was about to take a bath." I hesitated.*

*"You can take a bath in London or New York," Veronique mused. "But you can only visit the Villa d'Este when you are in Rome."*

*I stood in front of my closet and wondered what to wear. I was sure Veronique would be dressed in a perfectly cut Jacques Fath dress or Chanel suit. I imagine when she wakes up in the morning, her hair is perfectly coiffed and her skin is flawless.*

*I selected a beige Dior dress with a wide leather belt and Ferragamo pumps. I put on a wide straw hat and slipped on oval sunglasses.*

*"There you are." Veronique waved. She wore a turquoise*

Chanel dress with a matching jacket. "Sit in the front with me, the boys are talking business."

"You're driving?" I raised my eyebrow.

"Gregory doesn't have a license and Mel is a New Yorker, he never learned to drive." She hopped into the driver's seat of a shiny green Mini. "I love to drive on the motorway, there's no speed limit."

"There must be a speed limit," I said nervously.

Veronique started the ignition and shrugged. "If there is, I don't know what it is."


We drove through the outskirts of Rome onto the Appian Way. We stopped at a gas station and Veronique went inside to get a bottle of Coca Cola. Greg leaned forward and touched my shoulder.

"I hope you don't mind being kidnapped." He smiled. "Veronique thought it would be more fun if we had an even number."

For a moment I thought it was Greg's idea to invite me and I tried not to look disappointed. "I was about to take a bath."

"You'll have to make do with ham sandwiches instead of Hassler bonbons," Greg mused. "But I did pack a delicious Burgundy."

Veronique got back in the car and we entered the grounds of the Villa d'Este. Oh, Kitty, the gardens make Versailles look like a nursery garden. Everywhere you look there are fountains and sundials and tall birds of paradise. We passed fir trees and English gardens filled with yellow and white roses.

We explored the Hundred Fountains with its hanging plants and the Dragon Fountain with its stone dragons and the Oval Fountain with its marble nymphs. I ended up walking beside Mel. He's very sweet though quite serious. He seems to know everything about history and art and architecture.

"The villa was built for Cardinal Ippolito Il' d'Este in 1560," *he said as we entered the palace. The floor was gold and the ceilings were painted with intricate frescoes. "The cardinal was disappointed he didn't get the papacy so he hired Pirro Ligorio, the finest architect in Italy. The terraced gardens are the greatest example of late Renaissance style."*

*"Do they teach you that at Princeton?" I teased, glancing at the murals of wooden tables overflowing with green grapes and ripe cheese and pink roast beef.*

*"Every man should study great artists," Mel said seriously. "How else will they recognize beauty?"*

*We caught up with Greg and Veronique and spread a picnic blanket next to the fish ponds. It was heavenly watching the goldfish swim in the clear water.*

*We ate pancetta and tomato salad with goat cheese. There were green olives and figs and bunches of purple grapes. Greg opened a bottle of Burgundy and we talked about Rome and the movie business.*

*"Villa d'Este is nothing compared to Greg's spread in Beverly Hills." Veronique nibbled a grape. "He's got thirty rooms and a tennis court."*

*"Do you really?" I asked.*

*"My wife sends me pictures." He shrugged. "She redecorated it to resemble a Moroccan villa."*

*I glanced at Greg and realized he hardly ever talks about his wife. I was about to ask what she was like when Veronique announced she had a run in her stocking.*

*"I'm going to the car to get a new pair." She stood up.*

*"You keep extra stockings in your car?" I raised my eyebrow.*

*"Everyone should carry a first aid kit." She hurried across the lawn.*

Mel had a call scheduled to a producer in Hollywood and excused himself to find a pay phone. I glanced at Greg reclining against the picnic basket and blushed.

"It's a funny way to make a living," Greg said, eating a baguette. "Having a picnic in a sixteenth-century garden when most men eat peanut butter sandwiches at their desk."

"I suppose it is," I murmured, pulling daisies out of the ground to make a daisy chain.

"My mother made my father the same lunch every day, ham and Swiss cheese on white bread," Greg mused. "Every night she took his briefcase and handed him a martini, I haven't had dinner with my wife in two months."

"I'm sure she misses you," I mumbled.

Greg looked at me and suddenly changed the subject.

"Mel is sweet on you, you have to promise not to marry him."

"Why would I do that?" I smiled.

"Because you're twenty-four and think you want to be a movie star and have a big house in Beverly Hills. But in ten years you might wish you lived in a cabin in Maine or a loft in New York," Greg said earnestly. "But you'll be married with two towheaded children and a black Labrador and you can't change a thing."

"I don't think I'm ever getting married," I said glumly. "I'm going to be a lonely old spinster."

"There are lots of ways to be lonely," Greg replied. "Even in a house with thirty rooms and a tennis court."

Veronique and Mel returned and we ate jam tarts and miniature profiteroles. We toured the Grotto and by the time we drove back to Rome my feet ached.

I took the elevator to the Villa Medici Suite and turned on the bath. I sank into the bubbles and remembered what Greg said *about being lonely. I know I made the right decision by breaking up with James but it would be nice to have someone to come home to. I shall have to get a fluffy white poodle!*

*Audrey*

*Dear Kitty,*                            *September 1, 1952*

*We spent the whole day rehearsing the dance scene on the dock. I haven't danced in so long I felt like my ankles would snap. I miss it sometimes; give Madame Rambert a kiss for me!*

*I was changing in my dressing room when there was a knock on the door. I zipped up my dress and opened it.*

*"You're still here." Greg stood at the door.*

*"I was just changing." I ushered him inside. "My body feels like a pretzel."*

*"I haven't danced since I hurt my back in acting school," Greg began. "I wonder if you'd give me lessons."*

*"Me give you lessons?" I raised my eyebrow.*

*"Willy told me you were a great ballerina," Greg continued. "I don't need to be Fred Astaire, I just don't want to have two left feet."*

*"I was too tall to be a ballerina." I sighed. "You're a very good dancer."*

*"I need a refresher course," Greg replied. He wore a white collared shirt and tan slacks. "We could go to Harry's Bar and take a spin around the dance floor."*

*"Tonight?" I asked.*

*"I should have guessed you had plans." Greg turned to leave. "Perhaps another time."*

*I pictured whirling around the dance floor in Greg's arms and took a deep breath.*

"Tonight sounds wonderful, let me scrub off this makeup and put on a new dress."

Greg opened the door and smiled. "I'll meet you outside in thirty minutes."

I put on a cream Balmain dress and beige sandals. I coated my eyes with mascara and rubbed my lips with lipstick. I grabbed my purse and walked onto the set.

I saw Veronique smoking a cigarette. She wore an emerald green Schiaparelli dress with a gold belt. I followed her gaze and saw Greg talking to a blond woman in a black silk dress. She had pale blue eyes and a dimple on her cheek.

"They make a beautiful couple." Veronique let out a puff of smoke. "She's so petite, Gregory could fit her in his pocket."

"Who is she?" I asked.

"Greta Peck, the wife. She was at the summer Olympics in Helsinki and made a surprise appearance."

I remembered Greg's invitation to go dancing and blushed.

"They look so intimate," I blurted out, watching Greg kiss his wife on the mouth.

"Oh, dear." Veronique eyed me curiously. "Why don't you and I get a drink?"

"No, I . . ." I hesitated.

I looked up and saw Greg and Greta walking toward me. She smiled and extended her hand.

"You must be Audrey Hepburn. Greg told me so much about you," she said. "It sounds like you're going to steal the show."

"It's a pleasure to meet you, Mrs. Peck," I shook her hand.

"You make me sound like an old woman." She laughed. "Please call me Greta."

"Greta just got off the plane and she's famished," Greg said.

"We're going to eat pesto fettuccine at Alfredo's. Would you ladies like to join us?"

"Audrey and I are going to Harry's Bar." Veronique stubbed out her cigarette. "Maybe we'll catch up with you later."

We sat at a table in the back and drank Bloody Marys. Veronique ordered oysters and cocktail sauce but I wasn't hungry.

"You should have seen your face." She lit a cigarette. "You looked like someone stole your Easter candy."

"She's very pretty," I murmured.

"She's five years older than Gregory but she looks like a girl." Veronique sighed. "There's something to be said for never seeing the sun, Finnish women have beautiful creamy skin."

"They looked so close." I sipped my drink.

"They've produced three children in ten years." Veronique exhaled a thin trail of smoke. "In Hollywood they're like royalty. They have a chef and a butler and an Olympic-sized swimming pool. Everyone wants an invitation to the Pecks'."

"How do you know?" I raised my eyebrow.

"I interviewed Gregory last winter for Paris Soir," Veronique replied. "He told me everything about his marriage."

"He just . . . it sounded like . . ." I stumbled, flashing on Greg saying he was lonely.

"You do have a crush on our leading man," Veronique exclaimed. "It's a movie set, it's all make-believe."

"I don't understand." I frowned.

"If Gregory rambled on about barbecues and baseball games he couldn't give a good performance," Veronique continued. "He has to believe he's a tortured actor."

"Greg has been very kind." I nodded. "I'm glad he has a happy marriage."

"I'm sure it's not all champagne and chocolates." Veronique ground her cigarette into the ashtray. "But I doubt happy marriages exist, except on the screen."

"Don't you want to get married?" I asked, nibbling a handful of peanuts.

"I'm a writer." She bristled. "I'm not giving up my typewriter for a bottle of perfume and a fur coat."

Mel Ferrer arrived and we all had another round of drinks. Mel asked me to dance and we twirled around the dance floor until I felt dizzy. He is such a good dancer, I teased him he should join the American Ballet Theater! He asked if he could walk me home but I thought about what Greg said and shook my head.

Audrey

Dear Kitty,                                    September 2, 1952

This morning I was sitting in my dressing room eating a hard-boiled egg. There was a knock on the door and I stood up to open it.

"That doesn't look very appealing." Greg entered the room.

"It's Baroness Ella's hangover cure." I popped the egg in my mouth. "I drank too many Bloody Marys at Harry's Bar."

"Never trust a drink with celery, it only looks healthy." Greg slipped his hands in his pockets. "I'm sorry I had to cancel our dance lesson. Greta was just here for the night, I couldn't let her dine alone."

"She already left?" I asked.

"I was one stop on her itinerary," he explained. "She visited her designer in Paris and her mother in London. She has to be back in Los Angeles on Saturday for the premiere of High Noon."

"Veronique said you lead a very glamorous life," I replied. "Everyone wants to be invited to the Pecks' residence."

"Gary Cooper is a fan of my wife's Finnish cooking," Greg mused. "We often have Cary and Betsy and William and Ardis over. William fixes the best dry martini."

"Do you mean Cary Grant and William Holden?" I sucked in my breath.

"They'll be bowing at your feet after Roman Holiday comes out." Greg grinned. "You're going to win an Oscar the first time out of the gate."

"I wouldn't be able to utter one line without your and Mr. Wyler's help." I peeled another hard-boiled egg. "I can't imagine a life of cocktail parties and movie premieres. It sounds terribly fun."

"We have a good time as long as we're holding a scotch." Greg shrugged. "The trick is to never let the glass be empty."

There was a knock on the door and a man entered carrying a bouquet of red roses.

"Delivery for Miss Hepburn," he announced, placing the vase on the desk.

"It's from Mel." I blushed. "He met us at Harry's Bar."

"Is that so," Greg mused. "He's a very good dancer."

"He asked if he could walk me home."

I saw a funny look on Greg's face, as if he swallowed a snail.

"What did you tell him?" he asked.

"I took your advice and told him no." I smiled.

"Good girl." His shoulders relaxed. "Let's get on the set before Willy calls a search party."

We did the dance scene on the docks, and Greg held me so tightly I could barely breathe. When Mr. Wyler yelled cut I almost jumped. I had forgotten about the cameras and the lights, I thought we were the only two people in the world.

*Oh, Kitty, I know I'm being foolish, I can't possibly think about Greg in that way. He's older and sophisticated and Cary Grant plays bridge at his house! But you should have seen the way he looked at me when we danced; he has the kindest eyes I've ever seen.*

*Audrey*

Amelia put the letter on the bedside table and reclined against the pink and blue satin pillows. She thought about Audrey Hepburn's feelings for Gregory Peck and wondered if they were returned. Was it possible to fall in love with someone when you barely knew him?

She stood at the window and glanced at the sparkling Mediterranean. It would be lovely to hire a little boat and spend the afternoon exploring the inlets. But she didn't feel like being surrounded by spectacular yachts or gleaming catamarans, all she wanted was to find Sophie.

# chapter twenty-three

Amelia slipped on a yellow linen dress and white sandals. She tied a silk scarf around her head and put on oversized sunglasses. She grabbed her white Gucci tote and walked down the staircase to the lobby.

She spent the afternoon in her room; trying to think if she missed any clues. She finally glanced at the pink sky and realized it was evening. She would eat a quick plate of spaghetti before she caught her train.

She crossed the pink and white marble lobby and saw a man standing at the entrance. He wore a white collared shirt with the sleeves rolled up and tan slacks. He had a duffel bag slung over his shoulder and a leather watch on his wrist.

Amelia gasped and hid behind a palm tree. She didn't know why Philip was in Portofino and she didn't want to see him. She watched him approach the marble concierge desk and hesitated. She couldn't risk him talking to the concierge and learning her true identity.

"What are you doing in Portofino?" She approached him. "If you came to get more details for your exposé, Sophie isn't here."

"These are pretty fancy digs for a hotel maid." Philip whistled, putting his duffel bag on the floor.

"It was the only room available in Portofino. I used some of my savings. I had to come, Sophie is a good friend." Amelia blushed, glancing at the marble columns and gold inlaid ceiling. "Now she's missing and if I don't find her in twenty-four hours her lady-in-waiting will tell her father. You've ruined everything."

"I didn't have anything to do with it," Philip insisted, following Amelia onto the sidewalk.

"You keep saying that but I don't believe you." Amelia hurried toward the piazza. "It was printed in your newspaper."

"Sophie gave Adam the photo," Philip persisted. "She wrote the article herself."

Amelia stopped and turned around. She took off her sunglasses and felt her heart pound in her chest.

"She came into his office with a manila envelope and said she didn't want any money," Philip continued.

"Why would she do that?" Amelia asked. "She adores her father, she would never disgrace him."

"Maybe she's tired of being a princess," Philip mused.

"You don't know Sophie." Amelia bit her lip. "She takes her position very seriously."

"I haven't eaten anything except a packet of Signora Griselda's digestive biscuits." Philip touched her arm. "Why don't we talk about it over a plate of linguini marinara and a bottle of Chianti?"

They sat at an outdoor table at Ristorante Stella and sipped glasses of prosecco. Amelia gazed at the brightly colored buildings and striped umbrellas and thought it was the most romantic spot in Italy.

"It's like being in a mid-century fishing village." Philip glanced at the laundry hanging out of windows. "But with a very high price tag."

"We can get some fruit at the market," Amelia suggested.

"I didn't risk my life on the motorway to eat a bag of cherries." Philip grinned, studying the menu. "The fish soup and seafood ravioli sound delicious."

The waiter brought a basket of fresh bread and steaming bowls of soup. They ate Parmesan ravioli with calamari and mussels and prawns.

"I don't understand why you left my apartment." Philip buttered a baguette.

"I saw the photo of me and Sophie," Amelia replied. "I thought you were following us."

"Max takes photos of beautiful women and ancient monuments and churches." Philip shrugged. "He always has a camera slung over his shoulder."

Amelia took a bite of ravioli and wiped her mouth with a napkin. "I'm sorry I didn't believe you."

"I can hardly believe it myself," Philip replied. "The important thing is to find Sophie."

"Maybe Theo knows something. I'll ask him tomorrow." Amelia glanced at her watch. "I should go, my train leaves in an hour."

Philip reached across the table and took her hand. He turned it over and traced a circle around her palm.

"I borrowed Max's car, I'll drive you back to Rome."

Amelia glanced at his wavy hair and dark eyes and felt a weight lift from her shoulders. She picked up the menu and smiled.

"In that case we have time for dessert."

The waiter brought homemade lemon cake and vanilla ice cream. They drank coffee with Frangelico and nutmeg. Philip curled his hand around Amelia's fingers and she felt the sultry air on her cheeks.

They hiked up the path to the Hotel Splendido and admired the view. The Castello Brown loomed above them and the sky was full of stars. Amelia saw the twinkling lights of the motorway and the yachts bobbing in the harbor.

"The Frangelico was stronger than I thought." Philip pulled her toward him. "I don't trust myself behind the wheel of a car. Maybe we should leave first thing in the morning."

"Where will you sleep?" Amelia asked. "All the rooms in Portofino are taken."

"I was hoping I might get an invitation." Philip traced her mouth with his finger. "Considering I let you sleep in my apartment."

"As I remember the bed wasn't very comfortable," Amelia whispered. "The sheets were lumpy."

"I don't mind lumpy sheets." Philip kissed her on the lips. "I can even sleep on the floor."

"What kind of a hostess would I be," she murmured, "if I made you sleep on the floor?"

They crossed the lobby and climbed the stairs to the third floor. Amelia put her key in the lock and opened the door. She saw the white lace bedspread and her heart pounded in her chest.

Philip closed the curtains and unbuttoned his shirt. He slipped off his shoes and took off his watch. He walked to Amelia and kissed her on the mouth.

Amelia unzipped her dress and slipped off her sandals. She unsnapped her bra and placed his hand on her breast.

He tugged at her silk panties and Amelia caught her breath. She felt his fingers reach inside her and strained against his chest. She felt him push deeper until her body trembled. She let the pleasure well up inside her and carry her over the edge.

"You don't know how long I've wanted you," he whispered. "You're the most beautiful woman I've ever met."

Amelia's heart raced and she knew she had to tell him the truth. She opened her mouth but he kissed her softly on the lips. She kissed him back and ran her hands over his chest.

She lay on the white bedspread and pulled him on top of her. She clung to his back and pushed him to go faster. She held on to him until he came in one long exquisite shudder. She wrapped her legs around him and felt her body split open.

She listened to his soft breathing and tucked herself against his chest. She closed her eyes and blinked away the tears. It was too late to tell him the truth because she was already in love with him.

# chapter twenty-four

Amelia stood in front of Philip's blue Alfa Romeo glancing in both directions. She had gotten up early and ran down to the lobby to pay the bill. She stopped in the hotel gift shop and picked out a straw hat with a wide brim. She didn't think anyone would recognize her but she couldn't take the chance.

She would find Sophie and then she would tell Philip the truth. She pictured Sophie's white-blond hair and large blue eyes and frowned. Could she really disgrace her father and let down her lady-in-waiting?

"That hat looks wonderful on you." Philip approached the car, clutching two tall Styrofoam cups. "You look like a movie star."

"I bought it at the gift shop." Amelia flushed. "I wanted a souvenir of Portofino."

"I got double espressos, we'll need lots of energy," Philip replied, handing her a cup.

"We do?" Amelia raised her eyebrow.

"We have to drive back to Rome and find Sophie." He kissed her on the mouth. "And then we have to replay what we did last night."

"The delicious dinner and the evening stroll?" Amelia asked, tasting coffee and cinnamon.

"I was thinking about what happened afterward," Philip murmured, tucking her hair behind her ears.

Amelia felt a shiver run down her spine. She hopped into the passenger seat and fixed her sunglasses.

"Then we better start driving."

They drove out of Portofino and onto the motorway. Amelia gazed at the tranquil harbor and the green inlets and felt her heart turn over. It was so beautiful: the magnificent villas, the cliffs covered with purple and white daisies. She wished they could drive forever, with Philip's hand on her knee and the sun glinting on the windshield. She saw a group of nuns walking along the road, carrying a basket of fruit. Suddenly her eyes sparkled and her face broke into a smile.

"I know where Sophie is!"

"Where?" Philip asked.

"I'll show you." She grinned. "Just keep driving."


They wound through the Sabine Hills and approached the village of Toffia. Philip drove down the gravel path and Amelia recognized the stone building with small lead windows. She checked her lipstick in the mirror and fixed her hat. She opened the passenger door and leaned in the window.

"I think it's best if you wait here."

She walked to the narrow wooden door and knocked. She waited and knocked again. Finally she heard footsteps and a tall nun opened the door.

"Signorita Ann," the nun exclaimed. "What a pleasure to see you. Have you come to play with the children?"

"I'm looking for Sophie." Amelia smoothed her dress. "I thought she might be here."

"I haven't seen Signorita Sophie since she was here with the American doctor." Sister Lea frowned. "Would you like a glass of water before you go?"

"No, thank you." Amelia sighed.

She turned back to the car, feeling the hot sun on her shoulders. She was sure Sophie would be here, it was the perfect place to hide. She heard someone running and suddenly a little girl with blond curls threw her arms around her legs.

"Pretty lady! Don't go," Gloria exclaimed. "You have to play hide and go seek."

"I'm sorry, I have someone waiting." Amelia pointed to the car. "But it's lovely to see you."

"You have to play," Gloria insisted. "The pretty blond lady is hiding and I have to find her."

Amelia stopped and turned around. "Signorita Sophie?"

"We play games all day, hopscotch and ring around the rosy." Gloria nodded. "I always win hide and go seek, she won't hide in small places."

Amelia took Gloria's hand and walked to the convent. "Show me where to look and I'll find her."


"I can't believe Sister Lea lied that you weren't here," Amelia said.

"The nuns are serious about protecting people they care about from outsiders," Sophie replied. "That's how they survived the middle ages."

Amelia sat in the small reception room gazing at her friend. Sophie wore a white cotton dress and beige sandals. Her hair was knotted in a low ponytail and tied with a yellow ribbon.

"What are you doing here?" Amelia glanced at the threadbare brown sofa and stained glass window. There was a wooden coffee table with a tray of deviled eggs and a pitcher of lemonade.

"In the mornings I help the sisters in the vegetable garden; we're planting baby peas and butter lettuce and asparagus." Sophie put a deviled egg on a plate. "Then I prepare lunch and read and play with the children. I discovered Thomas Hardy—they have his complete works in the library."

"I mean what are you doing in Toffia?" Amelia asked. "I went to Portofino, Elspeth is worried."

"You went to Portofino to find me?" Sophie's eyes were wide.

"I thought Philip wrote the article about you." Amelia bit her lip. "I let slip that you were a princess when I was drunk. I thought you'd never forgive me."

"I had to write it." Sophie fiddled with her ponytail.

"I don't understand, how could you do something to hurt your father?" Amelia frowned.

"Lots of young royals spend the summer partying in Cannes or Monaco or Amalfi." Sophie shrugged. "It would create a small scandal but the alternative would be worse."

"The alternative?" Amelia raised her eyebrow.

"All I could think about was Theo." Sophie sipped her lemonade. "I was about to do something terrible."

"Does he know you are here?" Amelia asked.

"Of course not." Sophie shook her head. "He called the morning after we kissed and asked me to go to Pompeii to visit an orphanage. He promised we'd have separate rooms.

"I packed a dress and sandals and a toothbrush. I folded my lace underwear and bra and realized all I wanted was to go to bed with him." Sophie hesitated. "I couldn't let that happen, my father would never speak to me again."

"You could have told Theo you had to work and couldn't make it," Amelia said softly.

"But I wanted to go, I was falling in love with him!" Sophie exclaimed. "If I didn't run away I wouldn't have the strength to say no."

"Why not just go back to Portofino?" Amelia asked. "Why did you have to lie?"

"If Theo knew I lied about who I am, he'd never forgive me," Sophie replied. "I had to make sure it was over."

"You have to come back to Rome," Amelia insisted. "Elspeth said she'd give me twenty-four hours to find you until she tells your father."

"I am going back to Rome," Sophie said slowly. "I was leaving this afternoon."

"That's wonderful," Amelia beamed. "Philip is waiting outside."

"You don't understand." Sophie sat forward. "I lay in bed at night and thought about all the things I could do for the people of Lentz: build a state-of-the-art hospital, create an opera program for children, grow organic vegetables.

"I suddenly had all these ideas and it's because of Theo. When I'm with him I feel like I can do anything."

"Love makes you believe you can accomplish anything," Amelia murmured.

"You told me but I didn't believe you," Sophie nodded. "It's the greatest feeling in the world."

"What are you going to do?" Amelia asked.

"I'm going to tell my father I'll be the best queen Lentz ever had," Sophie declared. "But I'm going to pick my own husband."

Amelia gasped. "What will he say?"

"If he trusts me to rule the country, he has to trust me to marry the right man." Sophie bit her lip. "I want a husband and children and I won't live a charade."

"What about Prince Leopold?" Amelia asked.

"He's one of the wealthiest princes in Europe." Sophie waved her hand. "Girls will line up to be his wife."

"I'll tell Philip to make room in the backseat." Amelia smiled.

"What if Theo doesn't forgive me?" Sophie's mouth trembled.

"You're not going to find out playing hide and go seek with Gloria." Amelia stood up. "You have to ask him."

They drove silently back to Rome with Philip's hand resting on Amelia's knee. Amelia glanced at the villages with outdoor cafés and wished they could stop for a pizza margherita and a bottle of limoncello. But she felt Sophie dig her fingers into the back of her seat and knew they had to hurry back to the Hassler.

Philip pulled up in front of the hotel and Sophie jumped out. Amelia turned to Philip and hesitated.

"I should stay with her, she thinks Theo will be furious."

"Go on." Philip nodded. "Let's meet for dinner."

"Seven o'clock at Rosati?" Amelia's shoulders relaxed.

"I have to go home and beg Signora Griselda to iron my sheets." Philip kissed her lightly on the mouth. "Someone told me they're lumpy."

Amelia strode through the black and gold lobby and approached the elevator.

"Good afternoon, Miss Tate," Ernesto called. "How was Portofino?"

Amelia pictured the green cliffs and wooden fishing boats. She saw the brightly colored apartment buildings and whitewashed villas.

She remembered the scent of bougainvillea and hibiscus and fresh ground coffee.

"It was wonderful, Ernesto." Amelia smiled. "It's the most beautiful place in Italy."

She opened the door of the Villa Medici Suite and put down her suitcase. She flipped through the script and read her lines in front of the mirror. She pictured Philip's dark eyes and narrow cheeks and realized Sophie was right.

Suddenly she felt like she could do anything. Her eyes were brighter and even her smile was wider. She couldn't wait to get back on the set and play Princess Ann.

There was a knock on the door and she got up to answer it.

"The nurse said Theo wasn't at the clinic." Sophie entered the marble entry. "But I saw his Fiat in the alley."

"He could have stepped out for lunch," Amelia suggested.

"He never eats lunch unless we're together." Sophie sat on an ivory silk sofa. "How can I make him understand if he won't see me?"

Amelia studied Sophie's pale cheeks and white lips. She grabbed her straw hat and put on her sunglasses. "Wait here, I'll be right back."

She slipped out a side door of the Hassler and hurried down the alley. She entered the clinic and sat on a red vinyl chair. She heard the bell tinkle and saw the nurse with her metal clipboard.

"Can I help you?" the nurse asked.

"I need to see the doctor." She twisted her hands.

The nurse ushered her into a small room and Amelia sat uncomfortably on the wooden table. She heard the door open and saw Theo's blond hair and green eyes. He wore a white coat over blue jeans and had faint stubble on his chin.

"It's you." He folded his arms. "What do you want?"

"Sophie had a bad asthma attack," Amelia explained. "I gave her her inhaler but it's not helping, I'm very worried."

"Where is she?" Theo clutched his clipboard.

"At her suite at the Hassler." Amelia bit her lip. "Her breathing was ragged and her cheeks were white as paper."

Theo put down his clipboard and ran out the door. He raced down the alley and entered the gold revolving doors. Amelia followed him into the lobby and watched him disappear into the elevator. She waited until the doors closed and then she pressed the button to the seventh floor.

Amelia stepped out of the marble bathtub and walked to the closet. She had an hour until she met Philip and wanted to wear something glamorous and sexy. She flicked through cotton dresses and linen capris and found a lime green chiffon dress with a scooped neck. She paired it with gold Gucci sandals and a gold necklace. She snapped on her Cartier watch and added a few gold bangles.

She gazed at the vanity with its double marble sinks and white fluffy towels and jars of lotions and creams. Soon shooting would wrap and she'd go back to Los Angeles. She pictured Philip's dark eyes and white smile and shivered.

She was going to tell him she didn't mean to lie about who she was. It all started because she was exhausted from jet lag and had had too little to eat and too much champagne and wanted to explore Rome. She never meant it to go this far and she'd never lie to him again.

There was a knock on the door and she crossed the living room to answer it.

"I don't know what you did but I could kiss you." Sophie burst into the room. She wore a white linen dress with a silver belt. Her hair was knotted in a low bun and her mouth was coated with shimmering lip gloss.

"You look like you belong on the cover of *Vogue*." Amelia smiled, admiring her large blue eyes and thick dark lashes.

"I was curled up on the sofa reading *Tess of the D'Urbervilles* when Theo rushed into the suite." Sophie sat on a royal blue sofa and tucked her feet under her. "He took my pulse and stroked my forehead. He thought I had a terrible asthma attack."

"Is that so?" Amelia grinned.

"I tried to correct him but I burst into tears," Sophie replied. "By the time I stopped crying he was holding me in his arms and kissing me."

"Tears and diamonds are a girl's best friend," Amelia murmured.

"He said he should have known I was a princess because the first time he saw me he knew I was special."

"Go on." Amelia nodded.

"We talked about his dreams of building an orphanage and the responsibilities of being a princess," Sophie continued. "We're having dinner tonight at La Pergola."

"I'm glad," Amelia replied. "You are perfect for each other."

"I've never been on a real date; what if he wants to do more than kiss me goodnight?" Sophie asked.

"You'll get the hang of it." Amelia smiled. "You're doing great so far."

"I hope so." Sophie sighed, gazing at the silver tray of fresh scones and strawberry jam. "Since I fell in love I've barely had an appetite."

Amelia slipped on her sunglasses and gathered her purse. She imagined Philip waiting at Rosati and thought Sophie was right. Suddenly her stomach clenched and she wasn't hungry.

# chapter twenty-five

Philip crumpled a piece of paper and tossed it in the metal garbage can. He walked around his desk and poured a cup of black coffee. He sniffed it and placed it next to his laptop.

He had come to the office, determined to write the next article about Amelia. He kept picturing her in the Hotel Splendido. He saw her yellow dress and bare legs and white sandals. He remembered her slipping the key in the lock and inviting him into her room. He pictured her firm breasts and milky skin and wondered how could he possibly expose her in *Inside Rome*. He gulped the bitter coffee and felt his head throb.

"You look like you're dreaming about a college cheerleader you had a crush on." Adam entered the room. "I thought Yale cheerleaders were flat chested and wore glasses."

"I never went to football games." Philip closed his laptop. "I spent my time in the library."

"I got invited to the soccer World Cup by Sergio Levente." Adam poured a cup of coffee.

"Sergio Levente, the media magnate?" Philip asked.

"He read the piece about Princess Sophia and is interested in backing *Inside Rome*." Adam sipped his coffee. "But he won't invest unless we keep our circulation up."

"I'm working on the articles." Philip grimaced.

"You need to step up the schedule," Adam replied. "Get Amelia Tate to marry you by next week and I'll pay you twenty thousand dollars."

"Twenty thousand dollars," Philip spluttered.

"If Sergio invests I'll be able to hire a staff and cover Florence and Venice and Naples," Adam mused. "We'll change the name to *Inside Italy,* one day it might be *Inside Europe*."

"I'm meeting Amelia at Rosati's in an hour." Philip glanced at his watch.

"Buy her a dozen roses and a bottle of perfume." Adam reached into his pocket and took out a wad of euros. "And get better coffee. This shit will stunt your growth and put hair on your chest."

Philip crossed the Piazza del Popolo and approached Rosati's. He glanced inside and saw Amelia sitting at the window. She wore a green dress and her hair was pinned back with a gold clip. Her eyes sparkled and her mouth was coated with shimmering lip gloss.

"These are for you." He smiled, giving her a bouquet of yellow roses.

"They smell wonderful," Amelia beamed. "I was starving, I ordered a plate of pancetta and a bottle of Chianti."

"I wanted to change but I got stuck at the office." Philip glanced at his creased shirt. He gazed at Amelia's gold necklace and leather sandals and wished he'd put on a sport coat.

"You love the newspaper, don't you," Amelia mused, tearing a baguette.

"My office is the size of a sardine can and Adam can be abrasive." Philip grinned. "But he's passionate about what he does."

"You never told me why you left the *New York Times*," Amelia said.

"They kept hiring young kids and giving them big titles and little money." Philip frowned. "They folded my entire department into two guys straight out of journalism school."

"I'm sorry, that must have been terrible," Amelia murmured.

"I would have stayed even with a pay cut, it's all I ever wanted to do." Philip shrugged. "All the papers were being choked, why would anyone pay to read the news when it's free online?"

"I hardly ever read the paper." Amelia sipped a glass of Chianti. "But I promise to buy *Inside Rome* every morning."

"What did you do before you came to Rome?" Philip asked, eating ham and mozzarella wrapped in a fig leaf.

"I was premed at USC," Amelia replied. "My father is a surgeon and my mother is an anesthesiologist. I thought everyone's parents wore beepers and worked holidays and weekends."

"What happened?" Philip asked.

"I loved math but hated biology." Amelia shrugged. "I'm lucky, I could have spent eight years in medical school and then discovered I wasn't meant to wear a white coat. My parents love what they do but I didn't want to work in a hospital and sleep on an iron cot."

"What did you do instead?"

Amelia ate a bite of pancetta and dabbed her mouth with a napkin. Suddenly her cheeks were pale and she took a deep breath. "There's something I . . ."

"There you are." Max burst through the door. "I've been looking for you everywhere. Adam told me you were here, you have to help me."

"We're having dinner," Philip exclaimed, spilling his wine on the tablecloth.

"It looks delicious." Max glanced at the platter of soft cheeses and basket of olive bread. "But if you don't come with me I might be dead, and it's hard to enjoy a decent Burgundy when you've got tire treads on your forehead."

"What's going on?" Philip frowned.

"Let's go out the back and I'll tell you." He ducked behind the table. He bowed to Amelia and smiled. "My apologies for borrowing your boyfriend, I promise to return him. In the meantime try the swordfish in a lemon sauce, it's the chef's specialty."


"What the fuck are you doing?" Philip stormed when they entered his apartment. They had raced through the Piazza del Popolo to the Via del Corso. Max kept running until they climbed Philip's stairs and closed the door.

"I went to Lara's seventeenth-century palazzo, I wanted to tell her in person that I'm back with the countess." Max poured himself a glass of scotch. "The maid asked me to wait in the entry and I was surrounded by naked statues and frescoes of Roman feasts. Lara walked down the stairs in a red silk dress that was so tight I could barely swallow.

"I told her she was stunning and deserved someone who adored her. As I was leaving I saw a guy with gray hair drive up in a Maserati. He followed me out the gate and chased me through Rome." Max downed the scotch. "I finally pulled into the alley and hid the car in Signora Griselda's carport."

"The countess's Alfa Romeo is in Signora Griselda's carport?" Philip exclaimed.

"I didn't know what to do with it, I couldn't make it disappear."

Max poured another shot. "If Lara's husband caught me he'd wrap the fender around my neck."

"When will you stop chasing married women?" Philip paced around the room.

"I'm done with that," Max insisted. "I'm faithful to the countess."

"What about the count?" Philip asked.

"Mirabella says he's sixty and spends all his time at his silk factory in Umbria." Max shrugged. "He's glad the countess and I are together, it keeps away the gigolos."

"We're both in trouble." Philip sighed, pouring a glass of scotch and swallowing it in one gulp. "I think Amelia was about to reveal her identity."

"How do you know?" Max asked.

"We were talking about our pasts," Philip mused. "Suddenly her cheeks turned pale and she started to say something."

"You can't let her do that," Max insisted. "You have to ask her to marry you first."

"Adam upped the offer to twenty thousand dollars," Philip murmured.

"Twenty thousand dollars for her to say yes?" Max spluttered.

"An investor is interested in the newspaper." Philip nodded. "But how am I going to propose before she tells me the truth?"

"Tell her you have a deadline and don't have time to see her." Max paced around the room. "In the meantime you have to think of the perfect way to propose. You could make reservations at Imago and hire a violinist and a cellist. Or take a picnic to the Villa Borghese and have an airplane spell out 'Will you marry me?'"

"After tonight's dinner I can barely afford two slices of chocolate torte at Giolitti and a ring from a Cracker Jack box," Philip groaned.

"I forgot about the ring!" Max put his shot glass on the counter. "You need at least two carats, preferably surrounded by sapphires."

"How can I afford a ring like that?" Philip laughed.

"Convince Signora Griselda to hide my car." Max opened the door. "And I'll get a ring that would make the Duchess of Cambridge marry you."

"She's married to Prince William." Philip frowned.

"The right diamond can make a woman do anything."

Philip stood on the balcony, sipping his glass of scotch. He pictured Amelia's green chiffon dress and gold sandals. He saw the way she shrugged her shoulders and raised her eyebrows. He remembered the warmth of his mouth on her lips.

He walked inside and put the glass in the sink. He opened the fridge and took out a tomato and a head of lettuce. He spread mustard on whole wheat bread and added bacon and red onions. He placed the sandwich on a plate and realized he wasn't hungry.

# chapter twenty-six

A melia slipped on a white cotton robe and pink slippers. She sat on the four-poster bed and glanced at the yellow silk curtains. It was lovely to lie against the floral pillows and gaze at the Roman Forum and the Colosseum. It was lovely to sip a cup of English breakfast tea with milk and honey.

She remembered sitting across from Philip at Rosati's, eating pancetta and fresh bread. She remembered opening her mouth to tell him the truth and shivered. Tomorrow she'd go to the Campo de Fiori and buy prosciutto and ricotta cheese and baguettes. They'd take a picnic to Pinico Hill and she'd tell him everything.

She put her porcelain cup on the bedside table and glanced at Audrey Hepburn's letters. She picked up the top page and began to read.

*Dear Kitty,*                              *September 20, 1952*
*We are almost finished shooting and it reminds me of the last*
*days of school. You can't wait for summer but at the same time you*

*know you'll miss the friendships and the gossip and the boys passing notes.*

*Everyone has been in a good mood; even Mr. Wyler has been making jokes. He said if I could act like this in the beginning, we would have wrapped weeks ago. I'm not afraid of the lights or the cameras; I'm like a rose that finally bloomed.*

*This evening I approached the Hassler and saw a crowd of journalists on the stone steps. I thought they were waiting for someone famous like Humphrey Bogart or Katharine Hepburn. I entered the glass revolving doors and suddenly the camera bulbs flashed.*

*"Miss Hepburn, how do you feel about the rumor that you and Gregory Peck are having a romance?" a man in a gray suit asked.*

*"Is it true you plan on running away together after* Roman Holiday *wraps?" a woman in a black fitted dress demanded. "Where is your secret hideaway?"*

*Oh, Kitty, I was so shocked I thought I would faint! I remembered Gil telling me how important it is to be nice to journalists. I smoothed my skirt and gave them my widest smile.*

*"It seems you know more about our plans than I do," I replied. "Perhaps you can tell me where we're going."*

*"The odds are on Las Vegas." The woman glanced at her notes.*

*"Las Vegas!" I exclaimed. "Why would anyone go there? It's over a hundred degrees in the summer."*

*"So Gregory Peck can get a quick divorce and you can get married," piped in a reporter with dark hair and glasses.*

*"I'm afraid someone has given you the wrong information." I waved my hand. "I met Gregory Peck's wife and she is stunning. Mr. Peck plans to spend the rest of his summer camping with his family in Yosemite."*

"It's right here." The female reporter unfolded a copy of La Repubblica.

"Let me see that," I said, glancing at a photo of Greg and me sharing a gelato in the Piazza di Spagna.

"You don't need my copy." She shrugged. "It's on every newsstand in Rome."

I took the elevator to the Villa Medici Suite and closed the door. I picked up the phone to call the concierge but put it down. If I asked to speak to Greg every reporter in Rome would know I dialed his number.

I started reading the article but my stomach turned. How could the paper print such lies! Greg and I never talked about anything more than having a drink at Harry's Bar, and that's always with Veronique and Mel Ferrer.

I thought of Veronique and my shoulders relaxed. She would get to the bottom of this. I picked up the phone and asked to be connected to the operator.

"I need to speak to Veronique Passani," I said.

"We don't have a guest by that name," the operator replied.

"She must be staying at some hotel in Rome," I insisted. "She's a reporter for Paris Soir."

"There are dozens of hotels in Rome." The operator hesitated.

"Please, it's terribly important," I urged. "Tell her Audrey Hepburn must talk to her."

I paced around the living room waiting for the phone to ring.

"What's wrong?" Veronique's French accent came down the line. "I'm at the salon getting my nails done."

"Are you in Rome?" I clutched the phone.

"I just arrived, I've been in Paris," Veronique replied.

"I need to see you right away," I declared.

"I can hardly walk out with wet nails, Franco would be furious," Veronique snapped. "Have a glass of amaretto and relax, I'll be there as soon as the lacquer dries."

I remembered what Veronique said about journalists writing the truth and wondered if there was anything behind the story. Greg has been so kind since I ended my engagement but I would never dream of breaking up his marriage. And even if I did, he never tried to kiss me. Oh, Kitty, my thoughts keep turning like the carousel in the Bois de Boulogne. I can't wait for Veronique to get here!

Audrey

Dear Kitty, September 21, 1952

Veronique arrived wearing a dark green Dior dress and beige pumps. Her auburn hair fell to her shoulders and she carried a lizard clutch.

"I can't believe they wrote we're running away together." I showed her the newspaper. "I'm too embarrassed to show my face."

"Of course you're not running away." She folded the newspaper and placed it on the glass coffee table. She tapped a cigarette from her gold cigarette case and lit it with a pearl lighter. "We are."

"What did you say?" I spluttered.

"Gregory and I fell in love last winter when I interviewed him for Paris Soir." Veronique stood at the window. "It was his suggestion I spend time on the set and interview the other actors."

"But you said he was happily married!" I protested. "He loves his wife and he's crazy about his children."

"It's been a marriage in name only for years." Veronique exhaled a thin line of smoke. "Greta won't mind as long as she keeps her name and the mansion in Beverly Hills. But the boys adore their father, what chance would our relationship have if I was the woman who broke up their parents' marriage?"

"What are you saying?" I gasped.

"If the newspapers reported that Gregory Peck ran away with Veronique Passani, his children would never forgive me. But if Gregory had a romance with Audrey Hepburn that didn't work out, they would accept the woman who helped him recover."

"You wrote the article?" My eyes were wide.

"On-set romances happen all the time." Veronique shrugged. "This one went a little too far. When Audrey Hepburn returns to New York to play Gigi on Broadway, Veronique Passani will help Gregory Peck mend his broken heart."

"Does Greg know?" I asked.

"Of course not." Veronique laughed. "He's American, he isn't capable of subterfuge. It's a wonder the Americans helped us win the war, they would never have been able to fight in the resistance."

"But you said you'd never give up your typewriter to get married." I frowned, trying to stop my hands from shaking.

"The French know the most important thing in life is love." Veronique stubbed out her cigarette.

"Did you ask Greg to pay attention to me?" I demanded, flashing on the picnic and the horse and buggy ride.

"Don't be silly, Gregory admires you." Veronique shrugged. "You should be pleased, it doesn't hurt to have your name linked to one of the most sought-after actors in the world."

"I think it's terrible," I snapped. "What will his children say when he doesn't come home?"

"You're going to be a famous actress with designers begging to dress you and men falling at your feet," Veronique mused. "Some of us need to grab happiness in case it doesn't return."

"If you don't mind, I'd like to be alone." I stood up.

"I promise I will make his children happy," Veronique said softly. "Gregory is a wonderful father, he loves them very much."

Oh, Kitty, after Veronique left I threw myself on the bed. I pictured James in his Gieves & Hawkes suits and thought Veronique was right. I am lucky to be an actress and I've always had good fortune with men.

I dried my eyes and fixed my lipstick. I slipped on a white Chanel dress and ivory pumps. I put on silk gloves and pressed the button on the elevator.

"Miss Hepburn, do you have a comment about your love affair with Gregory Peck?" a reporter asked when the doors opened.

I looked at the reporter and took a deep breath.

"Have you ever been on a movie set? It's impossible not to fall in love." I sighed. "You fall in love with the fabulous location and the wonderful script and the glamorous clothes. I will always love Gregory Peck and William Wyler and everyone who made Roman Holiday possible. But the only thing I'm in love with right now is being an actress."

"Are you saying the reports that you're going to run away together are false?" the reporter persisted.

"I'm saying nothing on a movie set is real." I strode through the lobby and pushed through the gold revolving doors. "That's what makes it so utterly wonderful."

The reporters finally disappeared and I went to Sant'Eustachio and had iced coffee and a profiterole. I'm tired of eating plain pasta and sautéed vegetables, I craved sugar and cream.

I watched couples stroll along the Piazza Eustachio and remembered Greg talking about love. I was silly to imagine he was thinking of me when he just needed someone to talk to.

But, Kitty, I lied to the reporter when I said I'm only interested in being an actress. I want a man to talk to and laugh with and share chocolate torte!

Audrey

Dear Kitty,                                        September 24, 1952

Today we filmed the final scene where I meet the press in the royal palace and see Joe for the last time. I was so nervous; I hadn't seen Greg since La Repubblica printed the article. I sat in my dressing room waiting for Marie to bring in my gown.

Do you remember when we went to Convent Garden to see Margot Fonteyn in Sleeping Beauty? We couldn't keep our eyes off her; she was the most beautiful thing we'd ever seen. That's how I felt when I slipped on the Balenciaga gown. It's pink satin with delicate pearl buttons. Marie fastened the Harry Winston diamond tiara on my head and said I mustn't let it fall. Harry Winston lent it to Mr. Wyler and it cost thousands of dollars!

I stepped onto the set and saw Veronique Passani sitting in a chair. She wore a navy Chanel suit with a leather belt. Her hair was knotted in a low bun and she wore dark red lipstick.

I tried to avoid her but she approached me.

"I wanted you to see this before I give it to my editor." She handed me a sheet of paper. "It's my interview with you for Paris Soir."

I scanned the first paragraph and then read it out loud.

"Hollywood announces a new Myrna Loy or Katharine Hepburn is born every minute, but it is almost always studio hype. A real talent has emerged in Audrey Hepburn, the star of Paramount's Roman Holiday.

*"I spent a month observing Miss Hepburn and the slight, elegant girl is transformed on the screen. Her eyes are like saucers and her smile could light up Paris. I predict an illustrious career for the effervescent young star."*

*I put the paper down and looked at Veronique.*

*"You didn't have to write that," I murmured.*

*Veronique folded the paper and smiled. "A good journalist only writes the truth."*

*I entered the set and my stomach was full of butterflies. Greg stood across the room dressed in a dark suit and white shirt and black tie. His dark hair was brushed across his forehead and he was freshly shaved.*

*Kitty, I said my lines and my stomach rose to my throat. Greg looked at me so fiercely I thought my heart would break. You can say it was only acting, that he was Joe realizing he won't see Princess Ann again. But I know it was more than that, there is something between us I will never forget.*

*After Mr. Wyler said it's a wrap, someone popped a bottle of champagne. I don't like champagne, the bubbles make me blink and I get a terrible headache. But I was so giddy; I let the assistant fill my glass. I watched them roll up the red carpet and felt a tightness in my chest.*

*"You were wonderful." Greg approached me. "I haven't seen Willy so choked up since he won the Oscar for* Best Year of Our Lives.*"*

*"It was this gorgeous dress and these spectacular jewels." I shrugged. "Anyone could be a princess."*

*"I read the article in* La Repubblica,*" Greg mused, sipping his champagne.*

*"You'd think reporters have more important things to do than make up stories about an unknown actress." I blushed.*

*"Love and infidelity make great headlines but one of the best things in life is friendship," Greg replied.*

*"What do you mean?" I asked.*

*"It's rare you meet someone so beautiful and smart you know you'll be friends for life," he continued. "But when you do you cherish that friendship like a hothouse flower."*

*"I'd like to stay friends." I nodded.*

*"To our next picture together." Greg raised his champagne flute. "Somewhere it isn't so goddam humid your shirt sticks to your collar and the sandwiches aren't made of dry turkey and yellow American cheese."*

*I drained my glass and walked to my dressing room. I unbuttoned the pink satin Balenciaga gown and took off the Harry Winston diamond tiara and suddenly felt so happy. I played a princess and made a great friend, life is wonderful!*

*Audrey*

Amelia put the letter on the bedside table and walked to the window. She gazed at the twinkling lights of the Colosseum and the gold spires of Saint Peter's Basilica. She pictured Audrey Hepburn in her satin evening gown and diamond tiara saying life was wonderful.

Shooting was almost over and Sheldon was very pleased with her performance. She had explored the catacombs and visited the Vatican and tossed coins in the Trevi Fountain. She and Sophie ate lemon gelato at Caffé Greco and shopped at the boutiques on the Via Condotti.

But she couldn't enjoy the beautiful clothes or the delicious foods or the ancient sites until she told Philip the truth. What if he was furious and never wanted to see her again? She climbed on the four-poster bed and turned off the light. She pulled the ivory satin sheets around her shoulders and closed her eyes.

# chapter twenty-seven

Amelia drew back the yellow silk curtains and stood on the balcony. It was late afternoon and the sun gleamed on the red rooftops. She heard church bells ringing and smelled fresh roasted coffee and hibiscus.

She walked inside to her closet and slipped on an ivory silk dress and silver sandals. She tied a red scarf around her head and put on dark sunglasses. She and Sophie were going to sit at Gusto's and watch models stroll along the Via Veneto. Then she was going to come back to the Villa Medici Suite and rehearse until every syllable was perfect.

Philip left a message with Ernesto that he got a freelance assignment with a tight deadline. She missed him but she was happy to read her script and hear about Sophie's dinners with Theo.

She took the elevator to the lobby and saw Sophie standing in front of the gift shop. She wore a yellow Prada dress and gold sandals. Her hair was knotted in a low ponytail and tied with a yellow ribbon. She held a magazine in one hand and a packet of Life Savers in the other.

"I've never had butterscotch Life Savers before." She handed the packet to Amelia. "In Lentz we only had peppermint. I couldn't understand why they made a candy with a hole in it."

"That dress looks gorgeous on you." Amelia admired the narrow shoulder straps and thin gold belt.

"I feel naked but Theo said it makes my skin look like honey." Sophie crossed the black and gold marble floor. "Tonight we're going to the Modigliani exhibit at the National Museum."

They walked through the gold revolving doors and suddenly Sophie froze. She adjusted her sunglasses and hurried back to the lobby.

"You look like you've seen a ghost." Amelia frowned.

"Did you see the white Bentley pull into the driveway?" Sophie whispered.

Amelia glanced out the plate glass window and saw an ivory Bentley with a gold grill. It had a walnut dashboard and creamy leather seats.

"Bentleys arrive at the Hassler all the time." Amelia shrugged.

"Not ones with red and gold flags," Sophie hissed. "That's my father's car."

"Your father is in Rome?" Amelia raised her eyebrow.

"I talked to Elspeth this morning, she didn't say anything." Sophie twisted her hands. "He must have come to Rome to stop me from seeing Theo."

"Does he know about Theo?" Amelia asked.

"If Elspeth told him I was in Rome, she could have told him everything." Sophie sighed. "I was going to tell him soon, we just wanted some time alone together."

"What are you going to do?" Amelia watched the valet open the car door. A tall man with blond hair stepped out. He wore a navy blazer and cream slacks. He had a gold watch on his wrist and a yellow silk handkerchief in his pocket.

"I'm going to tell him Theo and I are in love and want to get married." Sophie strode toward the elevator.

"Where are you going?" Amelia asked, darting in the elevator.

"I can't meet him dressed like this." Sophie glanced at her yellow crepe dress and bare gold sandals. "I have to look like a princess."

Sophie emerged from her closet wearing a turquoise chiffon dress with a scalloped hem. Her hair was scooped into a bun and fastened with a diamond chopstick. She wore diamond earrings and a ruby necklace.

"That dress is stunning." Amelia gasped. It was cut below the knee and revealed Sophie's elegant calves. She wore ivory Gucci pumps and a ruby and diamond bracelet.

"It's Valentino," Sophie replied. "He was my mother's favorite designer. He visited the palace once a year with his new collection."

"You'll be wonderful." Amelia approached the door. "I should go."

"Please stay." Sophie touched her hand. "My father can be intimidating, he'll behave if you're here."

"Are you sure?" Amelia asked.

"Positive." Sophie nodded. Her eyes were wide and suddenly she looked like a girl on the way to her first communion rather than a woman about to be a queen.

"All right." Amelia nodded, sitting on a royal blue velvet sofa. "But if you want me to leave give me a sign."

There was a knock at the door and Sophie ran to answer it. King Alfred entered the marble foyer and Amelia sucked in her breath. Up close he looked like a movie star. He had thick blond hair and blue eyes and a cleft on his chin. His clothes were perfectly pressed and he smelled of Armani cologne.

"Father!" Sophie exclaimed. "What are you doing here?"

"Sophia, you look gorgeous." Alfred strode into the living room and glanced at Amelia.

"This is my friend, Amelia Tate," Sophie said hurriedly. "She's an actress shooting a movie in Rome."

Alfred took Amelia's hand and nodded. "I don't see many movies since my wife died, but she loved the cinema. You resemble a young Audrey Hepburn. We watched *Sabrina* a dozen times."

"It's a pleasure to meet you," Amelia stumbled. "Sophie talks about you often."

"Did Elspeth tell you I was here?" Sophie demanded.

Alfred turned to his daughter. "Of course not, Elspeth is incredibly loyal, she would never break your trust. Bernard has been keeping an eye on you."

Sophie's eyes flickered and she covered her hand with her mouth. "You had me followed?"

"Not followed, protected." Alfred smiled. "You're very precious to me."

"If you knew I was in Rome, why didn't you stop me?" Sophie asked.

"When I was twenty-three I sailed my father's yacht to Mykonos. There were no cell phones or e-mails, no one knew where I was," Alfred replied. "I caught my own dinner and ate paella and fresh figs and dates. At night I sat on the deck and read Hemingway and Dostoyevsky, it was the best month of my life."

"You let Elspeth think she was lying to you." Sophie frowned.

"It's important to have someone you can trust with anything." Alfred paused and looked at Sophie. "It wouldn't have been a rebellion with my permission."

"I've had a lovely time." Sophie bit her lip. "I visited the Villa Borghese and the Vatican and the Colosseum. I saw *Othello* at Opera

Roma and ate fettuccine at Alfredo's and bought shoes at Prada and Gucci."

"I haven't been to Rome in years." Alfred nodded. "But your mother loved to stock up on dresses and shoes and bags. We had to bring an extra car for her purchases."

"And I met an American doctor and fell in love." Sophie's eyes were wide. "He's handsome and kind and when we're together I feel like I can accomplish anything. I can't marry Prince Leopold."

King Alfred studied the crystal vase filled with pink and white tulips. He looked at Sophie and took a deep breath. "When I was twelve years old, friends of my parents visited the palace. I looked out the window and saw a girl standing in the rose garden. She had white-blond hair and blue eyes and skin like fresh cream. She glanced up and her face broke into a smile. It was the brightest smile I'd ever seen.

"I marched into my father's study and said I met the girl I was going to marry. Her name was Lady Fanny Windsor and she was ten years old." Alfred paused. "Twelve years later we were married in the Cathedral of Lentz and two years later you were born."

Sophie stood up and walked to the balcony. She turned around and her eyes were moist. "You said you had an arranged marriage."

"It was arranged by me." Alfred nodded. "My father understood that I would be the best king if I had the woman I loved by my side."

"Then why did you insist I have an arranged marriage?" Sophie demanded.

"Your mother was beautiful and bright and lit up every room," Alfred mused. "When she died I could barely function. If I didn't have heads of states waiting in the reception room, I wouldn't have gotten out of bed. I never wanted you to feel like that."

"You didn't want me to fall in love because you were afraid I'd get hurt." Sophie shivered.

"Parents have done worse things to protect their children." Alfred took Sophie's hand. "I can see in your eyes I was wrong. You're not a little girl; you're a mature beautiful woman. I hope you can forgive me."

"I lied about having the measles and made my lady-in-waiting keep my secret and printed a scandalous article in an international newspaper." Sophie's face broke into a smile. "I guess we're even."

"There's another person you have to tell," Alfred said slowly. "He's come a long way to see you."

Sophie's cheeks turned pale and her lips quivered. "What are you talking about?"

"Prince Leopold is waiting in my suite," Alfred replied. "I said I needed to talk to you first. Whether or not you marry him, you've been friends since you were five years old. You owe him an explanation."

Sophie looked at her father and took a deep breath. She thought of all the things she would have to do as queen: visit hospitals full of sick children, comfort farmers when they lost their crops, welcome foreign dignitaries. She smoothed her hair and smiled. "Of course, tell him to come up."

"If I had known you were going to be so beautiful, I would have insisted you wear the friendship ring I gave you when you were twelve years old," Prince Leopold said, nibbling a cucumber sandwich.

When Prince Leopold appeared at the door, Sophie had been so nervous she could hardly breathe. She glanced at Amelia but Amelia whispered she had nothing to worry about. He had short blond hair and green eyes and a long nose. He wore khakis and a yellow polo shirt and leather loafers.

Sophie sat on the blue silk sofa and thought of long afternoons spent running through the Palace gardens. She remembered capturing butterflies and carefully releasing them from the net. She pictured sharing a banana split with whipped cream and nuts.

"I should have called or written." Sophie apologized. "You didn't have to fly to Rome."

"I was coming to Italy for a conference." Prince Leopold poured tea into a porcelain cup. "And to tell you that I met someone. She's an intern specializing in pediatric cancer. I ignored my feelings for months, but it's like stopping an avalanche. Once you fall in love there's nothing you can do about it."

Sophie felt her shoulders relax and a warmth spread through her chest. "She sounds lovely, what's her name?"

"Alexandra, she's from California. She lives in shorts and T-shirts and has never tried fondue." Prince Leopold grinned. "But she makes me laugh and we never run out of things to talk about."

Sophie pictured Theo in his white coat and blue jeans. She saw his curly blond hair and green eyes and the cleft on his chin. She ate a bite of peach scone and smiled.

"I'm so happy for you." Her eyes were huge. "I met someone, too. His name is Theo. He works too much but he loves children and he wants to make the world a better place."

Leopold leaned forward and kissed Sophie on the cheek.

"He sounds perfect, I hope we are invited to the wedding."

After Prince Leopold left, King Alfred stood up and walked to the marble bar. He poured a shot of brandy and drank it in one gulp.

"We're in Rome, we must enjoy ourselves. I'm dying for a plate of Parmesan ravioli and a glass of Chianti." He turned to Amelia. "Would you join us for dinner?"

"No thank you." Amelia shook her head. "I have plans."

"Before we have dinner I'd like you to meet someone." Sophie smoothed her hair. "We're going to the clinic to see Theo."

Amelia crossed the black and gold marble floors of the lobby and walked through the glass revolving doors. She glanced at her watch and realized it was almost 7:00 P.M. She would go to Philip's apartment and ask him to join her for dinner. They'd sit at an outdoor café on the Piazza di Trevi and share a caprese salad and a bowl of linguini.

"Good evening, Miss Tate," Marco called. "You look beautiful tonight."

"Thank you, Marco, I love sunsets in Rome." Amelia beamed. "They're like a painting by Botticelli."

"Can I call a taxi?" Marco asked.

She glanced at the pink sky and the setting sun and the Spanish Steps in front of her. She inhaled the smell of bougainvillea and roasted chestnuts and gasoline.

"No thank you, Marco." She hurried down the steps. "I couldn't sit in traffic on such a lovely night, I'm going for a walk."

She crossed the Piazza di Spagna and strolled along the Via del Corso. She glanced up and saw a familiar figure standing in the Piazza di Trevi. He wore a white shirt with the sleeves rolled up and tan slacks.

"Ann, wait!" Philip called, striding across the piazza.

"I was coming to see you." Amelia gazed at his dark eyes and smooth cheeks and suddenly felt warm and happy. "It's such a beautiful evening I was going to drag you away from your assignment and ask you to have dinner."

"I finished the article, I'd like to do something special."

"Like what?" Amelia asked.

He put his arm around her waist and pulled her close. He kissed her softly on the lips and touched her chin. "You'll see."

They crossed Saint Peter's square and climbed the stone steps of the Basilica. Philip knocked on the double gold doors and slipped his hands in his pockets.

"It's after seven." Amelia glanced at her watch. "The tours are over."

The doors slowly opened and a guide in a brown uniform ushered them inside. Amelia gazed at the domed ceiling and the bronze columns and the mosaic floor and sucked in her breath.

"What are we doing?" she whispered.

Philip took her hand and smiled. "We're taking a private tour."

The guide led them to the side of the Basilica and into a secret passageway. Amelia heard her heels echo on the marble and saw walls covered with gold frames. She followed the guide into a rectangular room with rich oriental carpets. It had a gilt ceiling and walls painted with elaborate frescoes.

"These are the Raphael Rooms," the guide said. "They were chosen by Pope Julius to be his papal residence in 1513. The frescoes by Raphael are the finest examples of Renaissance art."

"They're breathtaking." Amelia gazed at a painting of Adam and Eve in the Garden of Eden. She kept walking and saw scenes depicting the School of Athens and the Coronation of Charlemagne.

"The Vatican museums are made up of two thousand rooms," the guide continued. "We could walk for nine miles."

They visited the Gold Room with its gold statues and the Niccoline Chapel with its murals by Fra Angelico and the Gallery of Tapestries. Amelia saw narrow spaces crammed with ancient Greek sculptures and ornate rooms filled with paintings by Perugino and Donatello and Caravaggio.

They entered wooden double doors and Amelia gasped. She glanced up and saw naked figures against a blue sky. There were plump nymphs and black serpents and baskets of ripe fruit.

"*The Last Judgment* was commissioned by Pope Paul the Third in 1535," the guide said. "Michelangelo built the scaffolding himself and used special paints that would be visible from the floor. It took him six years to complete and Cardinal Carafa wanted it removed because he thought the naked figures were obscene. Pope Paul prevailed and it is one of Michelangelo's greatest achievements."

Amelia gazed at the gold altar and ornate candlesticks and couldn't believe she was in the Sistine Chapel. She studied the sun and moon and the stars painted on the mosaic floor. She felt Philip's arm brush her shoulder and shivered.

They finally returned to Saint Peter's Basilica and the guide led them to a corner. They stopped in front of a marble statue of a woman holding her child.

"Sometimes it's hard to appreciate the Pieta with tourists crowding around her," the guide said. "Take your time, but please don't touch."

Amelia gazed at the statue she had studied in textbooks and her eyes filled with tears. She saw Mary's slender cheeks and graceful neck and billowing gown. She took Philip's hand and felt a warmth spread through her chest.

"How did you manage that?" Amelia asked when they emerged onto the steps. It was almost nine o'clock and the piazza was filled with couples strolling along the cobblestones. She heard violins playing and saw street vendors selling roasted chestnuts and sunflowers.

"Max's friend, the countess, arranged it." Philip grinned. "She tried to get an audience with the Pope but he is at his summer residence at the Castle Gandolfo."

"It was magnificent." Amelia breathed. "The frescoes are six hundred years old but they look like they were painted yesterday."

They strolled along the Via del Corso and crossed the Piazza di Trevi. She followed Philip up his staircase and stopped at his front door.

"I thought we were having dinner." Amelia frowned. "I haven't eaten since a slice of pizza Napolitano at lunch."

"We are having dinner." Philip opened the door. "Authentic Italian cuisine prepared by a personal chef."

Amelia walked inside and saw glass vases filled with yellow and white tulips. The round table was covered with a white linen tablecloth and set with gold inlaid china. There was a bottle of red wine and two crystal wineglasses.

"Where did this all come from?" Amelia gasped, admiring the flickering candles and silver tray of prosciutto and Edam cheese and smoked salmon.

"The countess lent Max the china and Signora Griselda provided the flowers; her cousin has a flower stall at the Campo de Fiori," Philip replied, walking to the counter.

Amelia sat on a wooden chair and waited while Philip filled their plates. There was stuffed chicken breast and risotto with black truffles. There was a platter of heirloom tomatoes and mozzarella with olive oil and basil and oregano.

"Signora Griselda gave me the recipe for risotto." Philip buttered a warm baguette. "She thinks not knowing how to cook is a greater sin than missing church on Sunday."

Amelia sipped her wine and took a deep breath. It was the perfect time to tell him the truth, while they were flushed from the private tour of the Vatican and the romantic setting and the delicious food.

She put down her glass and smoothed her hair. She looked at Philip and her eyes were huge.

"There's something I've been wanting to tell you," she began. Suddenly Philip knocked over her wineglass and red wine spilled on her skirt. She jumped up and dabbed it with a napkin.

"I'm such a klutz," he groaned. "If you go into the bathroom I'll find you something to wear."

"I'm fine," Amelia replied, gazing doubtfully at the red stain spreading over ivory silk.

"You don't want to ruin your dress." Philip frowned. "If you take it off, I'll try to remove the stain."

Amelia walked into the bathroom and closed the door. She glanced at her crumpled dress and her eyes filled with tears. Everything had been so lovely and now the mood was broken.

"You can wear this." Philip handed her a dress shirt and a pair of socks.

Amelia gave him the ruined dress and put on a white collared shirt. She slipped on yellow tube socks and entered the living room.

"I feel terrible." Philip hung the dress on the balcony and walked to the table. "I invited you to a romantic dinner and ruined your clothes."

"Don't worry about the dress." Amelia shrugged. "It was an accident."

"Luckily this restaurant doesn't have a dress code." Philip kissed her softly on the mouth. He put his hand under her shirt and caressed her breasts. "Because you look sexy in that shirt."

Amelia felt his mouth on hers and tasted tomato and olive oil and basil. She inhaled his citrus cologne and rubbed her palms against his chest.

He slipped his hand under her cotton panties and touched the wet spot between her legs. He kissed her on the mouth, digging his fingers deep inside her. She felt the warm liquid fill her up and bit her lip. She grabbed his shoulders, letting her body rise and tip and shudder.

She pulled him to the narrow bed and lay down on the mattress. She opened her legs and drew him on top of her. She wrapped her arms around his back, urging him to go faster. He pushed harder until they came together in one long, dizzying thrust.

Philip lay on his back and draped his arm around her waist. He gazed at the plaster ceiling and whispered.

"It may not be the Sistine Chapel, but there's nowhere I'd rather be in Rome."

# chapter twenty-eight

P hilip stood on the side of the Piazza del Popolo and squinted in
the mid-morning sun. He pictured Amelia's smooth breasts and
slender hips and wished he were lying next to her in bed. He imagined
her sitting at his dining room table, eating muesli and cut berries.

He thought about the articles safely stored on his computer. He
described their first meeting at the taxi stand and Amelia falling asleep
against his shoulder. He wrote about fishing her out of the Trevi fountain and making her eggs and bacon. He described the concert at
Hadrian's Villa and the restaurant in Trastevere. He wrote about picnics
and romantic dinners and their night in Portofino.

Every time he wrote about her brown eyes and wide smile he felt
his throat close up. He sat back in his chair and tapped his pencil on
the desk. He could go to her and admit he knew she was Amelia Tate.
He would tell her the whole story, how he hated lying to her but was
desperate to pay back his father. He would say he should never have
started it and hoped she would forgive him.

But he realized he knew so little about her. Actresses had on-set romances all the time. Perhaps he was nothing more than a distraction after she broke up with her boyfriend.

"Where were you last night?" Philip approached a wrought iron table in front of Canova. Max wore a creased yellow shirt and blue jeans. His blond hair touched his collar and he had faint stubble on his chin. "You were supposed to leave the diamond ring in my apartment. I was going to propose but Amelia said she had something to tell me. I had to distract her by spilling red wine on her dress."

"The count forgot his heart medication and came back from Umbria early." Max poured sugar into black coffee. "He found Mirabella and me in the kitchen making chocolate panna cotta."

"That doesn't sound incriminating." Philip sat in a chair and stretched his legs in front of him. He spread strawberry jam on a warm scone and took a large bite.

"She wasn't wearing anything but an apron," Max replied. "She made me wait in the Alfa Romeo, I felt like Bonnie and Clyde. Finally she hopped in the passenger seat and we tore out the gates. The count is a terrible driver, I lost him on the Via della Conciliazione."

"Where is the countess now?" Philip asked.

"Asleep in my bed." Max shrugged. "She said he'd calm down after he takes his heart medicine."

"The countess slept at your place?" Philip raised his eyebrow, picturing Max's small apartment with the glossy photos of beautiful women.

"I told her the photos were all for work." Max waved his hand. "I liked having her sleep over. We played strip scrabble, I don't care what decade she's in, she has the finest breasts in Italy. This morning we lay in bed and cuddled."

"Soon she'll be packing your lunchbox with a turkey sandwich and an apple and a chocolate chip cookie." Philip grinned.

"I did manage to get this for you." Max reached into his pocket and drew out a black velvet box. He opened it and revealed a large oval diamond flanked by two glittering sapphires.

"It's perfect." Philip sucked in his breath. "Where did you get it?"

"Mirabella's personal jeweler at Bulgari lent it to me," Max sipped his coffee. "It's a two-carat Griffe diamond on a platinum band. I only have it for forty-eight hours, you have to propose by tomorrow night."

"I left before she woke up. If I plan another romantic dinner she'll tell me who she is before we finish the soup." Philip felt a knot in his stomach. "She's like a deer caught in the headlights, she doesn't know which way to turn. Maybe I shouldn't go through with it, I don't want to hurt her. I'll tell Adam I proposed and she turned me down."

"Are you crazy? You're steps from the finish line!" Max exclaimed. "The countess received an invitation to the masquerade ball at the Palazzo Colonna. The Palazzo Colonna has been in the same family for nine hundred years and it is the most spectacular private residence in Rome." Max tapped his fingers on the porcelain cup. "Invite Amelia and tell her to meet you there. Ask her to dance and propose before she realizes who you are."

"Why isn't the countess going?" Philip asked.

"The count changed the locks and she doesn't have anything to wear." Max shrugged. "We'd prefer a quiet evening at home, we're going to make the lemon-honey semifreddo we learned at cooking school."

"How will I know Amelia if she is wearing a mask?" Philip frowned.

"I'll tail her from the Hassler," Max replied. "I'll text you and tell you what she's wearing."

Philip watched the sun glint on the diamond ring. He pictured gliding across the marble dance floor with his arm around Amelia's waist. He imagined her soft lips and smooth skin and floral scent.

"All right, I'll do it." Philip slipped the ring in his pocket. He felt the warm sun on his cheeks and his shoulders relaxed. "You're good at this, you should have been a spy."

"If I don't get a cut of that twenty thousand I may need to find a new career." Max drained his coffee cup. "You can't support two people on a photographer's salary."

Philip strode up the gravel driveway and glanced at the line of Maseratis and Ferraris. Valets in white jackets ran between silver Rolls-Royces and white Bentleys. Philip watched a couple step out of a low yellow Lamborghini and whistled.

He spent the whole afternoon rehearsing his proposal. He paced around his apartment rubbing the velvet box in his pocket. He pressed his best dress shirt and dusted his white dinner jacket and selected a black silk bow tie. Finally he called a taxi and inched slowly toward Quirinale Hill.

He entered the iron gates of the Palazzo Colonna and felt like he was in a private park. There were lush palm trees and vibrant birds of paradise. Philip heard crickets and frogs and the faint sound of violins.

"I'm supposed to meet someone but I got stuck in traffic." Philip approached a sentry in a white uniform. "Have you seen a young woman waiting?"

"I'm sorry, sir." The man took his invitation. "All the guests are already inside."

Philip put the mask over his face and stepped into the foyer. The hall had green and blue marble floors and gold inlaid ceilings. There were glittering chandeliers and paintings by Tintoretto and Albani and Bronzino.

Philip searched the sea of masks and thought maybe Amelia changed her mind. He crossed the grand salon and strode down a narrow hallway. He opened a door and entered a room with velvet walls and Oriental carpets.

He glanced at a woman sitting on a red and gold bench and his heart beat faster in his chest. He would have recognized Amelia even if Max hadn't described her dress. She wore a pink satin evening gown and ivory pumps. Her hair was held back with a diamond clip and she wore a thin gold necklace around her neck.

"It's such a beautiful room." Amelia looked up. "I've never seen such wonderful carpets, it's like the inside of Aladdin's lamp."

"It was the private apartments of Princess Isabelle. She entertained Queen Elizabeth in this room. She died at the age of ninety-six and toward the end of her life she filled the apartments with her greatest treasures."

"Are you a member of the Colonna family?" Amelia asked.

"I read the guidebook." Philip grinned. "The Colonna family have lived here for twenty generations, they still occupy rooms on the second and third floor."

"I'm not very good at parties," Amelia explained. "The music was too loud and there were so many people and it was so hot I couldn't breathe."

"If you don't like parties why did you come?" Philip asked, sitting on the bench beside her.

"I was supposed to meet someone but he didn't show up." Amelia shrugged. "If you'll excuse me, I'm going home."

Amelia stood up and her heel caught on the Oriental rug. She put her hand out to steady herself and Philip grabbed her arm.

"Please don't go." Philip took off his mask and dropped to his knee. "From the moment I saw you at the taxi stand, I knew you were special. When I told you love wasn't worth the effort I was wrong. I had never experienced love because now I know love is worth enduring anything. You are the most beautiful woman I've ever met and I want to spend my life with you." He drew the velvet box out of his pocket and snapped it open. "Ann, will you marry me."

"What are you doing?" Amelia gasped, tearing off her mask.

"Something I've wanted to do for three weeks." Philip grinned. "I'm asking you to be my wife."

"But it's so sudden," Amelia stammered. Her cheeks were pale and her lips trembled. "We hardly know each other."

"I know you like classic movies and Renaissance art and traveling in foreign countries," Philip began. "You're terrible at drinking champagne and have a knack for landing in difficult situations. But you have the most beautiful smile I've ever seen and when I'm with you I feel like I can accomplish anything. I want to spend the rest of my life learning your favorite colors and foods and books."

Amelia's eyes glistened and her hands shook. She looked into Philip's eyes and opened her mouth. "There's something I haven't told you . . ."

"Excuse me," a guard interrupted. "These are private apartments, they are off-limits to the guests."

"Can we have a minute?" Philip turned, his forehead creased in a frown.

Philip turned back to Amelia. She put her mask over her eyes and smoothed her hair.

"I need time to think." She walked toward the door.

"Where are you going?" Philip grabbed her hand.

"I have to be up early for work." She hesitated. "Can I see you tomorrow?"

"Of course." Philip nodded, letting go of her hand. "I'll see you tomorrow night."

Amelia opened the door and turned around. She removed her mask and her face broke into a smile.

"My favorite color is yellow."


Philip tossed his keys on the glass dining room table and loosened his tie. He pictured Amelia in her satin evening gown and white gloves and sucked in his breath.

He poured a shot of scotch and took the velvet box out of his pocket. He snapped it open and gazed at the glittering diamond. He fished out the yellow piece of paper and tossed it on the table. She had to say yes, or he would lose everything.

# chapter twenty-nine

Amelia hung up her pink satin evening gown and slipped on a cotton robe. She pictured the Princess Isabelle apartments with the gold ceilings and Oriental rugs and shivered. It had all been too much: Philip's proposal and the guard interrupting them and her heart hammering in her chest.

She poured a shot of amaretto and climbed onto the four-poster bed. She glanced at the stack of Audrey Hepburn's letters and lay back against the floral pillows. She picked up the last letter and began to read.

> *Dear Kitty,*                    *September 28, 1952*
> *Tomorrow morning I leave for New York. My trunk is packed and I bought* Vogue *and* Town & Country *and* Variety. *I will have fifteen hours on an airplane to catch up on the new collections and the fall theater season and Hollywood gossip.*
> *I wish I had time to stop in London but rehearsals for Gigi start in three days. I shall have to toss my suitcase in my new apartment*

*and race to the theater. I hope Gil hasn't rented something dismal;
I'm spoiled from the suite at the Pierre. I read in the* Observer *that
James is getting married and I'm happy for him. He needs a tall
blonde who he can parade at Ascot and Wimbledon.*

*Greg left this morning and I didn't say good-bye. You might
think I'm a coward but I knew if we met it would be as two actors
instead of Princess Ann and Joe. I hope we will stay friends but it
will never be the same. It's like the end of the performance of* Swan
Lake *when the corps de ballets step off their stage. The minute they
enter the dressing rooms they aren't swans, just ordinary girls in
white tutus.*

*I saw Veronique in the lobby of the Hassler. She wore an emer-
ald green Chanel suit and lizard pumps. I will always be jealous of
her glossy auburn hair and wide mouth and long red nails. But I
couldn't be French if I spent a year in Paris; I am a Dutch and English mutt!*

*I came up to the Villa Medici Suite and stood on the balcony. I
heard cars honking and people laughing and suddenly my heart
raced. I couldn't possibly spend my last night in Rome curled up in a
hotel robe and slippers.*

*I walked inside and put on a turquoise Givenchy dress and satin
pumps. I fastened diamond earrings in my ears and grabbed my
purse. Then I took the elevator to the lobby and asked for a taxi.*

*I entered the dining room of the Grand Hotel and gazed at the
crystal chandeliers and red velvet carpet and gold columns.*

*"Good evening, Paulo." I approached the maître d'. "Table for
one please."*

*"Are you dining alone, Miss Hepburn?" the maître d' asked.*

*"Don't worry, I have a good book for company." I smiled.*

*He escorted me to a table set with white china and gleaming* silverware. I looked up from the menu and saw a familiar figure across the room. He was very tall with large brown eyes and smooth brown hair.

"I wasn't sure that was you." Mel approached my table. "I'm by myself, do you mind if I join you?"

"Please do, it will make the maître d' happy." I nodded. "He thinks a woman dining alone is as scandalous as eating in your underwear."

"I thought you had left for New York," Mel said. He wore a gray suit with a white shirt and black tie. He wore a gold watch on his wrist and black leather shoes.

"I leave tomorrow morning, rehearsals for Gigi start on Wednesday." I sipped a glass of Burgundy. "I wanted one more night to enjoy myself."

"I'm happy you are still here," Mel replied. "I didn't get a chance to say good-bye."

"Tell me about yourself." I blushed. "How did you end up at Princeton?"

"I grew up in New Jersey," Mel began. "My father is Cuban and he is a successful surgeon and my mother is a socialite. No gala or benefit is complete until Mary O'Donohue Ferrer arrives in her fox stole and Tiffany diamonds."

"Why did you become an actor?" I asked, eating a bite of duck and baby peas.

"There are a few theories," Mel mused. "My father believes I wasted my Princeton education and my friends think it was to get women. Truthfully I didn't choose acting, it chose me. When I'm in front of the camera I don't feel like a Cuban-Irish mix who isn't smart enough to be a doctor or fast enough to be a basketball player."

"A basketball player!" I laughed.

*"I was six feet by the time I was twelve."* He sighed. *"I always dreamed of a career on the court but I tripped over my own feet."*

*"I wanted to be a dancer."* I nodded. *"But I was too tall and I didn't have the perfect turn out."*

*"I'm glad you weren't a dancer,"* he said slowly. *"The world would be dull without your smile lighting up the screen."*

*"Goodness, your friends were right."* I flushed. *"You are good with women, I shall have to be careful."*

*"On the contrary."* He shook his head. *"I'm usually quiet, you're easy to talk to."*

*We shared vanilla mascarpone for dessert and Mel suggested we go to Harry's Bar for an aperitif.*

*I sipped a Cognac and then Mel asked me to dance. Kitty, he is such a good dancer, it was like being in Madame Rambert's practice room with all those young men in leotards and tights. We danced to Frank Sinatra and Glenn Miller and Ella Fitzgerald.*

*This time when he asked if he could see me home, I agreed. He dropped me off on the steps of the Hassler and took my hand.*

*"Would you I mind if I looked you up in New York?"* he asked. *"I'm still determined to produce* War and Peace.*"*

*"You might wait until* Roman Holiday *comes out,"* I mused. *"I might be a terrible flop."*

*"Greg said you are going to be a huge star,"* Mel replied. *"He's never wrong."*

*"All right."* I hesitated. *"I'd like that."*

*I walked inside and he called after me.*

*"Greg also said you were beautiful and smart and too good for me."* He smiled. *"But I've never been good at following advice."*

*I took the elevator to the Villa Medici Suite and opened the door. I sat at my dressing table and pulled off my earrings.*

*I gazed at the twinkling lights of the Colosseum and pictured
Greg and Veronique running off together. I love being an actress
but I want more than that. I want a love affair that makes me want
to give up everything. I want a passion that makes it impossible to
eat and sleep and think.*

*I slipped on a silk robe and climbed onto the four-poster bed. I
remembered Mel guiding me around the dance floor and shivered.
I hope I see him in New York, you know I've always loved a man
who can dance.*

*Audrey*

Amelia put the letter on the bedside table and tied her cotton robe
around her waist. In a week shooting of *Roman Holiday* would be over
and she would return to Los Angeles. Even if she told Philip the truth
and he forgave her, how could they have a future together?

She pictured Philip in his white dinner jacket snapping open the velvet box. She saw the oval diamond and the small sapphires and the
platinum band. How could he want to marry her when they just met?
Then she remembered Whit striding out of Il Gabriello and disappearing up the Spanish Steps. They had been together for years but
they still broke up.

Love was a crazy combination of chemistry and attraction and luck.
Did it matter how long they knew each other or was the important
thing that they didn't want to be apart?

She flashed on Philip sitting at Rosati, sipping a tall iced coffee.
She saw quiet dinners in Trastevere and long walks on the Palatine
Hill. She pictured kissing in the Piazza di Trevi and having a picnic in
the Borghese Gardens.

She glanced at Audrey's letter and remembered telling Sophie she
couldn't live without love. She adored being an actress but she didn't

want to be alone. She needed the same things as Sophie and Veronique and Audrey: a husband, children, a home.

She jumped up and walked to the closet. She pulled on a cotton sweater and a pair of capris. She slipped on leather loafers and grabbed her purse. She had to tell Philip the truth, and she had to tell him she loved him.

She walked to the elevator and pressed the button. She waited for the doors to open and hoped that would be enough.

# chapter thirty

Amelia ran up the staircase and knocked on Philip's door. She waited and knocked again. She hesitated and finally walked inside.

The bed was neatly made and an umbrella stood in the umbrella stand. Papers were strewn on the desk with a cup of pens and pencils. Amelia saw a towel hanging on the bathroom door and clean dishes next to the sink.

She gazed at the gleaming toaster and coffeemaker and pictured waking up together on Sunday mornings. She imagined sitting at the round glass table eating scrambled eggs and bacon and whole wheat toast. She pictured drinking cups of fresh ground coffee with nutmeg and cinnamon.

She walked to the desk and pulled out a piece of paper. She would write Philip a note asking him to join her at Rosati's. Then she'd browse in the boutiques on the Via Condotti and buy a silk dress or some lace underwear.

She glanced at the dining room table and saw a stack of photos. She picked up a photo of Philip and her sitting at a café in the Piazza di Trevi. She was wearing a floral dress and Philip's arm was draped around her shoulder.

She flipped through the stack and saw a photo of them having a picnic at the Villa d'Este. There were pictures of them putting their hands in the Mouth of Truth and standing in front of the Castel Sant'Angelo.

Amelia heard the door open and turned around. She saw a man with wavy blond hair and blue eyes. He wore a yellow collared shirt and blue jeans and had a camera slung over his shoulder.

"You must be Ann." Max held out his hand. "We haven't been formally introduced. I'm Max, Philip's friend."

"Philip wasn't here so I was going to leave him a note," Amelia explained. "I don't understand, who took all these photos?"

"I did," Max replied, taking a peach from the wooden bowl. "Would you like a piece of fruit? The peaches are delicious."

"Why would you take pictures of us?" Amelia asked.

"I take pictures of everything; cats, flowers, children." Max bit into the peach. "I just took some great photos of nuns riding Vespas in Saint Peter's Square."

"But there are so many," Amelia insisted. "It's as if you were following us."

"I'm thinking of starting a wedding photography business," Max continued. "So many couples get engaged or elope in Rome. You are the perfect couple, the camera loves you."

Amelia flushed and turned to the desk. She picked up a piece of paper and read the first paragraph.

Hollywood Royalty or Hotel Maid?
When I played Good Samaritan to a Hassler hotel maid a few weeks ago, I didn't know she was really the actress Amelia

Tate. I rescued Miss Tate in the pouring rain when she hadn't money for a taxi. I shared my cab and when she fell asleep on my shoulder I carried her to my apartment.

Over the last three weeks, Miss Tate and I have developed a friendship but she still hasn't revealed her identity. During long walks and intimate dinners, she maintains the fiction she is an American learning Italian and working at the Hassler. Why would the actress predicted to be the next Audrey Hepburn pretend to be a maid? And what does her deception say about the moral climate of Hollywood?

Amelia dropped the paper and felt her heart pound in her chest. She glanced around the room and suddenly didn't know where she was. Everything looked different: the narrow bed, the plain brown sofa, the fire escape hung with Philip's dress shirts.

"Why did Philip write this?" Amelia asked.

Max scanned the paper and put it down. He paced around the room and ran his hands through his hair. "I can't tell you, I'll lose my best friend."

Amelia walked to the door and turned the key in the lock. She slipped the key in her pocket and sat at the dining room table.

"We're not leaving until I hear the whole story."

Max poured two glasses of scotch and handed one to Amelia.

"I was a photographer at your press conference," he began. "You looked stunning in that pink satin gown and white gloves. The next morning I showed the photos to Philip and he recognized you as the maid who fell asleep in the taxi." Max sipped his scotch. "It was my idea that he write a series of articles about a movie star pretending to be a hotel maid. Adam bought the articles for twenty thousand dollars."

"Twenty thousand dollars!" Amelia gasped. "This is my first starring role, no one is that interested in me."

"Adam upped the stakes a little," Max conceded. "He said he'd pay Philip twenty thousand if he could convince you to marry him without revealing who you are."

Amelia felt the room spin. She remembered Philip ripping off his mask and dropping to his knee. She saw him open the black velvet box and take out the diamond and sapphire ring.

"He bought a ring," she stammered.

"Borrowed it," Max corrected. "He has to return it tomorrow."

"Why would he do such a thing?" Amelia asked, her eyes filling with tears.

"Philip is the most upstanding guy I've ever met," Max replied. "He doesn't cheat at poker and he never takes a piece of fruit at the market without paying for it. He didn't see any other way out."

"Out of what?" Amelia frowned.

"After Philip graduated from Yale his father expected him to join Hamilton and Sons. Philip said he wanted to be a journalist and the old man demanded he repay his college tuition. If he couldn't start paying the loan in ten years, he had to join the company." Max paused and looked at Amelia. "He could never be a stockbroker, he has to be a writer."

"He told me he loved me," Amelia whispered. "He asked me to marry him."

"He thinks you're the nicest girl he's ever met," Max insisted. "He never wanted to hurt you."

Amelia pictured the room in Portofino with the white lace bedspread and silk pillows. She remembered Philip drawing her onto the bed and shuddered. She stood up and took a deep breath. She took the key out of her pocket and opened the door.

"Don't leave." Max jumped up. "Let Philip explain."

"You've explained everything perfectly. Please give Philip a message for me. Tell him thank you for rescuing me from the Trevi Fountain and showing me the Vatican and helping me find Sophie." Amelia smoothed her hair. "Tell him I had a lovely time and I never want to see him again."

Amelia ran down the stairs and through the Piazza di Trevi. She raced up the Spanish Steps and entered the gold revolving doors of the Hassler. She walked quickly to the elevator and pressed the button. She leaned against the mahogany paneling and burst into tears.

Amelia poured tea into a Limoges cup and added milk and honey. She gazed around the living room at the black and gold marble floors and the yellow silk curtains and the ivory silk sofas. She saw the crystal vases filled with yellow and white tulips and the sideboard set with a silver tray of scones and strawberry jam.

She remembered when she arrived in the Villa Medici Suite and it had all seemed like a fairy tale: the ivory Bentley that picked her up at the airport, the huge bouquet of pink and white roses. She had been so excited about being in her favorite city and filming *Roman Holiday*.

Now she glanced out the window at the Dome of Saint Peter's Basilica and the outline of the Roman Forum and felt like she couldn't breathe. How could she let herself fall in love with Philip? She remembered waking up in his apartment. She saw him standing at the counter, preparing fresh muesli and cut berries.

She put the cup on a white china saucer and walked to the balcony. She would finish shooting and return to Los Angeles. She would concentrate on reading scripts and finding her next role.

There was a knock on the door and she crossed the marble floor to answer it.

"I'm so glad you're here." Sophie entered the foyer. She wore white linen slacks and a yellow silk blouse. Her hair was knotted in a low bun and secured with a gold chopstick. "My father arranged a meeting with Pope Francis and I don't know what to wear. Should I wear the vintage red Valentino or the turquoise Dior?"

"You're meeting the Pope?" Amelia walked into the living room. She sat on a blue velvet love seat and tucked her feet under her.

"Pope Francis visited Lentz a few years ago," Sophie replied. "Theo is so excited he keeps changing his tie. I've been having the most wonderful time. Last night my father and Theo discussed building a children's hospital in Lentz. My father offered to donate the land and Theo knows a wonderful architect."

"I'm so happy for you." Amelia smiled.

"Theo asked my father for my hand in marriage," Sophie continued. "We're not officially engaged because he wants to propose with my mother's engagement ring but we started planning the wedding. It will be next summer in Lentz and I want you to be the maid of honor."

"You'll be the most beautiful bride, I wouldn't miss it."

"Without you I never would have had the courage to fall in love." Sophie's eyes were huge. "I almost kissed Marco for getting me a taxi and I paid the woman at the market thirty euros for a basket of cherries. I want everyone to be as happy as I am."

Amelia picked up the porcelain teacup but suddenly her hands shook and she spilled tea on her floral dress.

"Are you all right?" Sophie asked.

"Philip asked me to marry him at the masquerade ball. I was too flustered to reply but this afternoon I went to his apartment to say yes." Amelia wiped her dress. "I found an article he wrote about Amelia

Tate pretending to be a hotel maid. Everything was a lie: the night in Portofino and the romantic dinners and the moonlight strolls on Palatine Hill."

"He wouldn't have proposed if he didn't mean it," Sophie insisted.

"Adam was going to pay him twenty thousand dollars if I agreed to marry him without revealing my identity," Amelia explained. "I kept putting off telling him the truth because I didn't want to lose him."

"I saw him looking at you at the restaurant in Trastevere." Sophie frowned. "He was crazy about you."

"Lots of actresses fall in love on the set: Elizabeth Taylor and Richard Burton, Katharine Hepburn and Spencer Tracy, Nicole Kidman and Tom Cruise. Sometimes it lasts and sometimes it becomes part of the memory of the wonderful people and the delicious foods and the exotic location." Amelia's mouth trembled. "I can't think about Philip."

"You can't turn off your feelings for someone," Sophie shook her head. "It's like trying to dam a waterfall."

"I loved him and he lied to me about everything." Amelia let the tears spill down her cheeks.

"Theo and I are supposed to visit the orphanage in Pompeii." Sophie hesitated. "I'll tell him I can't go and we'll watch Italian movies with English subtitles."

"You must go." Amelia wiped her eyes. "Pompeii is fascinating."

"I told Theo I want separate rooms." Sophie blushed. "Now that we're getting married I don't want to spoil the wedding night."

"You two are perfect together." Amelia tried to smile. "I can't wait to be the godmother of six towheaded children."


Amelia walked to the marble bar and poured a shot of amaretto. She watched the sun set behind the Colosseum and pictured Audrey

Hepburn in an ivory Givenchy gown accepting her Oscar for *Roman Holiday*.

Maybe if Audrey had married James or run off with Gregory Peck she would never have been a famous actress. Amelia thought of all her wonderful movies: *Sabrina* and *Breakfast at Tiffany's* and *My Fair Lady* and shivered.

She saw herself gliding down the red carpet in a fabulous gown by Elie Saab or Oscar de la Renta. She imagined standing at the podium, thanking Sheldon and clutching the small gold statue. She pictured Sophie and Theo waving and clapping.

She finished her amaretto and walked inside. She walked into the bedroom and climbed onto the four-poster bed. She pictured Philip's dark eyes and smooth cheeks and felt her heart break.

# chapter thirty-one

P hilip knocked on Adam's office door. He paced around the small reception room and ran his hands through his hair.

"I was waiting for you to show up." Adam wore a striped shirt and khakis. "I figured either Amelia turned you down and you're hungover, or she said yes and you're deciding how to spend the money."

"The proposal was perfect." Philip entered the office. "Amelia was overwhelmed and asked if she could give her answer tonight. I could tell in her eyes that she is going to say yes."

"I'll call Sergio and tell him the deal is on," Adam beamed. "Maybe he'll fly us to his private island to celebrate."

Philip stuffed his hands in his pockets and took a deep breath. "I'm not going to write the articles, I'm in love with Amelia."

"What do you mean you're not going to write the articles?" Adam demanded.

"I'm going to tell Amelia the truth and ask her to forgive me." Philip paced around the room. "I don't care if I have to work for my father, I can't live without her."

"What if she says no?" Adam tapped the silver cigarette case and stuck a cigarette behind his ear.

Philip glanced at the red linoleum floor and the beige plaster walls. He saw the wooden desk and the metal garbage can and the framed photograph of Angelina Jolie. He gazed out the window at the Piazza di Trevi and felt a small pang in his chest.

"At least I'll know I tried." He walked to the door and turned the handle.

"That's the problem with women." Adam flicked the cigarette in the garbage can. "Even when we don't understand them they make us crazy."


Philip smoothed aftershave on his cheeks and slipped on a blue blazer. He put his keys in his pocket and grabbed a piece of paper. He was going to write Amelia a note asking her to have dinner at La Quirinale. Then he was going to buy her a bouquet of yellow roses or a silk scarf from Gucci.

He pictured her expression when he brought out the oval diamond ring. He saw her sparkling brown eyes and wide white smile. He knew she was going to say yes, it was written all over her face.

He opened the door and saw an older woman with blue eyes and auburn hair. She wore a pale yellow Chanel suit and white sunglasses. She carried a lizard-skin bag and had beige Ferragamo pumps on her feet.

"Mother, what are you doing here!" Philip exclaimed. "You're supposed to be in Bermuda."

"There was a hurricane, we caught the last plane out." Lily took off her sunglasses. "I think the jet lag caught up with me, I'm dying for a glass of water."

"Are you all right? You look a little pale." Philip poured a glass of water and filled it with ice.

"Your father insisted we take a nap but I couldn't wait to see you." Lily wiped her brow. "I forgot Rome in August is so humid, it's worse than New York."

"What are you doing in Rome?" Philip sat down opposite her.

"Your father was going to throw a big party for my birthday," Lily explained. "But then the hurricane approached and everyone scattered. I suggested we come to Rome, I can't think of anywhere I'd rather celebrate."

"Happy birthday." Philip kissed her on the cheek. "Now I'll have to buy you a present."

"It's not until tomorrow, one doesn't want to turn sixty a day early," Lily mused. "I'm going to buy myself a silk Versace dress and Bottega Veneta heels."

"You look wonderful." Philip nodded. "You could still walk the runway."

"That's why one has children, so they can pay you compliments." Lily gazed at Philip's blue blazer and tan slacks. "You're all dressed up, were you meeting someone?"

"I have an errand to run." Philip stuffed his hands in his pockets.

"I won't keep you." Lily waved her hand. "I wanted to see if you'd join us for dinner tomorrow night."

Philip pictured his father in his three-piece herringbone suit and tasseled shoes and frowned.

"You can't say no to your mother on her birthday," Lily pleaded. "I made reservations at Mirabelle, it has the best view in Rome."

Philip gazed at his mother's glossy auburn hair and remembered birthday parties when he was young. He saw pony rides in Central Park and ice-skating in Rockefeller Center. He pictured the private dining room at Tavern on the Green filled with blue and white balloons and a three-tier chocolate fondant cake.

"Of course I'll come to dinner." Philip smiled. "What time?"

"I'm so happy!" Lily exclaimed. "Your father can't eat sugar so there's no one to share my cake."

"We'll have beef tartar and wild salmon with Parmesan fondue and hazelnut mascarpone for dessert." Philip smiled.

"I feel festive already." Lily stood up and grabbed her purse. "I'm going to visit the boutiques on the Via Condotti and then I'm going to the hotel and take a bath. The bathtub has the most wonderful neck massager, when I step out I feel ten years younger."

Philip put the glass in the sink and heard the door open. He turned around and saw Max clutching a brown envelope. His cheeks were pale and he had fresh stubble on his chin.

"You just missed my mother," Philip said. "They flew in to celebrate her birthday, I have to join them for dinner tomorrow night."

"These are the rest of the photos of Amelia." Max slid the envelope across the table. "I thought you might want them."

Philip opened the envelope and saw a photo of Amelia strolling along the Via Veneto. There were pictures of her trying on leather sandals at Prada and white sunglasses at Fendi. There were photos of her and Sophie eating gelato at Caffé Greco and sitting on the steps of Saint Peter's Basilica.

"She has the loveliest smile," Philip sighed. "I'm going to ask her to dinner tonight, I know she's going to say she'll marry me."

"She was here yesterday evening," Max said slowly.

"She was here?" Philip raised his eyebrow. "Why didn't you tell me?"

"Mirabella is considering divorcing the count, we had to see a lawyer," Max replied. "Amelia saw the stack of photos on the dining room table."

"What did you tell her?" Philip asked.

"I said I was thinking of starting a photography business." Max shrugged. "Then she saw your article on the desk, she made me tell her everything."

"What do you mean 'everything'?" Philip said slowly.

"That you saw her photo at the press conference and recognized the maid who fell asleep in your taxi." Max gulped. "I said it was my idea to write the series of articles and Adam offered to pay you twenty thousand dollars."

"You told her that?" Philip sucked in his breath.

"She asked about the ring and I said you borrowed it."

"How could you?" Philip spluttered. "I just came back from the office. I told Adam I couldn't write the articles about Amelia, I'm in love with her."

"She locked the door and said she wouldn't leave unless I told her the whole story," Max said miserably. "I feel like one of those medieval knights, I want to die on my sword."

Philip paced around the room and stuffed his hands in his pockets. "It's not your fault, I should never have lied."

"You didn't tell me you were in love with her," Max moaned.

Philip pictured Amelia in her pink satin evening gown and white silk gloves. He saw her large brown eyes and small pink mouth.

"I didn't realize until a few days ago." He jumped up. "I have to go see her."

"I told her to wait and you'd explain everything." Max put his head in his hands. "But she said she never wanted to see you again."

\* \* \*

Philip entered the Hassler and crossed the black and gold marble lobby. He pictured Amelia's creamy skin and slender shoulders and felt like he had been punched in the stomach. He strode to the elevator and pressed the button for the seventh floor.

"Excuse me." Ernesto rushed over to him. "This is a private elevator, it is only for hotel guests."

"It's me, Ernesto." Philip turned around. "I need to see Amelia."

"Mr. Hamilton," Ernesto said stiffly. "I'm afraid you can't use the elevator."

"I know Amelia is staying in the Villa Medici Suite." Philip pressed the button. "I must talk to her."

"Please come to the concierge desk," Ernesto insisted. "Or I will have to ask you to leave."

Philip glanced at Ernesto's slick black hair and gold uniform. He stuffed his hands in his pockets and followed him to the marble concierge desk.

"You don't understand." Philip leaned over the desk. "There's been a terrible misunderstanding and I need to speak to her right away."

"Miss Tate left instructions that she did not want to see you," Ernesto replied.

"It's all a mistake." Philip rubbed his forehead. "If I can just talk to her I can explain."

"I'm sorry." Ernesto turned to his computer. "There's nothing I can do."

"You can give her a note." Philip grabbed a piece of paper.

"She said she does not want any more letters." Ernesto tapped on his keyboard.

Philip wanted to reach across the counter and grab a hotel key. He wanted to race to the elevator and shut the doors behind him.

"Ernesto, have you ever wanted something so badly you'd do anything to get it?" Philip searched his pockets and drew out a twenty-lire note.

"Our conversation is over." Ernesto glanced at the money. "I must assist other guests."

"I'll buy you a plane ticket to New York," Philip implored. "You can visit the Statue of Liberty and the Empire State Building."

"I do not want to alert security," Ernesto threatened.

Philip's shoulders sagged. He ran his hands through his hair and took a deep breath. "Miss Tate is the most beautiful woman I've ever met, don't you want her to be happy?"

Ernesto glanced up from his computer and shrugged. "I'm sorry, I cannot discuss Hassler guests."

Philip sat in a Louis XIV chair at the Hassler Bar. He reached into his pocket and drew out the black velvet box. He snapped it open and stared at the oval diamond ring. He put it on the table and signaled to a waiter.

"A dry martini please," he said. "No ice."

Philip entered Mirabelle and scanned the dining room. Wide windows overlooked the Vatican Gardens and the Villa Borghese. There were thick ivory carpets and crystal vases filled with white and yellow lilies. Philip saw tables set with gold inlaid china and gleaming silverware.

"There you are," Lily beamed. She wore a silver Dior evening gown. Her hair fell smoothly to her shoulders and she wore a diamond necklace around her neck. "Your father just gave me his present, isn't this necklace lovely?"

"You look beautiful." Philip kissed his mother on the cheek. He wore a white dinner jacket with a black tie and black slacks. His hair was brushed over his forehead and his cheeks glistened with aftershave. "You get younger every day."

"It's my new hair color. The stylist said it's the same color Sophia Loren wears." Lily patted her hair.

A tall man in a white dinner jacket approached the table. He had thick gray hair and gray eyes and a cleft on his chin. He wore a gold Patek Philippe watch and black leather Bruno Maglis.

"Philip, I'm glad you could join us." John held out his hand. "I was sorting out the wine with the maître d'. I asked him to uncork a bottle of 1986 Chateau Margaux."

"You didn't have to bring your own wine," Lily murmured.

"It's your sixtieth birthday." John sat on a high-backed velvet chair. "I've been saving this bottle for years."

"Your father had a whole birthday weekend planned." Lily turned to Philip. "A golf tournament at Southampton and a tennis match at St. George's and a dinner dance at the Elbow Beach Resort. Then it started raining and everyone left on their private jets."

"You should come to Bermuda next August." John tore an olive baguette. "The strongest business relationships are formed on the eighteenth hole of the Port Royal Golf Course."

Philip glanced at his father's steel gray eyes and flinched. "I've never been able to swing a golf club and I'm allergic to mosquito bites."

"I'd much rather celebrate my birthday in Rome," Lily interrupted, her cheeks flushing. "You must try the fresh goose liver with cherry brioche, it's a house specialty."

Philip watched while the waiter served creamy onion soup and rack of lamb with a raspberry crust. He gazed at his father meticulously cutting his meat and his stomach clenched.

"We received an invitation to Andrew Claxton's wedding," Lily said, eating a spoonful of risotto. "Didn't you room with him your second year at Yale? He's marrying Sarah Groton; she went to Smith and works at Sotheby's. The ceremony is going to be at Trinity Church followed by a reception at the Carlyle."

"It's important to marry the right person." John ate a large bite of lamb. "Your mother has always given the best dinner parties, she has impeccable taste."

"We were wondering about the girl you proposed to." Lily turned to Philip. "We don't know anything about her."

Philip held his wineglass so tightly he thought it would snap. He put down his fork and straightened his shoulders.

"You didn't come to Rome for your birthday," he seethed. "You came to see who I wanted to marry."

"You called and asked to borrow ten thousand dollars to buy a diamond ring. Your mother convinced me to wire the money even though we knew nothing about her." John frowned. "Of course we're curious."

"Don't be angry." Lily touched Philip's hand. "We're thrilled you want to get married but last time we were here you never mentioned you were seeing someone. It's easy to pick the wrong person when you're away from family and friends."

"I've lived in Rome for three years and I have great friends," Philip said icily.

"Friends you grew up with," Lily murmured.

"I don't mind lending you the money but you have to consider our position." John sipped his wine. "You'll be representing Hamilton and Sons at charity and society functions all over Manhattan. Your wife has to have a certain . . ."

"Class? Breeding? You make it sound like a dog show." Philip's eyes flickered. "Amelia is the most wonderful girl I've ever met. She has eyes like a young deer and the grace of a dancer. She's articulate and intelligent and her smile lights up a room."

"She sounds lovely," Lily murmured, eating taglierini and baby peas. "You should have brought her to dinner, we can't wait to meet her."

"I would have done anything for her but unfortunately she turned me down." Philip's eyes were dark. "I'm going to work at Hamilton and Sons because I'm a man of my word. But the minute I pay back your two hundred thousand dollars I never want to speak to either of you again."

Philip threw his napkin on his plate and pushed back his chair. He looked at his mother and frowned. "I'm sorry to ruin your birthday, but I just lost my appetite."

Philip walked along the Via di Porta Pinciana. The sky was a swath of black velvet and all of Rome lay at his feet. He saw the stone buildings of the National Museum and the gray ruins of the Pantheon.

He wanted to hail a taxi and go to the Hassler. He wanted to wait in the lobby until Amelia walked through the gold revolving doors.

He remembered what Ernesto said and knew he would call security and kick him out. He strode along the Via del Corso to his apartment. He climbed the metal staircase and opened the door. He loosened his tie and buried his head in his hands.

# chapter thirty-two

Amelia sat at a mahogany table in the Hassler Bar and picked at a silver bowl of pistachios. She glanced at women in shimmering cocktail dresses and men in white dinner jackets and wished Sophie was back from Pompeii.

She spent the evening browsing in the shops on the Via Condotti. She considered going to Caffé Greco and ordering linguini with scampi but she wasn't hungry. She walked back to the Hassler and entered the glass revolving doors.

Suddenly she didn't want to sit in the Villa Medici Suite and nibble a room service caprese salad. She didn't want to change into a silk robe and curl up with *Vogue* and a cup of English breakfast tea.

"You look familiar." A woman sat at the next table. She had auburn hair and wore a silver Dior evening gown. She had a diamond necklace around her neck and clutched a quilted Chanel purse.

"I'm Amelia Tate." Amelia blushed. "I'm an actress."

"I mainly see classic movies." The woman shrugged. "I'm a huge fan of Lauren Bacall and Grace Kelly and Audrey Hepburn."

"I'm in Rome filming the remake of *Roman Holiday*," Amelia replied, sipping a glass of amaretto and cream.

"Audrey Hepburn is my favorite actress!" the woman exclaimed. "When I was young I used to carry around a gold cigarette holder like Holly Golightly in *Breakfast at Tiffany's*. I've seen all her movies, I cry every time I watch *Two for the Road* and then I press replay and watch it again."

"She was very special," Amelia agreed. "I feel fortunate to be playing her role."

"You do look like her, you have the same wide brown eyes and narrow cheekbones," the woman mused. Suddenly she got up and walked over to Amelia. "Do you mind if I join you? I hate drinking alone, I feel like a character in a daytime soap opera."

"Please do." Amelia nodded, admiring her glossy hair and smooth skin. "I'm happy to have company."

"My name is Lily, it's a pleasure to meet you." The woman held out her hand. "I just turned sixty, it's the worst birthday I've had since Chanel discontinued Chanel No. 9."

"What happened?" Amelia asked.

"We had to evacuate Bermuda because of a hurricane," Lily began. "I didn't want to go back to New York, we always close the town house in August. We decided to come to Rome, our son lives here." She stirred her martini. "We met at Mirabelle for dinner and it started wonderfully. My husband gave me a diamond necklace and my son looked so handsome in a white dinner jacket and black tie.

"My husband has been pressuring my son to join the family firm for years." Lily sighed. "One can't help wanting the best for one's children: a beautiful home, a lovely family, the means to travel and enjoy gourmet foods and fine wines.

"A few days ago my son called and asked to borrow ten thousand dollars to buy an engagement ring. He met the most beautiful girl and wanted to spend the rest of his life with her." Lily explained. "It must have been terribly hard for him to ask his father for money, but true love will make you do anything.

"My husband hesitated but I insisted we send him the money. He accused us of coming to Rome to see if we approved of his choice." Lily frowned. "He got terribly angry and stormed out of the restaurant. I think he was upset because the girl turned him down."

Amelia sat quietly, stirring her drink. She gazed at the glass bottles lining the bar and the intricate murals covering the walls and the gold inlaid ceiling. She watched waiters in white jackets carrying trays of brightly colored drinks and men smoking thick cigars. She turned and looked at Lily.

"What's the name of your husband's company?" Amelia whispered.

"Hamilton and Sons," Lily replied. "It's a stockbroking firm on Wall Street. Have you heard of it?"

"I . . ." Amelia began.

"Are you all right?" Lily leaned forward. "You look very pale."

"I just remembered something." Amelia jumped up. "I have to go."

"I know why you look familiar," Lily exclaimed. "I saw your photo in Philip's apartment."

Amelia stood in front of her closet and picked out a white crepe dress. She fastened her hair with a gold clip and slipped a gold bangle around her wrist. She coated her eyes with mascara and rubbed her lips with pink lip gloss.

There was a knock on the door and she crossed the marble entry to answer it.

"We got back from Pompeii late last night and I didn't want to wake you." Sophie burst into the room. She wore a yellow linen dress and silver sandals. Her hair was knotted in a low ponytail and tied with a yellow ribbon. "I couldn't sleep all night, I couldn't wait to show you."

"Show me what?" Amelia asked.

"This." Sophie displayed a large square diamond flanked by two glittering rubies.

"It's gorgeous," Amelia gasped. "I've never seen anything like it."

"It's my mother's ring, my lady-in-waiting sent it to Theo." Sophie perched on an ivory silk love seat. "We took the ferry from Naples to Capri and had dinner at the Hotel Quisisana. It's the most gorgeous hotel, everything is pink and green and turquoise. After dessert the waiter brought a bottle of Dom Pérignon. I asked what we were celebrating and Theo dropped to his knee and asked me to marry him."

"What if you said no." Amelia giggled.

"I said yes before he finished asking the question." Sophie grinned. "After dinner we strolled to Ana Capri and danced in the moonlight."

"I'm so happy for you." Amelia smiled.

"I feel different being officially engaged, as if I'm already part of something bigger. I can't wait to show Theo the palace and the countryside." Sophie paused and glanced at Amelia. "Why are you all dressed up? It's barely eight A.M."

"I met a woman at the Hassler Bar, I was sitting by myself and she joined me," Amelia began. "She and her husband came to Rome to celebrate her birthday with her son. They got into a fight at dinner and her son stormed out of the restaurant. He was devastated because he bought an engagement ring and the girl turned him down.

"I asked her what was the name of her husband's firm and she said it was Hamilton and Sons." Amelia's eyes were wide. "I realized her son was Philip."

"You met Philip's mother." Sophie gasped. "I don't understand, you said Philip had to return the ring."

"He borrowed money from his father to buy the ring," Amelia beamed. "He wasn't lying when he asked me to marry him, he's in love with me."

"I knew he loved you." Sophie smiled. "But why didn't he tell you?"

"I told Ernesto I didn't want to see him." Amelia replied. "I'm going to his apartment to tell him I know the truth."

"We'll have a double wedding at Lentz Cathedral," Sophie exclaimed. "We'll invite European royalty and Hollywood celebrities. The Vienna Boys' Choir will sing and Pope Francis will give his blessing."

Amelia remembered when she discovered Sophie in the laundry basket at the Hassler. She remembered drinking glasses of Chianti and Sophie telling her she was a princess. She saw Sophie's suite littered with Fendi dresses and Prada sandals and Sophie saying she pawned a tiara.

"I can't have a royal wedding." Amelia gave Sophie a hug. "You're the real princess, I'm just an actress."

Amelia walked into the bedroom and grabbed her purse. She saw a stack of papers on the mahogany bedside table and suddenly had an idea. She selected a piece of ivory card stock and wrote:

*Dear Lily,*
*I discovered these letters hidden in an antique desk in my suite.*
*Audrey Hepburn wrote them over fifty years ago while she was*
*filming* Roman Holiday.
*You were right when you said Audrey Hepburn was a very*

*special actress. I learned so much about acting and love from read-*
*ing her letters. I've been wondering what to do with them. It didn't*
*seem right to make them public but I couldn't just tape them back*
*underneath the desk.*

*I hope you don't mind if I give them to you. Perhaps you'll know*
*where they belong. In the meantime, I hope you enjoy them as*
*much as I did. I know we only talked briefly, but it was a great*
*pleasure meeting you.*

*Amelia*

Amelia stuffed the letters in an envelope and walked into the hall-way. She pressed the button on the elevator and waited for the doors to open.

"Good morning, Miss Tate," Ernesto called. "You are up early."

"I have a few errands to run." Amelia approached the concierge desk. "Could you do me a favor?"

"I am at your service." Ernesto nodded.

"Could you give this to a guest?" Amelia handed him the brown envelope. "Her name is Lily Hamilton."

"It will be my pleasure." Ernesto took the envelope. "Can I get you a croissant or a glass of juice?"

"No thank you." Amelia waved her hand. "I'm not in the least bit hungry."

Amelia walked through the gold revolving doors and paused on the sidewalk. Bentleys and Jaguars lined the curb and valets carried Louis Vuitton cases and Gucci garment bags.

"Miss Tate." Marco approached her. "It is lovely to see you. Would you like a taxi?"

Amelia breathed in the scent of bougainvillea and azalea and French perfume. She turned to Marco and her face lit up in a smile.

"The weather is too nice to sit in a taxi, I'm going to walk."

She hurried down the Spanish Steps and crossed the Piazza di Spagna. She strode along the Via Condotti to the Piazza di Trevi. She pictured Philip's dark eyes and smooth cheeks and walked faster.

# chapter thirty-three

Philip gazed at the cardboard boxes filled with books and notepads. He glanced at the shirts laid out on his bed and the ties lining his dresser.

Signora Griselda said her nephew needed an apartment and he decided to return to New York. He pictured Amelia's brown eyes and wide smile and felt a pain in his chest.

"Isn't it a little early in the morning for redecorating?" Max asked, entering the apartment. He wore a yellow collared shirt and blue jeans. His hair was freshly washed and he carried a wax paper bag. "The countess and I made strawberry ricotta cannoli, I want you to try one."

"It's delicious." Philip took a bite of fluffy pastry and creamy ricotta cheese.

"Italian divorce laws are worse than slavery." Max opened the fridge and took out a carton of orange juice. "Mirabella gets nothing except her clothes and jewelry. Her uncle left her a pied-à-terre in Florence. We are going to live there and open a pastry shop."

"You're moving in with the countess?" Philip raised his eyebrow.

"We're getting married," Max corrected. "Mirabella doesn't believe in living together."

"Isn't that a bit sudden?" Philip frowned. "You're so young, what if you want children?"

"Mirabella is only forty-two." Max shrugged. "I'm crazy about her. All I want is to hear her laugh and smell her perfume."

"I'm happy for you." Philip nodded, stacking plates and silverware.

"Where are you going?" Max asked, glancing at the plane ticket on the glass dining room table.

"I'm leaving for New York." Philip looked at his watch. "My plane departs in four hours."

"What about *Inside Rome*?" Max asked.

"Adam will find other journalists." Philip shrugged. "I'll work at Hamilton and Sons until I pay my father back. Then I'll get a newspaper job in New York. It's time I wrote about gentrification in Brooklyn instead of the truffle festival in Sabina."

"Have you told Amelia?" Max sipped his orange juice.

"I tried to see her but Ernesto said she wouldn't talk to me," Philip said stiffly.

"You can't just give up." Max put down his glass. "What if I quit when the countess was furious at me for giving her daughter earrings? What if I let the count catch us when he chased us in the Alfa Romeo?"

"Even if I told Amelia the articles were a mistake and I'm in love with her, how could she ever trust me?" Philip asked.

"She lied, too," Max insisted. "She said she was a maid."

"But she didn't do anything to hurt me." Philip sighed. "I made a mess of everything."

Max reached into his pocket and drew out a wad of lire.

"Give this to Ernesto and demand he let you up to her suite." He handed them to Philip.

"This is a fortune." Philip examined the stack of notes.

"The countess sold a sapphire ring." Max shrugged.

"I can't take it." Philip shook his head. "You said all she has left is her jewelry."

Max walked to the counter and put his glass in the sink. He finished the cannoli and dusted sugar from his jeans. "The countess has one of the largest private jewelry collections in Rome."

Philip entered the Hassler and strode across the marble lobby. He saw Ernesto's slick black hair and gold uniform and hurried to the concierge desk.

"Ernesto," Philip called. "I need to see Amelia."

"I am sorry, I cannot allow that." Ernesto looked up from his computer.

"You don't understand." Philip drew the wad of lire out of his pocket and placed it on the counter. "It's about Amelia's health, I'm very worried about her."

Ernesto glanced at the thick pile of notes and gasped.

"If Miss Tate is unwell . . ." He hesitated.

"I'm sure I can help if you take me to her suite." Philip pressed the notes in his hand.

Ernesto stuffed the money in his pocket and wiped his brow.

"Miss Tate isn't here," he said.

"Where is she?" Philip asked.

"She had to run some errands." Ernesto shrugged. "She is leaving this evening."

"Leaving?" Philip sucked in his breath.

"Checking out." Ernesto consulted his computer. "Flying back to America."

"I see." Philip's eyes flickered. He smoothed his hair and stuffed his hands in his pockets. "Thank you, Ernesto. You've been very helpful."

Philip stood on the sidewalk and squinted in the bright sunshine. He pictured Amelia wearing oversized sunglasses and white sandals. He imagined her smiling and stepping into a taxi. He felt the air leave his lungs and a weight press down on his shoulders. He glanced at his watch and raised his hand.

Amelia rushed up the metal staircase and knocked on the door of Philip's apartment. She waited and knocked again. Finally she turned the handle and walked inside.

The red rug was littered with boxes and there was a stack of magazines on the wooden coffee table. White towels hung on the bathroom door and fresh sheets were piled on the bed. A woman with wiry dark hair stood on the narrow fire escape.

"Excuse me," Amelia called. "I'm looking for Philip."

"I am Signora Griselda." She wiped her hands on her dress. "I'm afraid you missed him."

"Do you know where he went?" Amelia asked.

"Signor Hamilton left for America," Signora Griselda replied.

"America." Amelia's eyes were wide. "He didn't say he was leaving."

"My nephew is taking the apartment," Signora Griselda explained. "Signor Hamilton is a very nice man, he said he would write me a postcard. I have never been to New York, I want to see the Statue of Liberty."

\* \* \*

Amelia trudged up the Spanish Steps and walked slowly back to the Hassler. She wanted to take off her sandals and collapse on an ivory silk love seat. She wanted to draw the curtains and drink a glass of cold limoncello.

"Miss Tate." Ernesto rushed over to her. "You are very pale, can I get you a glass of water?"

"I'm all right, Ernesto." Amelia tried to smile. "The sun is so hot, I felt a little light-headed. I'm going to go upstairs and take a cool bath."

"Mr. Hamilton was here." Ernesto hesitated. "He wanted to see you."

"Philip was here?" Amelia asked. "What did you tell him?"

"I said you ran some errands," Ernesto replied weakly.

"I have to find him," Amelia exclaimed. "Where did he go?"

"He didn't tell me." Ernesto shrugged. "Perhaps you can ask Marco."

Amelia ran onto the sidewalk and waved at Marco.

"Miss Tate, how lovely to see you again," Marco beamed. "It is a beautiful day. Would you like a taxi?"

"Did you see a tall man with dark hair?" Amelia asked.

"I see many guests," Marco replied.

"He has dark eyes and wears a lizard-skin watch," Amelia said desperately.

"The American!" Ernesto exclaimed. "He asked me to call a taxi."

"Where was he going?" Amelia felt her heart pound in her chest.

Marco rubbed his forehead. Suddenly his eyes gleamed and he smiled. "I remember, he went to Roma Termini."


Amelia stepped out of the taxi and walked through the tall glass doors. She glanced around the vast space and saw flashing signs reading Milan and Turin and Pisa. She saw men in gray uniforms and tourists rolling leather bags and canvas suitcases.

She searched the kiosks full of paperback books and the cafés selling iced coffees and packaged ham sandwiches. She was about to leave when she saw a man wearing a white collared shirt with the sleeves rolled up. He carried a black briefcase and flipped through a copy of *Time* magazine.

"Philip." She approached. Suddenly her cheeks burned and her heart hammered in her chest.

Philip closed the magazine and turned around.

He gasped. "Amelia, what are you doing here?"

"I went to your apartment," Amelia stammered. "Signora Griselda said you were going back to New York."

"I am." Philip nodded.

"Are you going to work for your father?" Amelia asked.

"My parents came to Rome for my mother's birthday." Philip hesitated. "It seems my mother told my father he has to stop telling me what to do. She said if he made me join the firm she would leave him."

"When did she say that?" Amelia raised her eyebrow.

"She called me an hour ago." Philip grinned. "Apparently she got quite drunk after dinner and told my father I was old enough to make my own decisions. I don't think he liked it but he would never survive without her."

"I met your mother by accident at the Hassler Bar last night," Amelia said. "She's a beautiful woman, I enjoyed her company very much."

"She's one of the smartest people I know," Philip agreed. "I'm very grateful."

"She said you borrowed ten thousand dollars from your father to buy an engagement ring." Amelia looked at the floor.

"I told Adam I couldn't write the articles, I never meant to hurt you. I realized I was in love with you and didn't care if I sold stocks or washed dishes as long as I could be with you." Philip took Amelia's hand. "But I guess I was too late."

"You're not too late." Amelia's eyes filled with tears. "I'm still here."

Philip drew her close and kissed her softly on the lips. He ran his hands through her hair and pressed her against his chest.

"Why are you at the train station if you're going to New York?" she asked when he finally released her.

"I wasn't ready to leave Italy yet," Philip replied. "I'm taking the train to Portofino."

"Portofino," Amelia whispered.

"I booked a room at the Hotel Splendido," Philip said. "I missed their seafood ravioli."

"I love Portofino." Amelia sighed, picturing the green inlets and the hills filled with yellow and purple daisies. "Can I come with you?"

"It's a very small room." Philip smiled.

"I can always sleep on the floor," Amelia murmured.

Philip wrapped his arms around her waist and kissed her on the mouth. He ran his fingers over her cheeks and touched her chin. "What kind of a host would I be if I made you sleep on the floor?"


They sat on hard leather seats and watched the train pull out of the station. Amelia gazed out the window and saw the Roman Forum and the Colosseum. She saw the spires of Saint Peter's Basilica and the lush gardens of the Villa Borghese.

"My agent sent me a script for a Broadway play," she mused. "It's a remake of *Gigi*."

"You'd be wonderful on Broadway," Philip said slowly.

"He thinks I'd be perfect for the Audrey Hepburn role." Amelia nodded. "She played Gigi right after she finished filming *Roman Holiday.*"

She felt Philip's hand on her knee and pictured long walks in Central Park. She imagined weekends exploring the Guggenheim and the Metropolitan Museum. She pictured Sunday mornings reading the *New York Times* and eating scrambled eggs and bacon. She turned to Philip and smiled.

"I've always wanted to do a play."

# acknowledgments

Thank you to my wonderful agent, Melissa Flashman, and my fabulous editor, Hilary Rubin Teeman, for your wisdom and enthusiasm. Thank you to everyone at St. Martin's Press: Hilary's fantastic assistant, Alicia Clancy, and my publicity and marketing team, Staci Burt and Janet Chow, and Elsie Lyons for another gorgeous cover. Thank you also to Jennifer Weis and Jennifer Enderlin for making St. Martin's my wonderful home.

And thank you to my family: My husband, Thomas, and my children, Alex, Andrew, Heather, Madeleine, Thomas, and Lisa, for bringing me so much joy.

1. Amelia is very reluctant to give up acting even though Whit doesn't approve of it. Should she be content to "get it out of her system" and return to studying medicine in order to save the relationship? Or should she continue to pursue her dream?

2. Amelia says she loves being on a film set—the lights, the costumes, the cameras—because it makes her feel alive. Is there something you feel so passionate about that you can't live without it?

3. Describe Sophie. Is she a throwback to an earlier time or is she a modern woman who puts her responsibilities before her own needs and desires?

4. Max says to Philip it is okay for him to lie to Amelia because she lied to Philip first. Is there ever a reason to lie in a relationship? If so, what situations would make you lie to a boyfriend or husband?

5. How do you feel about Philip? Is it understandable that he accepts Adam's challenge at Amelia's expense or should he give up his journalism career and return to Hamilton and Sons?

6. What lessons does Amelia learn from Audrey Hepburn's letters? Have you ever read a book or seen a movie that had a profound effect on your own life? If so, which ones?

7. When the novel opens, Max seems young and carefree. Describe how Max changes and grows throughout the story. How do you feel about Max at the end of the book?

8. The novel is full of descriptions of Rome. Do you think being in a foreign city affects Amelia's judgment? Would she have fallen in love so quickly if she were home in California?

St. Martin's
Griffin

9. Amelia often says that she can't live without love. Do you feel the same way or do you think one can be happy alone?

10. Audrey Hepburn was one of the most beloved actresses of the twentieth century. What else do you know about her? If you have seen any of her movies, describe how you feel about her through her letters compared to how she appears on the screen.